LORI COPELAND
Author of More Than 6 Million Books in Print!

MORE THAN SHE BARGAINED FOR

"Where are you going to come up with a husband on such short notice?" Slater demanded.

"Well, that's what I wanted to talk to you about...."

Slater's eyes narrowed suspiciously. "Now wait a minute. I certainly hope you're not thinking what I think you're thinking."

"What's that?" Jillane asked innocently.

"Getting me hooked up with your little scheme. Well, you can just think again."

"I can't see how it would hurt one tiny bit for you to help me out in a pinch—" she began.

"Oh, no!" He shook his head vehemently. "I don't intend to be anyone's husband, imaginary or otherwise!"

"Okay." She heaved a sigh of exasperation. "If you won't do it out of the goodness of your heart, let's get professional about this. Let me rent you for a week!"

LORI COPELAND

MORE THAN SHE BARGAINED FOR

LEISURE BOOKS **NEW YORK CITY**

A LEISURE BOOK®

April 1994

Published by

Dorchester Publishing Co., Inc.
276 Fifth Avenue
New York, NY 10001

Printed in the United States of America.

For Ofelia Delgadillo and Mary Grigg

More Than She Bargained For

Prologue

December 10

The last remaining vestige of the cold winter sun dipped behind the horizon as twilight settled gently over the bustling city. The streets teemed with early holiday shoppers and workers trying to make their way home to families and warm fires.

The two men who strode briskly around the corner huddled deeper into their coats as the chilling wind buffeted their tall frames. They stepped hurriedly into the small bar-and-grill on the corner just in time for the beginning of Happy Hour.

"Whew-ee!" Fritz Covell took his gloves off and good-naturedly slapped his partner on the back as they slid onto the bar stools and signaled for the waitress to bring two beers. "It's colder than a well-digger's rear in January out there today!"

Slater Holbrook grinned, picked up a handful of peanuts, and popped them into his mouth. Fritz hated cold weather and made no bones about it.

They sat drinking in the warmth of the room and talking about the day's work, sharing thoughts and private opinions as they had done so many times in the past. Slater Holbrook and Fritz Covell went back many years in their friendship. They not only worked in the same department at the phone company, but over the years they had become close friends as well.

As the twilight lengthened, their drinks grew more frequent and their conversation more sentimental.

"You know, Slater, I'm a happy man," Fritz announced with a long sigh. "I've got six wonderful kids and Marie. What more could a man want?"

"Nothing. You've got it all," Slater agreed, his hand dipping into the peanut bowl once more.

"You should try it, you know. You need a wife and kids, home mortgages, doctor bills, orthodontist bills—"

Slater laughed. "No, thanks. If you'll recall, I tried the wife bit and it didn't work. I'm happy just the way I am."

"I don't see how you can cite that short teenage marriage you had twenty years ago as a prime example of marriage."

"It was enough for me."

"Well." Fritz leaned over and draped his arm around Slater's neck, the effect of the last few beers beginning to show. "I can't do anything for you concerning the wife situation, but I'll tell you what I am gonna do, buddy. Marie and I were talking the other day, and we think it's time we had a will made."

Slater frowned. "Why do you want to do that? You aren't going anywhere for a while. . . ."

"I know, I know . . . but it's a good idea to have things covered if we do. Anyway, we both agreed we couldn't think of anyone we would rather see raise our children than you. Marie and I don't have any close family left. So, if you don't mind, we would like to make you guardian of our children . . . just in case anything ever happened. There would be no financial burden. The children are well taken care of by trust funds," he assured Slater.

Glancing at his friend, Slater was taken completely by surprise by his request. "Me? I don't know anything about raising kids," he protested with a laugh.

"What's there to know? All it takes is instinct and a lot of guts, and I know you have more than your share of both."

"Boy, I don't know, Fritz. . . ." There was nothing Slater wouldn't do for Fritz, but this was a sobering responsibility he was proposing.

"Come on, Slater. The chances of anything ever happening to Marie and me both is nil, but she would feel a lot better if she knew things were all set up. You know women. Always worrying about nothing."

"Yeah, I know." Slater relaxed and took a sip of his beer. He knew how much Fritz and Marie loved their children. Three boys and three girls. Actually, only the baby was theirs. The other five were adopted and came from various ethnic backgrounds. Up until a couple of years ago, they had thought they would never be able to have children of their own, so they began gathering available children from all ends of the earth. Then, when Marie found out she was pregnant, their happiness was complete.

Yes, the Covells had a beautiful family, and Sla-

11

ter could see why his friend would want protection for the children in the event of the unthinkable.

Sure, he would do this for Fritz and Marie if it would make them feel better. And, like Fritz had said, the chances of anything actually happening to them were almost nil. "Well, tell Marie to relax. I'd be proud to be named your children's guardian."

"Thanks, pal. We knew you would. That's why we had the will drawn up this morning." He tipped his glass in silent salute to his friend.

Slater looked at him patiently. "Why do I have the feeling I've just been set up?"

Fritz slapped Slater on the back once more and rose from the stool. "If you ever decide to have any kids, I'll return the favor." He glanced at his watch. "Hey, Marie should be picking me up any minute. We're going to do some Christmas shopping to-night."

Reaching for the bill, Slater rose with him, and they walked over to the cashier. "You getting that new bicycle for Joey?"

"Yeah." Fritz's grin widened. "They want an arm and a leg for it, but he's got his heart set on that particular one."

"Well, you're only nine once," Slater consoled, paying the bill and buttoning his coat.

They walked out into the crisp night air, greeted by the sound of sleet hitting the metal canopy over their head. "Looks like we're in for some bad weather." Fritz glanced up into the stormy sky and pulled his collar up closer. "Can we drop you somewhere?"

"No, thanks. I think I'll grab a sandwich, then go on home. I'm bushed." A dark sedan pulled up to the curb and honked. Slater raised his hand and waved at Marie. "See you in the morning."

"Yeah, see you tomorrow. Oh, hey! Remember our party Friday night. Marie said she would break your arm if you ruined her couples' party and showed up without a date!"

Slater grinned and waved him away as he started down the street.

Fritz slid into the car and leaned over to kiss his wife a warm hello. "Hi, woman."

"Ummm . . . you taste like beer! I bet you've had one too many, haven't you?" she accused affectionately. If he had, it would be unusual. Fritz was a very temperate man, and she knew that he and Slater's occasional drinks after work were harmless.

"Me? No way. But you'd better drive," he confessed sheepishly.

Glancing in the rearview mirror, Marie pulled slowly out into the line of traffic. For a moment the back wheels of the car failed to gain traction, and she looked at her husband anxiously. "It's beginning to get slick."

"Just take it easy, honey. We'll get something to eat before we shop, and then I'll drive home." Fritz knew his wife hated to drive when the roads were bad, and he berated himself for having had those last two beers.

The sleet was beginning to pelt down on the windshield now, glazing the roads and highways with a dangerous covering of ice.

Marie gripped the steering wheel of the car tightly and peered intently ahead of her.

"Kids all right?" Fritz asked, trying to lighten her mood as they crept along.

"Yes, but Tara has the sniffles. I called the doctor and he phoned in a prescription. We're supposed to pick it up on the way home."

"I hope she isn't getting sick," Fritz said, fretting.

"Oh, it's just the sniffles," Marie assured him.

"Did you send off the bill for the car insurance?"

"Mailed it on the way to pick you up."

"Good. Stop by the bank?"

"I did . . . oh, did you speak to Slater about the children?" she asked expectantly.

Fritz grinned and leaned over to kiss her again. "Yes, everything's all set. Slater sends his love and the message that you can stop worrying now. If anything should ever happen, he'll take the children."

Marie breathed a sigh of relief. "I know you think I'm being silly, but that does make me feel better," she admitted. She bit her lower lip pensively. "For some reason it's been on my mind almost constantly lately."

"Well, you can put it aside now and devote your full attention to me," he bantered. "By the way, have I mentioned that I think I'm in love with you?"

"Not since this morning," she returned perkily, tilting her head to allow him better access to her mouth. "But I have no objections to hearing it again."

"Umm . . . watch that truck coming out on the side street, honey." Fritz straightened uneasily as his eyes focused on the large vehicle that was making a frantic effort to stop.

Marie braked hard. The car swerved to the left as the truck slid through the intersection and headed straight for the sedan.

"Oh, dear God, Fritz! He's going to hit us!" Marie's voice broke as Fritz reached over and threw his arms protectively around her.

The sound of tearing metal and shattering glass stunned the people on the sidewalks as they stood and helplessly watched the collision of the two vehicles.

As the sounds of the horrible collision faded away, the air was filled with a deathly, paralyzed silence. Only the pelting sleet could be heard now as darkness surrounded the scene of the crash.

Fritz Covell's last thought before his life slowly drained out of him was one of gratitude . . . gratitude that Slater Holbrook still lived on and that his and Marie's children would have a father. . . .

CHAPTER ONE

June 12

Well, she had done it now.

Jillane Simms sank down on the sofa, her hand still feebly clutching the letter that had arrived in the morning mail.

Sue Talbot had changed her mind and decided to come to the class reunion after all.

Of all the rotten luck!

Only last week Sue had vowed she simply didn't have the time to make the trip to California and would have to bypass their tenth reunion. Now she was not only coming, but she also wanted to stay with Jillane and her new husband!

There had always existed a certain rivalry between Jillane and Sue. If anyone had asked why, neither one of them could have given a reasonable answer.

It wasn't that they were both raving beauties in their high-school days, because they were not. Oh, they certainly weren't unattractive, they just didn't offer anything unusual to a boy of sixteen or seventeen. At least, nothing that would make him want to leap off a tall building if one of them refused a date with him.

Still, the feeling of competition was always there between them. It was a sort of love-hate relationship, one Jillane found herself hopelessly trapped in. Somewhere locked in the deep, dark chambers of both women's minds there lurked a secret yearning to outdo the other.

When they graduated from school and went to work, that rivalry still continued to plague them. It seemed to Jillane that everywhere she went, she ran into Sue. Jillane would immediately begin to put on airs and pretend that her life was one big chocolate malted, when, in essence, alas, it was only a small dish of vanilla pudding.

Then a couple of years ago, when Sue received a promotion with her company and moved out of town, Jillane had breathed a huge sigh of relief. At last she could just be herself and make no effort whatsoever to impress anyone.

They still corresponded frequently, dutifully called each other during the holidays, and they never forgot to send each other a birthday present.

Gradually their letters and phone conversations were filled with more and more glowing reports on what they had been doing and how wonderfully life was treating them.

Jillane was dismayed to find that after each letter or phone call, her life had taken on ninety percent more glamour than it really had. She realized she was falling right back into the same old trap she had been in since the day she first met Sue Talbot.

She was particularly mortified after one of their more recent conversations, to find herself blithely

17

fibbing her head off about a newer, even *more* exciting life-style than before.

But, after all, if Sue could be driving a Jaguar and dating a president of an oil company who was simply mad about her and insisted on showering her with diamonds and furs, Jillane could be driving a silver Porsche and dating a world-renowned heart surgeon who just happened to cater to *her* every whim!

That little lie seemed to grow and grow, and when Sue had called one evening to gloat about her forthcoming marriage to the prized president, Jillane was flabbergasted to hear herself announce that she and the fabulously wealthy heart surgeon, Stanley Marcus, had impetuously eloped the week before!

Jillane knew how absurd and ridiculous she was being in her deception and she hated herself for it. But chances were that Sue would never come back to this town, so she would never find out about the lie.

In a few months Jillane would simply drop a letter in the mail explaining that she had become bored with Stanley and the hasty marriage had been a mistake. She would tell Sue that she was divorced now, but due to the *huge* settlement Stanley had insisted on giving her, she was independently wealthy and would never have to work another day in her life if she didn't want to.

Then she would quietly and discreetly taper off her communication with Sue and they would drift apart as so many of her high-school friends had done already.

She had been secure in the knowledge that Sue

would never find out about the wild, fraudulent statements she had been making. Since Sue's parents had decided to move out of town and closer to their daughter, Jillane had thought she was perfectly safe. There was nothing to bring Sue Talbot back.

Nothing, except this unexpected ten-year reunion!

What in the world was she going to do? Sue would come to town and discover that Jillane had been feeding her a line of bull ten feet long!

Well, she had to pull herself together and try to come up with a plan. *Now think, Jillane!*

Maybe things weren't as hopeless as they seemed. Actually, the only thing that she had to come up with before Sue arrived was a husband who was a famous heart surgeon, a few furs and diamonds, a Porsche, and a fabulous home overlooking a private lake.

Biting her lower lip, she glanced down at the letter before her and reread the closing lines.

". . . don't know exactly when I'll arrive, but sometime within the next week. I want to have plenty of time to run around and visit old acquaintances."

On second thought maybe she could just leave town and pretend she'd never gotten the letter? That might do it. Since there was a strike going on at the telephone company where she worked, she didn't have to be here until a week from tomorrow when she was scheduled to walk the picket line again.

Yes, that was her only choice. She would turn tail and run like the lily-livered coward she was and go

19

visit her parents who lived in Kentucky. She hated to leave Sue stranded, but at the moment, that was the only solution she could come up with.

The sound of the door bell interrupted her feverish planning.

Her little Yorkshire terrier, Petunia, came barreling out of the bedroom full speed ahead and beat her to the door. Seconds later the dog was jumping up and down and yipping excitedly at the top of its lungs.

If there was one thing that Petunia enjoyed, it was company.

Jillane opened her front door a crack, to find a tall man standing before her. "I'm from the telephone company, ma'am. I understand you reported some trouble on your line. . . ." He paused and looked at her more closely. "Jillane?"

Slater Holbrook leaned against the door frame and tried to catch his breath as the door opened a bit wider. A familiar face stared up at him. It was one of the women who worked at the phone company.

Slater took another deep breath. Having just walked up fifteen flights of stairs—no, he had walked up ten flights and *crawled* up the remaining five—he was reminded how out of shape he had become lately.

"Slater? Hi. What are you doing here?" Jillane swung the door open to let him in, a big grin spreading across her face. Slater Holbrook was in management at the phone company, and she had tried to catch his eye more than once since she'd gone to work there.

Petunia stiffened and started to growl, something she rarely did. Slater walked past the dog, eyeing it warily. "Will your dog bite?"

"Petunia?" Jillane laughed. "She wouldn't hurt a flea—" The words had scarcely left her mouth when the dog lunged at him and sank her teeth painfully into his ankle.

"*Petunia!*" Jillane gasped and tried to pry the dog off the poor man as he fought to get loose from the aggressive canine.

Petunia had never done anything like this before!

"Get her off me!" Slater was backing away, frantically trying to shake the furry ball off his foot.

"Petunia! You stop that this minute. . . . This isn't like you at all! Don't you see how naughty—"

"Will you stop trying to reason with the dog and just get her off me!"

The dog was shaking Slater's pant leg like a rag doll and growling ominously as Jillane finally managed to grab hold of her and force her teeth from the cloth of Slater's trousers.

"I thought you said she wouldn't bite!" he challenged.

"Why, my goodness! I don't know what's gotten into her!" Jillane apologized profusely. "She's never bitten anyone in her life!"

"She *just* blew her record," Slater noted irritably, trying to see how bad the attack had been.

"Please, I think you're scaring her," Jillane cautioned.

The dog whined and huddled closer in her mistress's arms.

Slater shot the dog a dirty look. "Scaring her!

21

She just about took my leg off, and you accuse me of scaring *her?*"

"I've already apologized for that. She must be feeling out of sorts today." Jillane patted the dog affectionately. "She won't do it again."

"I hope she won't be offended if I don't take your word for it. You're going to have to lock her up somewhere before I work on your phone," he announced flatly, still rubbing his smarting ankle. "Has she had all her shots?"

"Well, certainly! Did she break the skin?" Jillane glanced down at his ankle anxiously.

"No, I think she just barely nipped me," he conceded. "But I'm not about to let her at me again!"

This was just not going to be her day. Here she was, alone with Slater Holbrook. It was the perfect opportunity to gain some ground with him, and her dog decided to have him for lunch.

"You're a bad dog," Jillane scolded as she carried the cowering dog back to the bedroom. She placed her in the room and shut the door firmly. Returning to the living area, Jillane said, "There. She won't bother you again."

Slater grunted something under his breath. Why him? he thought miserably. As if the strike weren't enough to drive him crazy, the baby had been cutting teeth and had kept him up all night. And now this!

"I must say I'm a little surprised to see *you* here," Jillane confessed. "I thought with the strike going on I wouldn't be able to have the phone fixed for weeks," she admitted, feeling relieved that the commotion was over and her phone would soon be put back in order. She could be on her way to her parents' house by evening.

"We're trying our best to keep things running smoothly until the strike's settled," Slater acknowledged curtly.

Jillane knew that during the strike upper management was committed to filling the workload, a task that was often quite comical. In some cases it had been many years since the managers had worked in the field, but they valiantly carried on, praying that the strike would end soon and that they could get back to their normal routines.

Jillane carefully surveyed the man standing before her. So, fate had deposited Slater Holbrook on her doorstep. How interesting, even if it was poor timing.

His eyes were wandering around the room in search of the telephone he'd been sent to repair. Catching sight of the blue princess phone next to the sofa, he asked, "Is that the phone that's out of order?"

"Yes, it is," she returned brightly, hoping fervently that her hair was in some semblance of order and that she still had a trace of lipstick on.

"What's wrong with it?"

"It won't ring."

"Maybe Petunia knows what happened to it. She loves to chew on things," he noted irritably.

"Oh, I don't think so. She knows she would get in trouble for doing that."

Slater glanced at her sharply. "Maybe she just had another off day."

"No," she defended. "I'm sure she has nothing whatsoever to do with the problem. Maybe you should just take a look before you form any more opinions." It was plain that he wasn't in the best of moods today.

Muttering under his breath, Slater turned and stalked over to the phone.

As if he didn't have enough of a hassle without running into *her* today! This strike was about to get him down. He had had to work sometimes sixteen hours a day to keep up with the unaccustomed workload. And with his new family on top of it all, his nerves were beginning to frazzle.

"Why aren't you out there with your stubborn colleagues, walking the picket line?" he grumbled as he jerked the sofa out and crawled behind to examine the wiring.

"I walked it yesterday," she challenged. "I hope you're not going to try to harass me, Mr. Holbrook, because if you are, I'm going to have to tell on you." She meant it lightly, but he didn't take it that way.

"I wouldn't put it past you," he returned. "This whole strike's a bunch of nonsense. It could have been all over weeks ago and things settled back to normal if your union would listen to reason. Then I wouldn't have to be running all over town busting my rear to do a job I haven't done in ten years!"

"Oh, please stop." She was beginning to tire of his nasty disposition. "You're going to have me in tears in a few minutes over your sad story." In her opinion he was getting just what he deserved, and if it weren't for her empty wallet, she would hope the strike went on another month. "What's the matter? Don't you like new challenges?" Jillane couldn't help but gloat over his obvious dislike of his new duties. He was used to sitting behind a desk all day, giving orders instead of taking them.

"Love it!" he snarled in a muffled voice as he crawled deeper behind the sofa.

"Look." She came over to lean down behind the sofa and confront him. "I didn't have any inkling that *you* would be the one sent out here to repair my phone, so don't take it out on me. But, since you're already here, why don't you just get to work and stop feeling so sorry for yourself? You're not the only one who wants the strike over."

"All you had to do was vote for the very reasonable and fair contract the company offered in the first place," he pointed out stiffly.

"I am not the only person working for the telephone company," she returned evenly. "But it so happens that I didn't approve of some of the benefits they were offering, or should I say . . . lack of benefits they were offering."

"You have a good job and you're paid well for what you do. You people are getting to be a bunch of crybabies, always wanting more," he said without the least bit of sympathy for her plight. "If you went back to work tomorrow morning, you would never be able to make up what this strike has cost your pocketbook, Ms. Simms. Next time you're talking to some of your co-workers, you'd better point that out."

"I will, and next time you're speaking to *your* co-workers, you might remind them that just because they outrank us, we're no different from them. *We* enjoy the nicer things in life too. You know . . . little things make us happy, like being able to buy

25

groceries, buy shoes for our children, pay our utility bills, drive nice new cars just like they do. And, unfortunately, all those things keep costing more every year and our wages can't keep pace." She shrugged philosophically. "What are we supposed to do? Roll over and play dead when the company tosses a few meager crumbs in our direction?"

"You would be extremely upset if I told you what I wanted you to do," he snapped.

"Then I suggest you don't."

"What did you say this phone was doing?"

"It's not ringing. I can call out, but no one can call me."

He grunted something unintelligible and went back to work.

"Well," she announced in a breezy voice, "I think I'll go pack while you do your thing."

"You leaving town?"

"Yes, I think I'll loll around my parents' house for the next week or so," she told him with a yawn. "I really haven't anything else to do until the strike is settled, and from what I heard this morning, they're not even talking now. Guess that means you'll still be working your heinie off for the next few weeks, huh?"

She knew she was pressing her luck, but she couldn't pass up the opportunity to rub it in just a little.

"Looks that way. Then you plan on returning?"

"Yes . . . next week." She frowned. "Why?"

"Just thought you might have found a job you liked."

She was sorely tempted to boot him back farther underneath her couch, but she suppressed the urge. She might be jeopardizing her job by such a rash action, and she needed it too badly.

"I'll be in the bedroom if you need me," she informed him.

"I hardly think I will."

She took a deep breath and bit her lip. He was the one doing the pushing this time.

Leaning across the sofa, Jillane "accidentally" knocked over the vase of flowers that had been sitting on the table for the last week.

Slater sucked in his breath as the cold liquid seeped through his shirt and the stench of the rancid flower water threatened to make him gag.

"Oh, for goodness sake!" she cried in mock dismay. "How clumsy of me! Did I get you wet?"

Crawling out from behind the couch, he stood up, a murderous glare in his snapping gray eyes. "Why, yes, I believe you did."

"Tsk, tsk, tsk. That must be uncomfortable. And the smell . . . it's quite nauseating, isn't it?" she observed calmly.

"Quite."

"Oh, well, that after-shave you're wearing is surely strong enough to cover up the unpleasant odor," she assured brightly. She had been strangely attracted to his delicious smell from the moment he entered the room, but *he* would never know it. "I should have thrown those flowers away days ago," she conceded, reaching over to return the overturned vase to its original position. "Well, I'm sure you'll dry out in no time at all."

"Could I have a towel to help me along?" he prodded snidely, trying to ignore the feel of the nasty water trickling down his spine. He unhooked his tool belt and laid it on a chair.

"Well . . ." To his irritation she paused to think about his question. "Ordinarily I don't think you phone repair men are supposed to bother the customer with such personal requests, but I suppose since I need to wipe the water off the floor and table, anyway, I could make an exception in this case." She grinned wickedly. "I'll be right back."

As she scurried out of the room Slater unbuttoned his shirt and stripped it off impatiently. He started sopping up the moisture, grumbling all the time about that cotton-pickin', featherbrained female he was forced to endure on top of everything else.

The peal of the door bell interrupted his grousing. He glanced toward the hallway down which Jillane had disappeared.

The bell rang again, and he stepped out to the hallway and called out sharply. "Someone's at your door!"

There was no answer as the bell sounded once again.

"Oh, for heaven's sake!" He shot another worried glance at the front door. "Hey! Someone's at the door!"

Petunia had started to wail in the bedroom, and he could hear her nails clicking against the door as she ricocheted off the wood, trying to get out of the room.

Jillane was either goading him again or else she had gone stone-deaf, because she was refusing to answer his calls, he thought irritably.

The bell rang again, longer this time. He stalked

over to the door and jerked it open before the dog got out and came after him. "Yeah?"

"Oh, my . . ." The blond woman standing before him drew in her breath. Her eyes widened in appreciation as she took in the sight of Slater Holbrook's impressive bare chest. It was covered in a cloud of dark blond hair and looked as broad as the doorway he was standing in. "Uh . . . is this Jillane Marcus's residence?"

"Jillane? Yeah, sure, she lives here," he granted.

The blonde's face lit up radiantly. "Stanley!" She lunged forward, threw her arms around Slater's neck, and hugged him with undisguised zeal. "We meet at last! I'm Sue!"

CHAPTER TWO

"Who?"

"Sue! Sue Talbot . . . Jillane's friend from high school," she prompted. "Oh, Stanley, I can't tell you what a thrill it is to finally meet you!" Sue's grip tightened around Slater's neck. He staggered backward and tried to steady himself with the added weight clinging to his neck like flypaper.

"Jillane! *Get in here,*" he roared, wondering what the devil was going on now. Whoever this woman was, she obviously had mistaken him for someone else—and she certainly didn't have a shy bone in her body!

"Let me look at you, Stanley." Sue pulled back, and her eyes hungrily surveyed the masculine physique spread out before her like a royal banquet. Slater protectively clutched his soiled shirt in front of him as the woman's eyes literally devoured him.

"Uh-uh-uh-uh. Jillane has really outdone herself," she pronounced in awe.

"Jillane!"

Sue's brow raised slightly at the tone of desperation his voice had now taken.

"What do you want?" came an impatient female voice from the hallway.

"I think you'd better get out here," Slater called back, grinning lamely at a puzzled Sue. "You have company."

"Stanley, I can't tell you how happy I am to find you home," Sue proceeded as he hastily pulled his rumpled shirt back on. It had a most peculiar, almost offensive odor about it, Sue noticed. "Jillane has told me what a horrible schedule you work under. I thought it would probably be days before I got to meet her famous husband!"

Slater glanced up blankly as he was stuffing his shirttail in his pants and grinned weakly again. "Jillane!"

"Will you stop shouting, for heaven's sake! You're going to have the neighbors . . . *Sue!*"

Jillane had entered the room and stopped dead in her tracks as Sue turned around and gave her a dazzling smile.

"Jillane, dear! How wonderful to see you again." Sue crossed the room and embraced her friend warmly. "You look wonderful!"

"Thanks, you do too. . . ." As usual, Sue looked stunning, Jillane thought, surveying her in a near state of shock.

"I was just telling Stanley how marvelously thrilled I am to meet him," Sue exclaimed, turning her attention back to Slater. "Why, he's everything you said he was, Jillane. How in the world did you ever trap such a hunk of man!" She smiled up at Slater and possessively looped her arm through his.

Jillane cast a panic-stricken glance in his direction as he opened his mouth to correct her obvious misconception.

31

"Slate . . . Stanley, darling!" Jillane stammered, rushing over to drag him away from Sue's clutches. "Oh, my goodness, this is Sue . . . you know, my very dearest friend whom I've spoken to you about on numerous occasions!"

"I know she's Sue, but who in the hell is Stan—"

Jillane shot him a desperate look, praying that he would go along with her for the moment and keep quiet. "Sue's here to attend our ten-year reunion. Isn't that nice?"

"Super. But, who's Sta—"

Jillane pinched him painfully in the ribs to silence him.

Slater grimaced and shot her a murderous glare, but, mercifully, he didn't finish his twice-aborted question.

"I—I must admit, I didn't expect you so soon, Sue," Jillane stammered. "I only received your letter this morning."

"Really?" She looked puzzled. "That's strange. I mailed it over a week ago."

Jillane's heart sank. Of all the times for the post office to screw up, *why* did it have to be now?

"I hope I haven't inconvenienced you?"

"Oh!" Jillane gave a carefree laugh. "Not at all. We are thrilled to have you." She stepped closer to Slater and pinched him again. "Aren't we, dear?"

"Well, I must admit, I thought I was in the wrong place at first, but the cabdriver assured me that this was the address I had given him." Sue looked around the small apartment, and Jillane could have sworn she saw her wrinkle her nose for one brief moment.

"My goodness! I bet you did! It just occurred to

me that I didn't tell you about selling our house and building a new one, did I?"

"No . . ."

Jillane hazarded a glance to see how Slater was taking all of this, and as she feared, he was staring at her with his mouth slack.

"It's just all happened so quickly, hasn't it, Stanley?" Before "Stanley" could answer, she rushed on. "Our house by the lake sold practically overnight, and since my lease hadn't run out on this apartment yet, we were forced to move back here until the new house is finished."

"Oh? Well, I'm sure this is quite a comedown from what you've been living in," Sue noted sympathetically. "Your home overlooking the lake sounded quite impressive."

"Oh, yes. Quite. But we love it here. It's so . . . down to earth."

Sue's eyes told Jillane that she clearly agreed. "When do you expect your new home to be ready for occupancy?" Sue turned her attention back to Slater.

Once again he was forced to answer lamely. "I really couldn't say." He turned to Jillane. "Could I speak to you in the kitchen for a moment?"

"Certainly . . . dear. Will you excuse us, Sue? Stanley will be leaving for work shortly, and he had something he wanted to discuss with me before he left. Please make yourself at home. I'll be right back."

"Don't worry about me. I'd like to freshen my makeup and just sit and rest for a while. I think I have jet lag. Do you have surgery scheduled for today, Stanley?"

Slater turned to Jillane. "Do I have surgery?"

"No, just your usual rounds at the hospital," she prompted.

Slater turned back to Sue obediently. "No, no surgery. Just my usual rounds at the hospital."

"I find your work so . . . so fascinating," Sue crooned. "Don't you find it utterly stimulating?"

"Only when my screwdriver hits the wrong connection."

"Beg your pardon?"

"Stanley! Look at the time!" Jillane shoved him through the kitchen doorway before he could say another word and slammed the door.

They both turned to face each other in a huff of anger. "You want to tell me what the devil was going on out there?" Slater demanded impatiently.

"Please . . ." Jillane glanced apprehensively toward the doorway. "Lower your voice. Sue will hear us!" she pleaded.

"I don't care if she hears us," he said heartlessly. "That was the craziest conversation I've ever heard in my life! *Who* is Stanley?"

"I don't know a Stanley."

"What do you mean, you don't know a Stanley? You were talking as if you were married to him!"

"Well, I am . . . or I'm supposed to be," she admitted glumly.

"What was he? Your fiancé?"

"No. Not really."

"Your lover?"

"Mmmmm . . . no, not that either."

"Hey, why don't we just stop playing twenty

questions and *you* tell me who the dickens that woman out there thinks I am."

"Stanley Marcus."

Slater slammed his hand down on the kitchen counter and leaned his head against the cabinet doors in exasperation. "You just said you didn't know a Stanley!"

"I don't. He's just my imaginary, world-renowned, heart-surgeon husband. I made him up," she confessed wearily.

"You what?"

"You heard me. I made Stanley up. He doesn't exist."

"Well, that lady out there sure seems to think he does!"

"I know. I'm in big trouble." Jillane sank down on one of the kitchen chairs and stared bleakly out the window.

Slater leaned against the counter and crossed his arms, turning his eyes upward. "Why me, Lord?"

Jillane hazarded a cautious glance to see if anyone had answered him, then returned her gaze to him. "I know this all seems strange, but I can explain."

Although the last thing in the world Slater needed was another delay in his work schedule, he could sense that she needed someone to talk to more.

"Five minutes. I'll give you five minutes, then I'm leaving," he warned.

So, for the next few minutes Jillane confessed all the wild fabrications she'd made up and had led Sue to believe for the past two years. Slater listened attentively, finding some of the material outrageous and unbelievable at times, not hesitating to tell her so.

"That has to be the most childish thing I have ever heard," he told her irritably as she finished.

"I know. There just didn't seem to be any way to stop the lies," she argued. "I knew what I was doing was wrong and immature, but Sue has always been able to put me on the defensive. You met her . . . it won't take you long to find out everything she has is *always* better than anyone else's—or so she implies—and I just got tired of always feeling like I'm the inferior nobody."

"A person who would make you feel like you had to lie about your life isn't worth the time of day," Slater noted. "Why would you let her drag you down to her level?"

"I guess I'm not a very nice person, either, or I wouldn't have."

"Well, whether you're nice or not is beside the point. It's time for the lies to stop. You're going to have to go out there and tell her that your life is every bit as good as hers, only you aren't married to a heart surgeon, you're not in the process of building a new home, and the Porsche was something you're only hoping to own someday."

"I can't do that!" Jillane pleaded. "Don't you see? She would laugh me right out of town!"

"She doesn't even live here anymore!"

"But we both have the same friends, Slater. I would *die* if I went to the reunion and she told everyone what a farce I am . . . and you mark my words, she would do it in a blink of an eye!"

"I thought you said she was your friend!"

"We are! But, we're really not, either," she admitted.

"This doesn't make one bit of sense." Slater ran his fingers through his curly, dark blond hair. "If you both have the same friends, they are going to tell her you're not married."

"No, they won't. I haven't kept in close touch with the people I went to school with. And, besides, the majority of them have all moved out of town and will only be back here for the reunion this weekend." She sat up on the edge of her chair and faced him. "Oh, don't you see? If I can only bluff my way through these next few days and send Sue home without ever finding out about my little fibs, I promise I'll never tell another lie as long as I live!"

"I don't see how you could possibly do that. Where are you going to come up with a husband between now and when you walk out of this room?" Slater snorted.

"Well, that's what I was sort of wanting to talk to you about. . . ."

His eyes narrowed suspiciously. "Now wait a minute. I certainly hope you're not thinking what I think you're thinking."

"What do you think I'm thinking?"

"I think you're thinking that you're going to get *me* hooked up with this little scheme, and you can just think again!"

"You're not married," she challenged. She knew he wasn't. It was a well-known fact around the company that Slater was a bachelor, and by all outward appearances he planned to stay that way.

"No, and I'm here to tell you that I don't intend

to be, either, imaginary or otherwise!" he announced flatly.

"Is that a firm no?" she ventured hesitantly. It certainly sounded like one, but it wouldn't hurt to make absolutely sure.

"Shall I spell it out for you? N-o. No. I will *not* become involved in your madness."

"Well, look, did I ask you to become involved?" she snapped.

"No, but I could tell by the look on your face that you were getting ready to."

"I can't see how it would hurt one tiny bit for you to help me out in a pinch," she pointed out. "Sue already thinks you're Stanley. You would only have to carry out the deception for one measly little week, and you wouldn't have to be around more than a few hours each day," she stressed. "Sue knows that Stanley has a hectic schedule, and she wouldn't think anything was wrong at all if you just put in a brief appearance once a day and spent a few nights here. And that shouldn't be too hard since you're having to work so much overtime. Now, would that kill you?"

"Probably. If it didn't, those fifteen flights of stairs every day would."

"Those stairs only bother you because you're so out of shape," she noted crossly.

"Whatever the reason, I'm not doing it." He recrossed his arms stubbornly. Why he was standing here wasting his time talking to her was beyond him. He still had to finish the day's work and go through the applications he had for yet another housekeeper before he could get some badly needed sleep.

"Okay." She heaved a sigh of exasperation. "If you won't do it out of the goodness of your heart, let's get professional about this. Let me rent you for the week."

"You have *got* to be kidding!" he said incredulously. "Rent me!"

"That's right. I'm desperate, Slater! Surely even you can see that. Now, I'm willing to pay you one hundred dollars to pose as my husband for one week. The only thing you would be expected to do is stick your head in the doorway once in a while and smile. Now admit it. You're not dumb enough to pass up such easy money."

His arms dropped back to his side in disgust. "That does it. I'm getting out of here."

Jillane stood up and blocked his exit. "You are bound and determined to make this hard on me, aren't you? All right. Name your price."

"I don't have a price!"

"Everyone has a price," she corrected, pushing him down into one of the chairs. "Now think about it. Don't you have something you've really been wanting to buy? I know you guys in management make a heck of a lot more money than I do, but surely you can't have everything in the world you want," she reasoned patiently, keeping a firm hold on him to keep him seated.

Slater struggled to get out of her grasp, forcing her to plop down on his lap to hold him in place.

His gray eyes looked at her indignantly. "What do you think you're doing? Get off my lap!"

"I will. Just as soon as you listen to reason."

"You are not going to 'rent' me, even if we sit here all weekend," he warned.

She had to admit that he was cute. He had blond curly hair, a thick, blond mustache, and the nicest eyes she had ever seen . . . if only fire hadn't been shooting out of them.

"Would you like a nice little vacation somewhere?" she tempted, batting her eyelashes flirtatiously. Maybe she could use feminine wiles to persuade him.

"No."

"How about some new clothes?"

"No."

"Season tickets to your favorite baseball team?"

He faltered somewhat. "No. Besides, my favorite team is the Yankees," he taunted.

Gad. That ruled that one out. California and New York were a little too far apart to tempt him with that morsel. She'd have to try another approach.

"Mmmmm . . . I bet with all this overtime you've been having, you've had to miss seeing a lot of games, haven't you?"

His eyes narrowed. She had hit a sore spot with that one. Slater was an avid baseball fan, and he *had* missed four games already due to his work, and the strike was nowhere near over yet.

Jillane brought her face closer to his, her eyes growing devious. "How about a videocassette recorder so you can tape the games and watch them later?"

"A videocassette recorder?" His face grew thoughtful. That would be nice. He had been thinking about buying one, but he had so many other obligations at the moment and he hated to

40

let go of the money. "What kind?" he ventured hesitantly.

"Any kind you want."

"Could I have a videocassette recorder?" He named an expensive brand.

"How much is it?" It didn't really matter. She would have to charge it and make payments on it for the next few years, but it would be worth it if she could get him to agree.

"I thought it didn't matter. I thought you were desperate."

She stiffened with resentment. He had her under a barrel and he knew it.

"It doesn't. You can have the VCR *if* you'll agree to be Stanley Marcus just until Sue leaves."

"Oh, brother. It's tempting . . . but no, I can't." Slater sighed heavily. He would not sell himself for a videocassette recorder, no matter how badly he wanted one.

"Well, for heaven's sake, why not!" she rebuked.

"Because the whole idea is mind-boggling." The last thing in the world he needed was another kid to look after, and if he took on this job, that's exactly what he would have—in the form of Jillane Simms.

"Now look, Slater." She eyed him straightforwardly. "Obviously I'm desperate. There *has* to be something you want or need. Just name your price." She fully realized that she was leaving the door wide-open for all sorts of propositions but decided that she could always backtrack if anything unsavory came up.

"Nope, nothing. I'm telling you the truth. I'm a happy man. There isn't one thing I want except for

41

a reliable housekeeper and a million dollars, and I know you can't give me either of those."

Jillane lifted her brow. "A housekeeper?"

"Yeah, preferably one with nerves of steel. The fourth one this month just walked out on me."

"Are you that hard to work for?" She knew he could be a little testy at times, but enough to go through four housekeepers in one month?

"I'm not hard to work for," he denied. "It's my six kids who tend to make them a little edgy."

Six kids! Jillane immediately slithered off his lap. "You have six children?" Brother! Granted, she was desperate, but not desperate enough to get tied up with a man with six kids! "Well, it was worth a try. Thanks for listening," she dismissed abruptly.

Noticing her swift change of mood, Slater's cynical grin tugged at the corners of his mouth. So, she was like all the other women he had met in the past few months. When they found out that Slater Holbrook had a whole batch of kids, they lost interest pronto. Deciding that it would be fun to watch her squirm for a minute or two, he inquired innocently, "Did I say something to upset you?"

"Oh, no. I just realized what a pest I'm making out of myself. When did you get six kids?" she added suspiciously. "I was under the distinct impression that you were a bachelor." She couldn't imagine how that little fact had escaped office gossip! Before he could answer, though, she quickly decided that she really didn't care how he got them. He had them, and that was all that mattered. "My, look at the time. You're really running late now." She edged toward the doorway. She might as well get back in there, confess to Sue, and get it over with.

"Well"—Slater leaned back in his chair and casually pulled a cigarette from his shirt pocket, devilishly ignoring her effort to dismiss him—"I figure I'm already running two hours behind, so what's another few minutes? You old enough to smoke yet?" He politely extended the pack of menthol filters to her.

"I'm old enough to do anything I want," she snapped, shaking her head in refusal. "Just how old do you think I am, anyway?" It irked her, the way he was treating her like a child.

"I don't know. Nineteen . . . twenty?"

"Twenty-eight!"

He was momentarily surprised. "You don't look it."

"Thanks, but I can assure you I am, so stop treating me like one of your children."

Slater shot her a lazy grin. "You seemed to tense up a bit at the mention of my children," he remarked, snapping his lighter shut and taking a long drag off the cigarette.

"I can't imagine why you would think that," she murmured guiltily.

"You like children?"

"They're all right. My goodness. Just *look* at that clock. It *is* getting late."

"You don't *sound* as if you like children." He seemed determined to carry on the conversation that she was determined to end.

She glanced at him uneasily. "I do like children . . . I mean, I like other people's children. I come from a family of ten myself."

"Other people's children?" He sensed her uneasiness concerning the subject and pressed onward.

"Yes. Other people's children. Personally I don't want any myself," she confessed.

"How interesting." He took another drag off his cigarette.

"Well, don't look at me as if I'm some sort of freak," she protested, trying to ignore the condemnation she read in his eyes. "It just so happens that I come from a large family, and I'm a little tired of sacrificing my privacy, that's all. If *you* wanted six children, I'm happy for you. But don't try to make me feel guilty because I like sleeping in my own bed and having a bathroom all to myself for the first time in my life."

"How interesting," he repeated.

She nervously checked her watch again. "You'd better be rushing off."

"Listen." He was about to slit his own throat, but he was powerless to resist the temptation. Besides, she would never accept what he was about to propose, so he would be off the hook with a clear conscience and on his way. "I've been thinking about our conversation earlier." His smile was positively angelic.

"You have?" Her smile was lame, to say the least. He wouldn't! He just couldn't be so cruel as to propose some sort of compromise if she would consent to being his housekeeper!

"Yes, I've decided on something that I really want. Your services as a housekeeper."

"Uh . . . I've decided I'd better tell Sue the truth," she admitted hastily. "You were right.

44

That's the only logical thing to do. Tell the truth and face the music." She laughed.

"True. And Sue and *all* your friends will probably laugh about it for months to come," he agreed, laughing with her.

Jillane's face fell a mile.

"I can't be your housekeeper," she snapped. He had his nerve!

"Why not? You said *anything* I wanted. And that's what I want. A housekeeper."

"I said that before I knew you had *six* children," she defended. "Heavenly days! Haven't you ever heard of moderation, Mr. Holbrook?"

His grin widened. "This is going to blow your mind completely, Ms. Simms, but I didn't father a single one of them."

Her mouth sagged. "You're joking. What happened? Did your wife walk out on you and leave you with all *her* kids?"

"No. My best friend and his wife were killed in an automobile wreck. I was left as the children's guardian."

She gasped. "They left you with all that responsibility?"

Slater stiffened with resentment, all the mirth draining out of him now. "I love those children, Jillane. They are a handful, but they're very special to me."

Jillane immediately felt guilty for being so flip. "I'm sorry . . . it just seems strange to think that you have six children and not one of them is yours. . . ." Her voice trailed off weakly.

"Well, I feel like they're all mine, and at the moment I need a housekeeper. Mom and Dad are staying with me right now, but they're both getting old and can't stand the hassle. They want to go home. So you and I might be able to work out a deal until I can find a permanent housekeeper . . . that is, if you're still interested?" He loved to see the way her face had gone a sickly green; it would be interesting to see just how desperate she really was.

Jillane bit her lower lip pensively. Six children. Could anything be worth dealing with six children? She glanced over at Slater and her stomach fluttered. On the other hand, it wouldn't be so unpleasant to be in his company for the next few weeks. Maybe she should check this out further before absolutely refusing.

"How old are they?" she ventured hesitantly.

"All the way from nineteen to two and a half, but the nineteen-year-old is getting married in August," he added.

"And if I agreed to this, how long would it be for?"

"I really couldn't say. I'm in the process of looking for someone right now, but with the strike going on and all the extra hours I'm putting in, it could take a few weeks. But I don't see why that should be any problem. You're not doing anything right now but walking the picket line, are you?"

Hummm . . . a few weeks . . . six kids . . . mountains of laundry . . . cooking for an army . . . clutter, messes, and complete chaos . . . She just *couldn't!* Her eyes unwillingly went back to his rugged good looks and lingered wistfully. Wellll, maybe she could.

His former good humor returned when he saw

the look of distress flooding her features. "Well, I can see you're not interested." He shrugged. He had had his fun, and the time was right to leave.

She calmly stepped in his path as he rose from the table and headed for the door.

"Just a few weeks?"

He backed away warily. "Yeah . . . a few . . ."

"And you'll be a convincing Stanley Marcus if I do this?"

"Now look . . ." Surely she wasn't going to accept his offer. "Telling the truth is far better—"

"I'll do it," she cut in decisively. "I'm beginning to get a little bored doing nothing, anyway. Of course, you'll have to pay me the same salary you would pay a permanent housekeeper, but it will be worth it if you'll help me get through this week. Besides, I could use the extra money until the strike's over."

"You're really going to accept this offer?" His face was every bit as sickly-looking as hers was.

"Certainly." She smiled weakly. A few weeks wouldn't be all that bad, and since she was used to a large family, she could stand it . . . for a few weeks. "But you have to live up to your end of the bargain," she warned. "Sue is never to suspect that you are anyone but Stanley Marcus, heart surgeon."

"I can't believe this." He sighed in disgust at the way his plan had suddenly backfired. She *was* desperate! "Okay, I will be Stanley Marcus, if all I have to do is put in one appearance a day," he relented. That probably wouldn't kill him. With the hours he was working, he would barely have time to lie down and catch a little sleep before it was time to be back on duty. And it *would* take the pressure of finding a housekeeper off him for a few days.

"I may require a little more effort on your part than that," she ventured, "but I'll try to keep it to a minimum. Since your parents are with the children, can you come back here in the evenings for the next week and sleep—"

"I don't know about that. This thing could get out of hand real fast. . . ." Glancing at her blossoming curves, he was suddenly reminded that he wasn't talking to one of his kids now. "I'm not at all convinced we should get into any of this."

Jillane's face turned stormy. "Well, don't look at me as if I'm trying to proposition you!"

"Then why do you want me to come over here and sleep with you?"

"I didn't mean for you to 'sleep' with me! For heaven's sake! Where would you get a screwball idea like that? I only meant . . . Sue would think it strange if you didn't stay here nights," she finished helplessly.

"Oh." He at least had the decency to look a little ashamed of his far-out assumption. "Well, I just wanted to be clear on what you meant. And another thing. I'll agree to hanging around here some this week, but I refuse to tell any direct lies. If Sue wants to think I'm Stanley Marcus, that's her problem, but I'm sure not going to tell her I am."

"That's up to you. But you can rest assured that your virtue is perfectly safe with me. And, if I have to take care of *your* house and children, you have to at least be decent to me in front of Sue. After all, we're supposed to be newlyweds, and if you go

48

around snarling at me the way you have been, she'll know something's wrong."

"Don't give me any reason to snarl and I won't," he said curtly.

"I have never given you a reason to snarl. You, Mr. Holbrook, are a born snarler. Face it. Now, Sue will be wondering what's taking us so long. We'd better get back out there."

Slater looked at his watch and checked the time. "Thanks to you I'm running another hour behind," he snarled.

She smiled pointedly. "See? You're snarling again. Is my phone fixed?"

"Yes, I'd just finished when you spilled the water down my back."

"That was an accident."

"Sure it was."

They walked out of the kitchen together to find Sue just emerging from the bathroom. "There you are, you lovebirds!"

"Yes." Jillane gave a carefree laugh and hooked her arm through Slater's. "Stanley just wanted a few minutes alone with me, didn't you, dear?"

"If you say so."

"Dear, I hate to ask, but before you leave, would you go down and get Sue's luggage and bring it up for her?"

Slater's face paled. "Up all those stairs?"

Jillane smiled at Sue. "He still isn't used to those stairs. I keep telling him that they're such marvelous exercise!"

"Oh, that would be so thoughtful of you, Stanley!" Sue exclaimed. "I left them in the foyer downstairs. There are four large bags and three small ones."

Slater looked aghast. "How long did you say you were staying?"

"Only a week. I'm afraid Arnold would have a fit if I were gone any longer," she purred.

"How is Arnold?" Jillane inquired politely, not really wanting to hear about Sue's *fabulously* wealthy president of an oil company fiancé.

"Wonderful, dear, simply wonderful. I can't wait until you meet him. He wanted to come with me, but I'm afraid his time is never his own. You know how it is . . . meeting with his stockbrokers . . . his banker . . . his accountant."

"Oh, yes. Stanley has the same problem. His time is definitely not his own, either," she said, empathizing with Sue.

Slater looked at her and shook his head in disbelief at the hot air floating around the room. "I'll get the luggage."

Thirty minutes and two trips up the stairway later, he sagged against the door frame and wheezed in exhaustion. "I . . . gasp . . . gasp, think that about does it . . . gasp."

"Thank you, dear. You're such a gentleman." Jillane walked over and pecked him on the cheek perfunctorily.

"If you . . . gasp . . . say so . . . gasp . . . dear."

"I say so." She pushed him away and turned back to Sue. "Well, Sue. You and I can get reacquainted while Stanley runs on to work."

"Is there anything else . . . gasp . . . I can do for you . . . dear?"

50

"No. I think that covers it, Stanley."

"Well." He stepped forward and draped his arm around her waist. "Come and kiss daddy good-bye. He's off to make another million."

Before Jillane knew what was happening, he pulled her up close and kissed her.

Sue watched with envy as he drew Jillane closer to his broad frame and hugged her affectionately . . . just like any newlywed bridegroom would do.

When they parted a few moments later, Jillane gazed at him, stunned.

"Anything else, dear?"

"No, nothing else . . . dear," she parroted weakly.

"Good. See you later." He turned to Sue. "So happy to meet you. I do hope you and . . . my lovely wife have a nice visit," he stated with excessive politeness. "But now I really must get to work."

"I understand, Stanley." Sue's small hand covered his. "I'm looking forward to spending more time with you."

"Thanks. It should be interesting for all of us." He lifted her hand and kissed it lightly, then winked at Jillane before he hurriedly slipped out the front door.

CHAPTER THREE

Good heavens! What had she gotten herself into this time? Six children and Slater Holbrook would be all it would take to push her over the edge in the next few weeks. With any luck at all he would reconsider and not come back this evening. With *any* luck . . .

As the evening wore on, however, Jillane became more nervous, going over to the window to peer anxiously down to the street.

By ten o'clock, only the deserted street with its one dim streetlight glowing eerily in the gathering fog met her worried eye.

"You're acting like the typical new bride." Sue laughed as she set aside the magazine she had been reading and stretched lazily. "Although I must admit that if I were married to that delicious hunk of man, I would be anxious to see him come home, too."

The two women had talked nonstop after Slater had left the apartment a few hours ago, catching up on all the gossip. But now they were both talked out. They had taken their baths and were in their loungewear, waiting for Jillane's "husband" to return. Since the hour was growing so late, Jillane was about to throw in the towel and confess the whole story.

She sighed morosely and let the curtain drop back in place. How was she going to tell Sue that "Stanley" was not coming home?

Oh, she could always fall back on the excuse that an emergency had arisen at the hospital and he couldn't get away. Sue would certainly believe that, but would one more lie be worth the effort? And what happened when he didn't come home tomorrow night, either, or the next . . . or the next? It would be hard to convince her friend that Stanley spent all his time in surgery.

Wouldn't it just be easier to tell the truth and get it over with?

That evening, Jillane had carefully avoided telling Sue anything that wasn't the truth during their long conversation. She was aware that she had sounded pretty evasive at times, but she had decided from now on that she was going to be as truthful as possible. It wasn't hard to see what a hopeless predicament she had gotten herself into by deceit, and she promised herself that if she got out of this mess without being made to look like a fool, she would never tell another lie as long as she lived.

"I really hope I won't inconvenience you and Stanley by staying a week or so, but I did so want to look up some of my old friends." Sue broke into her thoughts.

"No, not at all," Jillane assured. "We're happy to have you. I only wish Arnold could have made the trip with you."

"Arnie is such a doll." Sue sighed as she toyed

53

with a short strand of her stylish blond hair. "I can't wait until you meet him. He isn't as good-looking as your Stanley, but he's such a gentleman . . . and so rich too."

"I'm sure he's very nice," Jillane murmured.

"Oh, he is. And so rich."

"Yes, I believe you've mentioned that before." By now Jillane was sick and tired of hearing about Arnold's bank account. "Are you sure you wouldn't like a cup of tea before you go to bed?" An unseasonable cold snap had descended on the town, and it was becoming quite chilly in the room. "A fire would feel good tonight."

"I didn't realize it got this cold here in the summer."

"Oh, it doesn't. This is unusual."

"Well, I think I'll pass on the tea. What time does Stanley usually get home?" Sue yawned. "I'd like to say good night to him before I turn in."

"I don't know. It varies."

"I'll bet you live an exciting life. Do you and Stanley socialize a lot with the upper crust?" Sue's eyes had taken on a look of gleeful expectation as she thought about all the millionaires Jillane undoubtably rubbed elbows with every day.

"Not really."

"Oh, now, come on!" Sue sat up on the edge of her seat and grinned knowingly. "Don't be so modest. A man in Stanley's position would have to know some pretty influential people."

Jillane turned from her vigil at the window and took a deep breath before she spoke. "Sue. I . . . I don't know how to tell you this, but . . ."

54

Her courage threatened to fail her once more as Sue glanced expectantly up at her. "Yes?"

"It's about . . . Stanley. He isn't . . ."

"Isn't?" she prompted, sitting up straighter.

"He isn't—"

The sound of the door bell prevented her from going any further. She closed her eyes and took a long, deep breath. *He isn't going to let me down after all,* she finished silently.

"Who in the world could that be at this hour?" Sue wondered.

"I'm afraid it's Stanley."

"Ringing the door bell?"

"He's probably forgotten his key again," Jillane hedged, making her way to the door.

Slater was propped against the doorjamb, fighting to regain his breath after climbing the long flight of stairs.

"Hi . . . gasp . . . gasp."

"Hi. I was beginning to get worried about you."

"Why?"

"Because it's getting so late and I thought . . ." She glanced over her shoulder to see if Sue was listening.

She was.

". . . I thought you might be unable to get back home tonight."

"No. I just got tied up. A couple of emergencies came in and I had to help." He summoned the strength to push himself up straighter and enter the apartment.

"Oh, Stanley. There you are!" Sue rose from the sofa and made her way over to greet him. "I think you wife was about to send a posse out after you."

Slater's smile was weary as he slipped off his jacket and tossed it on the nearest chair. "I'm sorry I'm so late, but it was business. . . ."

"You look simply exhausted." Sue sympathized, and Jillane had to agree with her. He looked as if he were about ready to drop in his tracks.

"Have you had anything to eat?" Jillane inquired sympathetically.

"I don't think so . . . at least, not since breakfast."

"Come on in the kitchen and I'll see what I can find," she offered.

"Thanks, but I think I'll just take a shower and hit the sack. I have to be back on duty by seven in the morning," he yawned.

"So early?" Sue clearly looked disappointed. "I was hoping we could all have breakfast together."

"That would have been nice," Slater murmured politely, and looked to Jillane for quick salvation.

"Why don't you go on to bed and I'll be in shortly," Jillane offered hurriedly. "I'll just turn out the lights and help Sue make up her bed."

"Fine."

All three stood staring at each other uneasily.

"Well, aren't you going . . ." Jillane prompted.

"Yeah. Which way?"

She'd completely forgotten that he had no idea where her bedroom was.

"Oh! Well, since the sofa makes out into a comfortable bed, I thought Sue could sleep here and you and I would go ahead and sleep in our room."

"I wouldn't think of putting you out of your own bed," Sue said, crooning. "I don't want to be any trouble at all."

"No, no, you're not," Slater reassured hastily. "I'll just sorta mosey on down the hallway and try to find my bed." He smiled bravely.

"I'm sure you can't miss it, dear. It's the same old room two doors down on the left that we've always slept in," Jillane offered.

While Slater casually ambled off in search of his room, Jillane helped Sue make up her bed.

"If you need anything, just let me know," Jillane invited. "I'll tell . . . Stanley to try to keep from disturbing you in the morning when he goes to work."

"I really like him," Sue said for what must have been the tenth time since she had gotten there. "He seems so . . . so casual and down-to-earth. Why, I figured he would be wearing those expensive Italian suits and dressing to fit his image, but here he is just as casual as casual can be."

Jillane's smile was weak. Yes, Stanley was dressed rather modestly in a pair of jeans and a plaid shirt. She knew this was only Sue's snooty way of asking "What the devil is he doing dressed like that," instead of coming right out and saying, "What the devil is he doing dressed like that?"

Leaning closer, Jillane whispered mysteriously. "I've been meaning to warn you . . . he's rather eccentric at times. So, if he happens to do or say anything that doesn't particularly make any sense, just overlook it." She smiled patiently. "You know how these . . . wealthy men can be at times."

Sue's eyes widened. "How exciting! He's really eccentric?"

Jillane nodded solemnly. "He really is." And to her that was the honest truth.

"Oh, my," Sue breathed reverently. "How thrilling."

"Well, if you don't need anything else, I'll be running along," Jillane announced. Slater was probably standing in her bedroom, wondering what to do next.

"Oh, don't worry. I'm just fine. Run along to your husband."

"Good night."

"Good night."

When Jillane approached her bedroom door, she paused when she saw that it was closed. She had visions of walking in on Slater half undressed. Surely he was planning on spending the night here or he would never have come back, so she hesitantly tapped on the door.

Seconds later she opened the door a crack and cautiously peeked in. "Oh, dear. Petunia!"

She had completely forgotten that the dog was in the bedroom when she had sent Slater in there alone.

"Good. It's you." Slater glanced up in relief from his position on the bed where the dog had him cornered.

Jillane hurried into the room and locked the door behind her. "Gosh, I'm sorry, Slater. Why didn't you yell?" She rushed over and picked up the growling bundle, putting her firmly in her basket next to the bed.

"I tried. You two were talking a mile a minute and didn't hear me!" Once again his voice sounded irritated and out of sorts as he shot Petunia a dirty look. "That dog hates me."

"She does not. For some reason you just seem to

put her on the defensive," Jillane protested, looking fondly at the little dog who had settled down obediently and gone right to sleep.

She had to bite back a giggle as she noted Slater's large, masculine frame cowering in the middle of her frilly yellow bedspread. He looked like a clump of ragweed sitting in a daisy patch.

"I see you found the bedroom," Jillane said conversationally. She shifted around on one foot, wondering what she should do next.

The realization that she was alone in her bedroom with a man who would be staying with her for the next week suddenly hit her, and her knees turned weak. What had she let herself in for? She barely knew him! What if he were some sort of pervert who would try to take advantage of the situation she had nearly forced him into?

For a few moments she frantically searched her mind for any information she knew about Slater Holbrook. Unhappily she confessed to herself that she knew very little other than the office gossip, which really couldn't ever be counted on.

He was quite a bit older than she was. That she knew. If she were to guess, she would have to estimate him as being somewhere in his late thirties. She thought she had heard that he'd been married once, but she had no idea to whom or what the circumstances were for the breakup. He had a reputation for being a loner, or at least he had never made any overtures toward the women in his department. Because of his apparent inaccessibility to the opposite sex, some of the women at the phone company had declared open season on him simply because he was a challenge. As far

59

as Jillane knew, no one had bagged him as yet, and since she hadn't actually heard anything derogatory about him, she supposed she would be safe in his presence.

"I know you must be tired and want to get to bed. Feel free to use the bathroom first," she invited politely.

"How are we going to work this sleeping arrangement?" he asked, looking around warily. One bed. That's all there was in this room to sleep in. Why had he ever let her talk him into such a ridiculous mess! He could boot his rear end from here to Texas if it would do any good, but it looked like he was stuck with the situation for a while, whether he liked it or not. Several times that evening he had tossed around the idea of backing out of the whole arrangement but had finally admitted to himself that he was as desperate as she was. "There's only one bed in here."

"I've been thinking about that." She plopped down next to him on the bed and crossed her legs. "I suppose since I'm not working and don't need my rest quite as much as you do, I should be the one to sleep on the floor in a sleeping bag."

"That might be all right for one night," he reasoned, "but for a whole week?"

"Yes, that's true. One week would be a nightmare." Her face turned pensive. "We could rent a rollaway bed, but Sue would know something was wrong if we did that."

"Why don't I just stay a couple of nights and then use the excuse that I've been detained at work?" he suggested wearily. "I hate to leave Mom and Dad alone with the kids for a week." He fell back on the bed and stretched out with a sigh. "Boy, this feels good."

"Now, you promised you'd stay here, Slater," she reminded. "I've been thinking about this arrangement. I'll find time to slip over to your house and help your parents with the children until Sue leaves if you'll keep your word and stay here nights."

"All right. All right, I'll stay here. But I'm not going to try to work the hours I'm working and sleep on the floor," he murmured in a drowsy voice. "So, I guess you'll be the one with a backache . . . or I might take turns with you," he relented. "I guess that wouldn't kill me."

"Why should either one of us have a backache?" she reasoned. "This is a king-size bed. There is plenty of room for both of us to sleep here and not even come close to each other."

One of Slater's eyes popped open. "Both of us sleep in this bed?"

"That's right. We are two mature people. Just because we sleep in the same bed doesn't mean we have to act like some sort of animals," she rationalized. "Up until a few years ago I didn't know what it was like to sleep in a bed by myself, so you aren't going to bother me any."

"True, but I think this is just a little different. . . ." His voice sounded skeptical.

"Not to me it isn't." She sighed in disbelief. "Are you afraid I'm going to try to accost you, Mr. Holbrook?"

"You?" He laughed. "You don't look old enough to know the meaning of the word."

Jillane tensed and sat up straighter. She realized

that she didn't look as old as she was, and she resented the fact that he had to keep mentioning it. Granted, in another few years she would undoubtedly welcome the comment but not now. "I *told* you. I happen to be twenty-eight years old."

"Oh, right. Twenty-eight." He sounded as unimpressed as he felt.

"Well, how old are you, Methuselah?"

"Too old to let myself get involved with a twenty-eight-year-old," he acknowledged wryly.

Jillane's curiosity was getting the better of her. Just exactly how old *was* he?

"You're not forty yet," she challenged.

He grunted and closed his eyes once more.

"Are you?"

"Does it matter?"

"No . . . I just wondered."

"Well, don't. It's none of your business."

She looked at him and smiled slyly. So, he was one of those vain men afraid of losing his youth.

"You don't look bad for your age," she said grudgingly. No matter how old he was, he still looked darned good, and he probably knew it. He was just fishing for a compliment, and she had taken the bait like an idiot and given him one.

"I didn't have time to go by my house and get a toothbrush or change of clothes." He changed the conversation abruptly, growing tired of the subject. "I just had time to call Mom and tell her I would probably be scarce for the next week."

"Oh. I think I have an extra toothbrush," she offered, "but I'm afraid I don't have any men's clothing around."

"I'll run by the house in the morning and

change clothes before I go to work." Forcing himself off the bed, he headed for the bath off to the left side of the room.

While he was showering Jillane turned back the bed and creamed her face. When he came out from the bathroom a few minutes later, she glanced up, and her face turned a bright red. He was wearing nothing but his underwear and a devilish grin.

"Something wrong?" He looked at her expectantly, daring her to make a fuss. If he was going to be forced into staying here for a week, he was going to be comfortable.

"I . . . I . . . you . . . you . . ."

"What . . . what . . ." he taunted.

"You . . . you're not dressed!" she stammered weakly.

His face turned pink as he glanced down hurriedly. "I most certainly am!"

"You're in your underwear!"

"Ms. Simms, I like to be comfortable when I go to bed, and as far as I'm concerned, I'm overly dressed. I usually sleep in the buff."

"Oh."

He walked over to the bed and got in on her side as Jillane's eyes unwillingly trailed across the room with him. He was all man, there was no doubt left about that. His body looked like one of those jocks on television, advertising after-shave or underwear.

Oh, well. She shrugged her shoulders and grinned to herself wickedly. She guessed she could stand it. Disappearing into the bathroom, she brushed her teeth and then left the bedroom. She was back a few minutes later, carrying a small dish in her hand.

"You are on my side of the bed," she said curtly.

Slater grunted and rolled over to the opposite side. He critically surveyed her with one eye. She had done her hair up in a ponytail and with the oversize football jersey she was wearing, she looked like a twelve-year-old waif.

"Where are you going? To be on *Let's Make A Deal?*"

"No, why?"

"You look like one of those kooky contestants who tries to get on the show."

She shot him a dirty look. "I like to be comfortable when I go to bed too."

She set the dish on the nightstand. Walking over to the window, she raised it up partway as Slater stuck his head underneath the covers.

"Good grief." Slater's head immediately popped out from beneath the blanket. "What are you doing?"

"Getting some fresh air. I can't sleep in a stuffy room."

"Do you know what the temperature is out there?" he asked incredulously. "It must be in the forties!"

"I don't care what temperature it is," she said curtly. "I always sleep with a window open."

Jerking the blanket up tighter around his head, he grumbled something to himself and shut his eyes once more.

Jillane sat down on the bed and kicked off her scuffs. Tucking her legs underneath her, she picked up the remote control and turned on the small portable television sitting on the dresser. Then she picked up the dish on the night table.

"TV bother you?"

Another grunt was the only answer she received.

Moments later the air was alive with the sound of sucking, the tart, tangy smell of lemons, and the sound of Johnny Carson.

Slater came back out from under the covers again and sat up in disbelief. "What in the devil are you eating?"

"Lemons."

His face puckered involuntarily, and his mouth began to water.

"I always eat lemons at night," she explained. "Want one?"

"No!"

"Am I bothering you?" She looked at him apprehensively. "I can turn the TV down lower," she offered.

He lay back down and punched at his pillow irritably. Even though he didn't say so, she knew she was bothering him.

With a resigned sigh she put her bowl of lemons back on the nightstand. "I'll just turn it off . . . okay?"

There was no sound from his side.

Leaning over him, she switched on the oscillating fan beside the bed. It started whirring loudly. As the blades turned it made a funny sound—tick, tick, tick—a soothing sound that would always put her to sleep instantly.

Slater sat up once again, his hair blowing wildly about his head. He shot her a withering glare.

She smiled lamely. "I can't go to sleep without a fan on, either."

"Doesn't the window thrown wide-open provide enough fresh air for you?"

"It isn't the fresh air. I just need the sound of the fan to go to sleep," she explained. "If it isn't on, I just lie here all night with my eyes wide open."

"Oh, brother!" He lay back down and pulled the blankets up tighter around his face. The room had dropped at least fifteen degrees in the last five minutes.

"If you get cold, you can turn on your side of the electric blanket," she encouraged, switching her control on to the number-seven setting. "That's what I do."

As the apartment settled down for the night, Slater lay staring up at the ceiling. The wind was whistling through the window, the fan was ticking away, and the light on his side of the electric blanket clicked on and off with annoying regularity.

Was he really this desperate?

He couldn't help but wonder how his nice, sane life had taken such a drastic turn in a mere matter of months. He loved his new family, but he was still in a period of adjustment. He had to admit, six kids could play havoc with a bachelor's way of life. If only he could find a reliable housekeeper and get his life back on an even keel. Well, for the next few weeks he would try his very best to put up with this arrangement until he found someone to help. Surely he could make it.

He shivered and pulled the blanket up tighter around his neck. That is, if he didn't die of pneumonia first.

CHAPTER FOUR

"Now look. I think if we're going to make this thing work, we're going to have to lay down a few ground rules." Slater was almost in a stupor the next morning as he sat at the breakfast table slumped over his coffee cup. He felt as though he hadn't closed his eyes the entire night, and he was decidedly grumpy from lack of sleep.

"Didn't you sleep well?" Jillane kept her voice at a low whisper, so she wouldn't wake Sue as she bustled around the kitchen fixing his breakfast. She couldn't imagine why he wouldn't have. She had slept like a rock.

Slater spooned another teaspoon of sugar into his coffee. "No, I didn't sleep well. All that blowing and whirring and clicking nearly drove me up a wall."

"Well, maybe we can work something out, but I have to have the fan," she warned, slapping pieces of sliced chicken on whole-wheat bread.

He took a sip from his cup and surveyed her rumpled appearance. She was wearing an old green housecoat that had seen better days, red knee socks, and a bulky blue sweater that nearly swallowed her.

"You didn't have to get up with me," he said, turning his gaze away from her stunning attire.

"Oh, that's all right. I'm happy to do it." Tearing off a hunk of lettuce, she patted it firmly on the sandwich. For a long moment she stared at the sandwich proudly. "Gee, that looks good," she said. "I think that's what I'll have for breakfast."

He glanced up at her, his stomach rolling over at the mere thought. "You'd eat a chicken sandwich for breakfast!"

"I sure would! It's a lot better than the cold pizza I'm usually stuck with," she theorized.

Seconds later she handed him a brown paper bag. "Here."

He eyed the bag sleepily. "What's that?"

"Your lunch." She smiled. "I fixed it for you."

"You didn't need to go to all that trouble," he protested. "I always grab a hamburger close to where I'm working."

"This will be more nourishing," she dismissed. She picked an orange up off the table and slipped it in the bag. "Be sure to eat your fruit."

"I don't like fruit."

"It's good for you."

"But I don't *like* fruit."

"Eat it, anyway."

He sighed and took another sip of his coffee. He wasn't going to sit here and argue with her, but he wasn't going to eat the orange, either. "What's on your agenda today?" he asked, trying to change the subject.

"I'm not sure. Probably just a lot of running around." She padded over to the chair opposite

68

him and sat down. "Do you have any idea what time you'll be home this evening?"

Taking a final drink of his coffee, he pushed back from the table and stood up. "Not really. I can give you a call later today when I see how things are going."

"Okay." Jillane stood and helped him slip on his jacket. "Sue and I will probably visit friends until four or so, but I thought if you got home in time this evening, we could go over to your house. I'd like to meet the children."

"I should be back before six if nothing big comes up," he promised. "But what about Sue? How do we explain our absence to her?"

"Oh, don't worry about Sue. She's already made plans to have dinner with Nettie Lawrence this evening. She and Sue were extremely close when they were in school."

"Won't they expect you to join them?"

"No, Nettie and I could never stand each other. She's too snooty," Jillane scoffed. "But it will be nice for Sue and her to visit. They're a lot alike, you know. Besides, I thought I might have a small dinner party Friday night and have Nettie and her husband to dinner before Sue leaves."

Slater shook his head and picked up his lunch. He had to admit that her reasoning left him a bit blank at times. "If the three of you have such a hard time getting along, it sure seems to me that you are going to a heck of a lot of trouble to have a miserable time this next week."

"For heaven's sake, why? We're all friends!"

He gave up. "I'll see you around six."

"Oh, wait a minute. I want to give you a key to

the apartment." Rummaging through the drawer next to the telephone, she came up with an extra key and handed it to him. "There. Now you can come and go as you please."

Slater absently stuck the key in his pocket and pushed the kitchen door open. Jillane followed behind, tiptoeing through the front room with him to the door. He immediately proceeded out the doorway and slowed down only when he heard her clear her throat in warning. Glancing up, he saw her motioning with her eyes toward Sue, who was just beginning to stir.

"Uh . . . good-bye, dear," Jillane prompted brightly.

"Oh, yeah. Good-bye." He leaned over and placed a kiss on her mouth. What would it be like to really be kissed by him, Jillane idly wondered as their mouths parted seconds later. "Have a nice day."

"I'll try. Be sure to eat your fruit. It's a good source of vitamin C."

"Right. And you have a nice day, dear."

"Right."

Moments later he disappeared out the door, and Jillane closed it firmly behind him and turned to face the day.

Actually the day went more smoothly than she would have expected. After breakfast the two women dressed and started on their rounds. From then on it was a succession of quick stops to visit with friends they had not seen since school days. The hours flew by and except for the fact that Jillane's conscience kept nagging at her to come clean and tell Sue the truth, it had been a fun day. There were numerous times when she had been on the verge of telling Sue that her life was not what it seemed, but then "Arnie with the big, fat checkbook" would surface, and all Jillane's good intentions would go right down the drain.

By the time Sue left to have dinner with Nettie Lawrence, Jillane was a bundle of nerves. She had just taken a shower and was in the bedroom dressing when she heard the key turn in the lock.

Slater was in the door before she could scurry over to retrieve her dressing gown. For a moment they both froze as his eyes narrowed, then focused on her slim figure clothed only in a pale, beige teddy.

"Uh . . . hi," she murmured. "I was just dressing."

"Hi. I'm a little early," he said, apologizing. He tried to get his eyes to move away from the soft, tempting swell of her bustline, but they suddenly wanted to linger where they shouldn't. The thought immediately hit him that she'd been right on target the night before when she'd informed him that she was not a child. She certainly wasn't, and with a sinking feeling, he realized that this was only going to complicate matters if he wasn't careful.

At any other time Jillane would have felt a certain shyness that a man she barely knew would be seeing her in this nearly unclothed condition. But, strangely enough, she didn't feel timid around Slater at all. It seemed rather natural. After all, if he could parade around in front of her in his jockey shorts, then he would have to allow her a few such

71

niceties without complaining. On the other hand, she wasn't sure he would view her nearly naked state as rationally as she did.

"Would you mind handing me my robe?" she asked hesitantly. The way he was looking at her sent goose bumps racing up and down her spine. Either her imagination was playing tricks on her or he had suddenly grown much more handsome since she had seen him this morning, and that worried her. The last thing she needed was to become involved with Slater Holbrook and his six children, but she could tell it was going to be hard to avoid it. Admittedly the children were the crux of the problem. In all honesty she knew it would be relatively easy for her to fall for a guy like Slater. Not only was he sexy, masculine, and extremely attractive, but also he was beginning to be rather nice about this whole arrangement. Of course, he could afford to be nice, since she would be the one to come out on the short end of the stick. But, still, she would have to keep her guard up against any personal feelings developing between them.

"Slater . . . my robe?" she reminded him.

"Oh, sure." He glanced around and saw the robe on a nearby chair. "Is that it?"

"Yes, thank you." She waited until the robe dangled limply in his hands. He approached her, his eyes traveling slowly over her body.

"What's that thing you have on?" he asked cautiously.

Jillane glanced down at her attire, then back up to him. "A teddy."

"A what?"

"A teddy. It's sort of a one-piece . . . bra and . . . panties."

He extended the robe to her with a shy grin. "Oh, great idea. I like it."

"Thanks." She returned his grin and slipped the robe on, trying hard to not read anything personal into his words. The teddy was new and it *was* nice, and he was only trying to be polite.

"The shower's all yours if you want it," she offered as she sat down at her dressing table and started applying her makeup.

"Thanks, but I think I'll wait until we get over to my house. I didn't get a chance to drop by this morning, so I'll need some clean things. Has Sue already gone?"

"Yes, she left around twenty minutes ago."

Slater sat down on the bed and watched her as she carefully applied a thin coat of eyeliner to her upper lid. "How was your day?" he asked conversationally.

"It went all right . . . except my conscience is killing me," she confessed. "I came close to blurting out the truth several times today, but then I would always lose my nerve at the last minute. How was yours?"

"Busy as usual." He lay back on the bed and stretched out for a few moments.

"Anything new concerning the strike?"

"Not that I've heard."

"Darn. I hope it doesn't go on much longer," she said, fretting. "I'll run out of money by next month."

"You're forgetting your new job," he parried. "You'll get filthy rich on my hard-earned money."

"Yeah, sure I will," she scoffed. "Besides, I don't plan on working at my new profession long enough to collect more than a few paychecks from you. Are you hungry? I can fix you something before we go." She tinted her cheeks with a light peach blush and frowned. "I think there are the remains of a chicken casserole in the refrigerator."

"Thanks, but Mom insisted we have dinner over there tonight. I hope you don't mind."

"No, I don't mind." Anytime she could get out of cooking was fine with her.

"She said something about eating out by the pool."

"Sounds good." Jillane dabbed a touch of color to her lips and stood up. "I'll be ready as soon as I slip on some clothes."

In a few moments she appeared from the bathroom wearing a mauve shirtdress and matching pumps. She walked back over to where he lay on the bed. "Could you get my zipper, please?"

He looked a bit surprised by her request but immediately moved to sit up on the side of the bed. "I never was very good at this sort of thing," he apologized, trying to get his large fingers to manipulate the small hook and eye adorning the dress. His gaze meandered down her feminine curves and ended on her bottom, where his eyes unwillingly paused. She wasn't the skinny thin so many women were keeping themselves nowadays, and he liked that. Somehow he knew she had a certain softness that would make a man want to hold her in his arms and he'd know without a doubt that he was holding a woman. Too bad she was so darn young, he thought. "There. That ought to do it."

"Thanks." She walked over to the dresser and picked up her purse. "Well, I'm ready to meet your family. How do I look?"

"Fine," he assured her, and tried to get his mind on other things. "We'd better get a move-on. She warned me that the meal would be on the table by six-thirty."

"Slater, what did you tell your parents about me?" Jillane inquired as they started down the long flight of stairs. Obviously he couldn't tell them the truth.

"As little as possible," he confessed. "I told them I thought I'd found a temporary house-keeper for the next few weeks and they could make plans to go home soon if it all worked out."

"Good. And I'm sure it will all work out," she predicted optimistically as they walked out the front door. "All we have to do is make it through this week, then it's all downhill from there on."

She had been giving the subject a lot of thought. If she could just make it until Sue left, then the rest of the bargain would come easy. She was used to a large family and the every day problems she would be confronted with. And it would be for just a few weeks at the most. Then she could go back to her old way of life with the fervent promise that she would never tell another lie as long as she lived!

"Is this your car?" she exclaimed. Slater had stopped before a late-model sports car and was opening the door for her.

"Yeah." He grinned. "I called this my B.K. car."

"B.K.?"

"Before kids," he explained as she got in. He closed her door and went around to the driver's side. "I've had to buy a beat-up old station wagon so we can all go somewhere at the same time. I only drive this one on dates now."

"Oh." Jillane glanced around her and wondered when he'd last used it. "It's very nice."

The drive to his house was filled with idle conversation, most of it relating to news of the strike . . . or lack of news. The bargaining committees were still at an impasse, and it looked as if the strike was going to be a lengthy ordeal.

When the car turned in the drive of a sprawling, two-story brick home, Jillane was definitely impressed. The neighborhood was in one of the newer, more exclusive districts of town, and she knew it cost and arm and a leg to live there.

"Wow," she breathed reverently.

Slater chuckled and drove the small car up the circular drive. "I know it's a bit ostentatious for a man like me, but because of all the upheaval in the short span of their lives, I thought it best to keep the children in an environment they were familiar with," he explained. "We all had a painful period of adjustment, but it was made easier for the children to keep them in a place where they had had some of the happiest memories of their lives. So, I went in hock up to my eyeballs and bought Fritz and Marie's house after their deaths."

"It's beautiful," she remarked, her eyes drinking in the beautiful landscaping surrounding the house. There were just enough trees and flowers to make it look homey, yet elegant at the same time.

76

As they got out of the car the sound of children's laughter filled the air. "They must all be in the pool," Slater remarked as he took her arm and led her to the oak, double-entrance doors of the house.

"Isn't it a little cool for swimming?" Jillane asked worriedly. The temperature was cooling down, and it was still a bit breezy.

"They're all a bunch of water ducks regardless of the weather," Slater explained, holding the front door open for her.

As they stepped in the marble entryway the sound of a woman's voice greeted them above the din of clatter from poolside. "Is that you, Slater?"

"Yo!"

"We're out here."

Slater turned to Jillane and grinned. "No kidding."

Jillane had to laugh. It sounded like feeding time at the zoo as they made their way across the spacious living area and out to the pool.

The minute Slater stepped through the doorway, he had two wet bodies clamoring around him to get a first hug. Jillane noticed that in addition to the two children hovering around Slater, there was an older girl stretched on a towel at the end of the pool reading a book. A boy who looked to be a little younger was doing elaborate flips off the diving board, and a baby was gurgling happily in a playpen. An older woman was cooking hamburgers on an open grill.

"Hi, Mom. How's it going?" Slater greeted.

"Just fine!" she assured him, flipping the meat over systematically. "We ran out of ice. As soon as

77

your father returns from the store we'll be ready to eat." She smiled at Jillane. "Hi, there!"

Jillane timidly returned the smile. "Hi."

"Fleur's over there engrossed in her book," she told her. "Fleur! You have company!"

The pretty young French girl glanced up, and her face went blank. "For me?"

"She's with me, Mom," Slater corrected her hurriedly.

"Oh . . . well, my goodness. Of course." She laughed. "I just assumed you were Fleur's friend."

"That's all right." Jillane smiled.

Kneeling down to greet the smaller children clamoring around his leg, Slater gathered them in his arms and squeezed them affectionately as they each tried to babble out their own piece of news for the day.

"Eben hit a home run today," Wong, a delicate-looking Vietnamese girl, announced excitedly. "It went clear-r-r over the back fence!"

"No kiddin'?" Slater was duly impressed. "You really hit it over the back fence this time, Eben?"

The small, frail boy's grin was shy but decidedly proud. "Oh, it was nothin'. I just gripped the handle with both hands like you showed me, and it went sailin' through the air."

"It was too somepin," Wong insisted. "He hit it real hard!"

Slater chuckled and gave her an affectionate pat on her bottom as she scampered off to jump in the pool once more.

"Hey, kids! Everyone front and center," Slater ordered. "I want you to meet someone."

There was a lot of splashing and giggling as the

children hastened to do as they were bid. Seconds later there were five children and a friendly St. Bernard obediently lined up in a row in front of the new arrival. The baby, peering out of the bars of the playpen, watched intently as Slater began the introductions.

"Children, I'd like you to meet Jillane Simms." He looked at Jillane and smiled. "Jillane and I work for the same company, and due to the strike, she has some extra time on her hands. So she has graciously consented to be our new housekeeper for the next few weeks."

All eyes landed on Jillane and studied her thoughtfully.

"She won't make it any longer than the rest of them did," Eben pronounced fatalistically.

Slater leveled a stern look in his direction. "She *will* make it, until I can find someone permanent to take her place. Understand?" His authoritative gaze took in the entire group.

"She's not going to be here for keeps?" Wong looked at her guardian expectantly.

"No, not for keeps," he explained. "Your grandmother and grandfather need to get back home, and since I'm working unusually long hours right now, Jillane has offered to fill in until I can find someone who wants the job permanently. Now, I want all of you to promise that you will do your share of the work around here and keep things running smoothly until other arrangements can be made. Okay?"

There were nods from the children as they continued to study the new, unexpected addition to the family.

Satisfied that they would all do their part to keep harmony, Slater let out a relieved sigh. "All right. Let's start with the introductions." His arm went around the Vietnamese girl. "This is Wong. She's seven years old and a big help around here."

Jillane smiled and took the small hand extended to her. "Hello, Wong."

"And this is Eben. He's six."

A cold, wet hand clasped hers, accompanied by a grin with two front teeth missing. "Hi!"

"Hi."

"And this is Joey. He's nine."

Solemn brown eyes coolly surveyed Jillane's outstretched hand as she made her way down the line of curious faces. When the Indian boy failed to take her hand, she moved on to the next child with a quiet nod of her head.

"And this is Caleb. He's our sixteen-year-old," Slater informed her.

"Driving yet?" Jillane asked with a friendly grin.

"Two whole weeks," he said proudly.

"And three whole fender benders," Slater teased.

"Ah, Slater, those could have happened to anyone," Caleb said, protesting.

"And this is our princess, Fleur," Slater continued. "She's getting married in—"

"Exactly two months, four days, and two hours," Fleur supplied helpfully, taking Jillane's hand. "Thank goodness this time Slater's found a housekeeper who isn't such a grouch." She paused and looked at Jillane expectantly, "You're not a grouch, are you?"

"Not very often," Jillane returned truthfully,

clasping her hand with a squeeze. "I'll try to keep my grouchiness to a minimum," she promised with a knowing wink.

"This furry creature is Hercules. He's the biggest baby in the family." Slater rubbed the dog's ears affectionately. "And, last, but never least, we have baby Tara, who's two and a half years old." Slater reached over and took the dark-headed child with bright blue eyes out of the playpen. "Say hi to Jillane, Tara."

Fat little arms waved in the air as she grinned widely and gurgled. "Hi! Hi! Hi!"

Jillane took Tara's hand and shook it playfully. "Hi to you!" she said with a laugh.

"And to round it all out, this lovely lady standing next to me is their grandmother, and my sainted mother, Fay Holbrook, and she would kill me if I told you how old she is," he joked. "Dad will be back from the store in a few minutes and you can meet him."

Jillane nodded and smiled again. "Hi."

"So, welcome to Fort Holbrook." Slater grinned at her hopefully. "What do you think?"

Wong, Eben, Joey, Caleb, Fleur, Tara . . . and Slater Holbrook.

What did she think?

She thought she was in for a heck of a lot of trouble!

CHAPTER FIVE

The apartment was empty when Sue returned from her dinner date that evening. It was just a few minutes after eight, and she had to admit that the evening had not gone well. It seemed to her that Nettie had changed so much from their high-school days that she barely recognized her any longer.

She sighed and kicked off her shoes. Well, she guessed she had changed too. Everyone changed whether they liked it or not. All except Jillane. She seemed to be the same happy-go-lucky girl with everything going her way that she had been ten years ago.

Sue walked over to the sofa. For a few minutes she contented herself with a magazine, but that soon lost all its attraction. Idly she wondered where Jillane and Stanley were this evening. They seemed so happy together. A sudden wave of loneliness for Arnold swept over her as her mind conjured up her fiancé. Arnie was her foundation in life. He always seemed so levelheaded and in complete control of life, traits Sue desperately wished he could teach her. What a person had or didn't have was the very least of his concerns. He was more than happy with what life had given him and looked forward to each day with an enthusiasm that left Sue breathless. The mere thought of him made her shiver with anticipation as she leaned her head back on the sofa and tried to remember what his lips felt like on hers. It wasn't hard to do. She could almost taste him, almost feel the touch of his mouth caressing and teasing . . . until shafts of longing surged through her.

What was she doing here? she wondered unhappily. If it hadn't been for her insane desire to come to this reunion and meet Jillane's fabulous "Stanley," she could be in Arnie's arms right now instead of only dreaming about it. And if Arnie had any idea what a sham she was portraying, he would probably never speak to her again, let alone take her in his arms!

A niggling guilt tugged at her once more. Why was she doing what she was doing? Especially since she had made up her mind prior to the trip to come here and confess to Jillane what a complete liar she had been for the last two years and to make her amends. For the life of her she couldn't understand why she and Jillane always seemed to be competing with each other! She honestly liked Jillane, for heaven's sake, and wished her nothing but the best. She had been a loyal friend to Sue more times than she could remember, and now that they were grown women, Sue valued her friendship even more, so why was she still lying to the poor girl?

So Sue wasn't going with an oil executive with a gargantuan bank account. So *what* if she was engaged to plain old Arnold Jones, who owned a gas station and had to work darn hard for his money? He was still one of the most honest, sincere men she had ever met, and she would love him no matter what his bank account was! Did it make him any less a man just because he wasn't a jet setter and filthy rich like dear Stanley? Of course not!

If all that were true, then why didn't she just tell Jillane the truth and go home to that wonderful man and get on with her life?

She honestly didn't know.

For some crazy, inexplicable reason she was driven to continue her charade while she was here. But one thing she was going to promise herself: the minute she returned home, she was going to air express an overnight letter to Jillane and confess all her sins. If Jillane wanted to end their friendship, then Sue would get just what she deserved.

Picking up the phone, she dialed the number of Arnie's station and waited while the beeps and clicks connected her to him. She knew he would still be there even at this late hour.

"Jones Standard!"

"Arnie? Hi, it's me."

"Sue? Hold on a minute, honey. There's so much noise here I can't hear you."

A few seconds later he was back on the line in quieter surroundings. "Hi, sweetheart. What's up?"

"Oh, nothing," she replied wistfully. "I was just thinking about you."

There was a soft chuckle on the other end of the line. "I've been thinking about you all day too. Are you having a good time?"

"I suppose so. Jillane and Stanley are very gracious hosts," she admitted, "but I miss you."

"Good. I miss you too."

"And, I love you very, very much," she added, hoping she could ease some of the guilt she was feeling.

"That's always good to hear." His voice was tender, but she sensed that he wasn't alone, or he would have told her of his love for her.

"Are you alone?"

"No."

"I thought so." She laughed as she pictured him shyly trying to carry on a conversation with his girl while one of his employees listened. Arnold was as passionate as the next man, but he wasn't one to flaunt it to the whole world. Somehow that always made the moments when he was telling her how much he loved her so much more special. "Aren't you going to tell me you love me too?" she teased.

"No, but you know I do . . . a hell of a lot," he returned sincerely.

"Oh, Arnie, I wish I were there with you!"

"Hop on the next plane and I'll meet you at the airport," he urged.

"No, I can't do that," she conceded. "It would look strange to Jillane."

"Whatever you say, but it's sure a nice thought."

"I know. Well, I won't keep you," she returned softly. "I just wanted to hear your voice."

"You are still coming home Sunday?"

"Yes. The dance will be Saturday night. There's a picnic Sunday, but I think I'll skip that and catch an early plane."

"You know how sorry I am I can't be with you,"

he apologized. "If Mac weren't in the hospital, I would have gone with you."

"Oh, that's all right. I understand, darling." If it hadn't been for the fact that his partner had picked this time to have a hernia operation, Sue wouldn't have thought about coming in the first place. Her charade would have been discovered immediately if Arnie had come with her!

"I'm looking forward to meeting Jillane and Stanley," Arnold was saying. "Maybe we can fly up there late this summer and visit them."

"Yes, that would be nice." She was hedging now. "But they're in the process of building a new house right now, so I don't know if that would be convenient. We'll just have to see."

"It's something to think about," Arnie said, coaxing her. "We might even make it a honeymoon trip. How would you like that?"

"We'll talk about it," she promised.

"Good girl. I'm going to have to go now, honey. I have a car on the grease rack." His voice grew softer, more intimate as he leaned in closer to the phone. "Call me again tomorrow?"

"You know I will."

"You know what? Sunday suddenly seems an awful long time from now," he murmured.

"I know. I love you, Arnie."

"Okay. Me too. I'll talk to you tomorrow."

There was a fine mist of tears in her eyes when he finally hung up the phone. She sat for a moment hugging the receiver close to her breast, pretending it was him. Moments later she willed herself to replace it in its cradle and wipe at her streaming eyes.

Fumbling for a tissue in her purse, she told herself that Jillane would never go to half as much trouble to impress a friend!

A greasy blob of hamburger landed in Jillane's iced tea glass, spraying the liquid all over her face and dress. Baby Tara's accompanying gurgle of mirth left no doubt where the missile had come from as Jillane calmly picked an ice cube out of her lap and put it on her plate.

"Tara!" Fay affectionately swatted the baby's hands. "How many times have I told you, don't throw your food!"

A big pucker formed on the baby's face as she picked up another piece of meat and crammed it in her mouth. "Yummy food!" She giggled.

"I'm sorry, dear." Fay extended a bowl to Jillane with a polite smile. "More potato salad?"

"No, thank you, Mrs. Holbrook. I think I've had enough."

"Fay, dear. Just call me Fay. Fleur, don't tell me you're through eating already!" she scolded. "Why, you've barely touched your plate again."

"I told you Grandma, I have to take off five pounds before the wedding," the young woman protested as she rose from the table. "If it were up to you, I'd walk down the aisle looking like Miss Piggy."

"At least you'd be healthy," Fay pointed out. "You women nowadays keep yourselves so skinny, a good wind could blow you away! At least finish your milk, dear."

"Slater." Fleur groaned hopelessly. "Do I have to?"

"She looks healthy enough to me, Mom." Slater grinned at the nineteen-year-old conspiratorially. "She can have a snack when she gets in from her date with Johnnie."

"John! For heaven's sake, not Johnnie," Fleur corrected. "You make him sound like a baby!"

"I'm sorry, I stand corrected. John," Slater said with an impish wink at his father. "But he sure looks like that kid down the street who used to deliver our newspapers, and I could swear his name was Johnnie."

"John only delivered papers to help pay his way through college," she returned airily, not at all perturbed by his goading. She breezed by his chair and dropped an affectionate kiss on his forehead. "I'll be in my room wasting away if anyone should call." She winked at Fay, picked up her glass of milk, and downed it hurriedly. "If I can't fit into my wedding dress, it's all your fault!"

The other children finished the last of their dinner, then bolted away from the table as Fay rose and started to wipe the baby's hands.

"Here, let me," Jillane offered.

"Why, thank you. That would be helpful."

"I'm going over to Allen's to help him work on his car," Caleb called.

"Don't stay out late," Slater warned. "And, for gosh sakes, watch where you're backing. One more wreck and your insurance is going to go through the ceiling."

"Ah, come on! This is summer vacation," Eben objected. "Can't I stay out till at least midnight?"

"Ten o'clock," Slater stated firmly.

"I can't believe this," the boy grumbled. "I'm

sixteen years old and you still treat me like a baby. I'm going to be the laughingstock of the whole town. The other kids get to stay out till midnight!"

"All right. Ten-thirty and not a minute later," Slater said, yielding.

Eben and Wong noisily raced for the swing set as Caleb accepted his fate and ambled off. Joey elected to go over and sit beside the pool by himself.

Jillane had noticed what a quiet and reserved little boy he seemed to be and made a mental note to ask Slater about him later on.

"Dad, let's you and me go take a look at the tomato plants," Slater suggested, pushing back from his own plate. "They probably need to be watered."

"I staked up a few today," Hubert told him as they wandered off the patio. "Now, you're gonna have to watch them more carefully when I leave, son. They're gonna get pithy if you're not careful."

"I will, Dad, I will." Jillane heard Slater pacify the older man as they walked to the back of the yard. "The last thing I need right now is a roaring case of pith."

Jillane cleaned the baby's sticky face and played a quick game of patty cake with her before she set her in the playpen once more. Tara was an adorable child and seemed to have such a sweet nature. Moments later Jillane busied herself in the cheerful kitchen, helping Fay stack the dishwasher.

They were soon chattering away as they took the opportunity to become acquainted with one another. As they worked Jillane found herself telling the older woman all about herself and the fact that

89

she had come from a large family also. Fay revealed that she and Slater's father, Hubert, lived in a small town about two hundred miles away. Hubert had retired from the insurance business a few years ago, and other than traveling to see their son and new grandchildren regularly, they pretty much took life easy now.

"I noticed the children seemed to have adjusted well to your whole family," Jillane marveled. "They even call you Grandma."

Fay's weathered face fairly beamed as she rinsed the final skillet and handed it to her. "Isn't that nice! I can't tell you how much that pleases Hubert and me. Slater gave them their choice of what they wanted to call us, and they chose Grandpa and Grandma."

"I notice they call Slater by his first name instead of Dad."

"Yes. I think the smaller ones will eventually call him Dad, but they've had too many moms and dads in their lives to call him that yet. They can't help but be confused." She chuckled. "Slater wants them to do what they feel most comfortable with."

Before they knew it, the kitchen was back in its immaculate order, and Jillane felt she had known Fay Holbrook all her life.

"You must work twenty-four hours a day," Jillane complimented as she folded her dishcloth and draped it over the towel rack. "You would never know six children lived here." From what she had seen the house was in perfect order and lovingly kept.

"Well, I must admit they're a handful for me, but

Slater makes them all pitch in and do their share of the work. No one seems to complain too much. They're really a good bunch of kids."

"Grandma Holbrook! Can you come up here and help me with this hem?" Fleur's voice drifted down the stairway as Fay and Jillane applied lotion to their hands.

"Oh, my. If I have to climb those stairs one more time today, I don't think my old bones will make it." Fay grimaced.

"Why don't you go see to the baby?" Jillane offered. "I guess since I'm going to be the new housekeeper around here, I might as well get broken in right."

"Would you?" Fay's face beamed gratefully. "I would surely appreciate it."

"No problem." Jillane hurried up the stairs as Fay went back outside to check on the children.

Slater and Hubert had come back from checking the tomatoes and were draped comfortably in lawn chairs discussing the strike.

"Would you gentlemen like something cold to drink?" Fay inquired pleasantly.

"No, thanks, dear, nothing for me. What about you, son?"

"No, I'm fine." Slater glanced around. "Where's Jillane, Mom?"

"She went upstairs to help Fleur put a hem in one of the new dresses she bought today. She'll be along soon."

Slater leveled a solemn gaze on his mother. "Well, what do you think of her?"

"She's very nice, but how old is she? She doesn't look much older than Fleur," Fay said uneasily.

"She's twenty-eight," Slater hastened to defend.

"She is? She certainly doesn't look it."

Slater's mind drifted back to earlier that evening when he'd walked in on her getting dressed. He tried to push away the titillating memory. "Well, believe me, she is."

"Well, she certainly seems able to get along well with the children," Hubert remarked as he scraped out the bowl of his pipe and refilled it with tobacco. "That should be to her advantage."

"Why wouldn't she?" Slater mused. "She's almost a child herself."

Hubert chuckled and cast a wry glance at his son. "Now I wouldn't go so far as to say that. She's unquestionably a lovely young woman, and I think the consideration here is not so much if she'll be able to do the job but whether or not you can remember she's just the housekeeper," he plied discreetly.

"Lands, I'd be tickled to death if your son would take serious note of a woman," Fay said, chiding. She reached over and handed Slater the baby. "I've about given up on him marrying again."

"Good. What's it going to take to shove you over the brink?" Slater playfully buried his face in the baby's stomach, making her giggle with glee.

"Now, I'm serious, Slater. You need to marry and give these children a mother."

"Mom, let's not go into that again," he pleaded. "The kids and I get along just fine. We don't need a mother figure around here. Besides, what woman in her right mind would want to marry a man with six children who weren't even his? That would leave very little room to have children of her

92

own," he reasoned, "and I can't picture any woman wanting to get in that situation."

"But I worry about you, dear."

"Well, don't. I'm doing great . . . ouch!" Tara dug her fingers in his curly hair and yanked painfully. "Let go, you little dickens!"

Hubert struck a match and lit his pipe thoughtfully. "Don't worry about the boy, Fay. Someday some woman is going to get in his hair just like Tara's doing, and he won't have a chance. He'll end up marryin' her in spite of himself."

Fay heaved a resigned sigh and resorted to one of her old tricks: talking over Slater's head as if he weren't sitting two feet away from her. "I certainly hope so. Maybe this Jillane will be an incentive for him to settle down. . . ."

"Now hold on, you two!" Slater's head popped up defensively. "Let's not get crazy. IF I were going to marry, I certainly wouldn't have to resort to robbing the cradle. I *have* six children, thank you, and that's all I need."

Hubert shook his head. "You're in for a big surprise there, boy," he prophesied. "She's no child."

"Jillane has consented to be my housekeeper until I can find a permanent one, that's all. Don't go reading anything romantic into this," Slater returned gruffly.

"Must have had to pay her a goodly little sum to get her to take the job," Hubert mused. "It's a big job for one person."

"She's being paid well, plus the fact that I'm doing her a little favor in return. It's strictly on the up-and-up."

93

Hubert chuckled and took a long puff on his pipe. "I'm not doubting your word, son."

Slater shook his head tolerantly. "Jillane can start helping you some this week, Mom, then take over permanently next Monday."

"That should work out perfectly. We'll be able to go home and check on the house, then return in August for Fleur's wedding," she noted in a pleased voice.

"Don't know why that girl couldn't have done things like most people do and get married this month," Hubert observed thoughtfully. "I thought all women wanted to be a June bride."

"Now, dear, you know that Johnnie only has a few days off from school until the middle of August. They want to have at least a couple of weeks with each other before fall semester begins, so that's why they selected August as their wedding date."

"John, Mother. Not Johnnie," Slater warned.

In a few minutes Jillane and Fleur came out to join the others. Fleur whirled around the pool dramatically, showing off her new dress and Jillane's perfect hemming job.

"Am I lovely?" she demanded.

"I can hardly keep from drooling all over myself," Slater drawled. "Johnnie will go out of his gourd when he sees you in that."

Fleur glared good-naturedly at him and went back to her preening.

The rest of the evening was spent in a family-type atmosphere. At one point Jillane found herself helping Wong do her English homework for summer school the next morning. All the children seemed open and receptive, all except Joey, who managed to keep a cool distance from her.

"I like your family," Jillane announced as she and Slater drove out of the driveway amid friendly waves and shouts of good-bye. "The next few weeks aren't going to be so hard," she said in a relieved tone.

"I think they like you too," he complimented.

"I'm sure they did . . . all except Joey. What makes him so aloof?" she prompted.

"He's that way with everyone. He's had a lot of tough knocks in life and he doesn't trust anyone."

"Not even you?"

"No, not even me."

Jillane turned and put her arm on the back of the seat where she could face him. "For heaven's sake, why? You seem to have a marvelous relationship with the children."

"Joey's lost a lot of people he's loved in his nine years. His first mother died when he was barely two. His father couldn't care for him, so he was passed on to his grandparents. They were elderly and both died before he was five. From then on he was in six different foster homes before Fritz and Marie adopted him. Of course, when Fritz and Marie died, his world was turned upside down again. I've tried my best to give him extra love, but it's just going to take time."

"You think he's afraid to love again?"

"Wouldn't you be?"

"I don't know. I don't think I'd ever be afraid to love, but in view of his circumstances, I suppose I *would* hesitate." They rode in silence for a few minutes while Jillane thought about what he had said.

"Slater, why haven't you ever married?" she asked quietly. She had heard rumors that he was divorced, but she wasn't sure they were true.

For a moment she didn't think he was going to answer her question. He concentrated on the traffic, and his face took on a certain stubborn tilt to it, which she knew could mean trouble. "I was married for a short time. I didn't care for it," he stated simply.

"You were?" Not one to be discreet, Jillane's curiosity was peaked. "How long?"

Slater scowled. "Does it matter?"

"Yes. I sort of like to know a little about the man I'm sleeping with." She grinned impishly, trying to keep things light.

He snorted and turned his eyes back to the traffic. "I know you're teasing about that sleeping bit, but don't let anyone else ever hear you say that."

She frowned. Granted, she was teasing and wouldn't have made such a statement in anyone else's presence, but did he have to be so offended by the thought?

"Is that such a repulsive idea . . . you sleeping with me?" she challenged coolly.

"It was a short teenage marriage," he returned calmly.

"What was?"

"My marriage."

"That wasn't the subject of discussion," she pointed out.

"It was until you decided to change it."

"Well, I'd just like to know—not that it makes any difference to me, mind you—but what would

96

be so awful about sleeping with me? A lot of men would view that as a pleasure, not a punishment."

"It lasted six months before we admitted we had both made a mistake. We decided we had been too young to really know what we wanted in a mate," he continued, as if they were both still on the same subject. "She went her way and I went mine, and I haven't heard or seen her since."

"What would be so horrible about sleeping with me?"

"From then on I decided I didn't need that kind of hassle in my life again, so now I just love 'em and leave 'em. It's a lot more simple that way."

"Name me one good reason. Just one," she persisted.

"I wear a size sixteen and a half shirt, size ten and a half shoe, like my steaks rare and my coffee black. A good John Wayne movie and a piece of chocolate pie is my idea of a lot of fun." He pulled up in front of her apartment and shut off the engine. They both got out and walked to the front door as she pointedly ignored him. He continued to carry on his side of the conversation. "I hate to fly, and I never sleep past nine in the morning because it gives me a headache." They began their long ascent up the stairway. "I hate climbing stairs, and apartment buildings that don't have elevators in them," he added with a wheeze as they finally reached the fifteenth floor. "Now, does that pretty well answer your first question."

"Perfectly." They paused in front of the door as he withdrew his keys from his pocket. "Now, kindly answer my second one. What would be so crummy about sleeping with me?"

For a moment their eyes met in an obstinate gaze.

"For one thing, you're too young for me," he said bluntly. "For another, I'm only trying to protect your reputation."

"Poppycock! I'm not too young for you. I'm twenty-eight!"

"And I'm a heck of a lot older than that."

"So? Have certain parts gone out on you?"

He grew instantly defensive. "Certainly not!"

"Then what's the problem?"

His eyes narrowed. "Are you actually propositioning me?" he asked incredulously.

She felt her face turn beet-red. "Certainly not!"

"Then what's the purpose of this discussion?"

Now that she thought about it, she wasn't sure. "Well, it's just—"

"Just what?"

"Just . . . well, darn! I'm *not* a child, Slater, and I resent your thinking of me as one."

Once more their gazes met and held for a moment. Jillane felt her pulse flutter. She had no intention of becoming involved with him intimately, so why was she pushing the subject?

"Look." His gaze softened. "I just think it's best if we try to keep this strictly on a business level," he defended. "I'm more than aware that you're a lovely woman, but let's be honest about this. You wouldn't want to get involved with me on a permanent basis, and we both know it."

"Well, maybe not permanently," Jillane was forced to admit. "Oh, not that I don't find you attractive." She paused, and smiled at him sheepishly. "You want to know something funny? I've been trying to get your attention at the office for the last six months, but you never gave me a second glance."

He shifted his stand uncomfortably. "Oh, yes, I did."

"You did?" She peered at him expectantly, trying to control the surge of joy she had just experienced at his confession.

"Sure I have. You have this one blue dress you wear every once in a while that clings to . . . well, anyway, I've noticed you," he said, conceding once more. "But, I still don't think we should let this develop into anything personal."

Jillane was frantically trying to remember what dress he was referring to so she could wear it in his presence more often. "Oh, well . . . sure . . . I agree. I think you're absolutely right. I could probably find myself attracted to you, but I really don't think I . . ." Her words trailed off lamely as she searched for words to find a tactful way to say she wasn't interested in a ready-made family at this point in her life.

"You couldn't handle me and six children?" he finished. "That's perfectly understandable. Not a whole lot of women could."

"That sounds pretty selfish of me, doesn't it? But I came from such a large family, and even though I love all my brothers and sisters dearly, I've always dreamed of the day I could have my own peace and quiet . . . although"—she paused and thought for a moment before she actually closed all doors—"that doesn't necessarily mean my feelings concerning this subject are carved in stone."

"Well, let's face it. In addition to all my drawbacks you *are* entirely too young for me," he argued. "Since we're being honest with each other, I'll have to say, yes, I can't help but notice that you're a damn nice-looking woman, and it would be easy to let myself become intimately involved with you for a few weeks. But since there's obviously no future for us, why bother?" Jillane felt he wasn't being sarcastic, only honest. "I really can't see compounding the situation with a meaningless affair."

Jillane grinned. "Mr. Holbrook, I think you've misunderstood my intentions. I wasn't inviting you to have an affair with me. I only wanted to know why you would find it so unappealing."

This time his smile made her pulse do erratic flip-flops. "I wouldn't. Maybe when you turn thirty-five or so, we'll talk about it."

"But then you would be seven years older, too, and definitely over the hill," she reasoned innocently.

"Never over the hill, honey." He winked suggestively. "Just older."

Maybe it was the constant reminder that he was still thinking of her as a child, or maybe it was purely for selfish reasons alone, but Jillane felt obligated to prove a point. She leaned forward and gave him a kiss that was as far from a child's kiss as California was from New York.

For a moment he stiffened with surprise at her unexpected aggressiveness, but seconds later she was smug with the satisfaction that he was offering no resistance. When they parted seconds later, he gave her a stern look and firmly set her back from him. "Now that was a crazy thing to do."

"You're too stodgy, Mr. Holbrook," she accused lightly, surprised to find how much she had enjoyed the kiss.

"I thought we'd just agreed to keep this thing neutral!"

"It was just a neutral kiss," she said, defending herself.

Just the slightest tracings of a grin tugged at the corners of his mouth now. "Well, I suppose that since the damage has already been done, we might as well explore this thing further."

"Uhmmm." She tipped her face up to his and grinned impishly. "I suppose."

He feigned a frown. "You're shameless, little girl."

She had no idea where all her boldness had suddenly come from, but it was there in full force. "I know, but humor me, Methuselah," she coaxed.

With a slow, lazy movement he pulled her back in his arms and really kissed her this time. The feel of his lean body pressed tightly against hers sent her senses spiraling. For the first time she realized what a dangerous situation she could find herself in if she weren't extremely careful. Slater Holbrook could become intoxicating with just a small sip of his charms.

His mouth opened more fully over hers, sending hot shafts of desire coursing through her as he continued to deepen the kiss. She found herself pressing intimately against him, her arms wrapped possessively around his neck.

They were both breathless and a little surprised

101

at their instant arousal, when he finally let her go many long minutes later.

"I think we'd better break this up," he murmured huskily, "and get back to business."

"Not yet." She sounded very much like a little girl now as she pulled his mouth back down to hers for another long, quenching drink. He kissed her exactly as she hoped he would: soft, then firm, then demanding. . . .

"You still think I'm too young for you?" she prompted in a soft whisper when he reluctantly broke the embrace.

"I'm trying to." He groaned painfully.

"Now admit it, Slater. I think you enjoyed that," she taunted affectionately. "And I know I certainly did."

"Well, put it out of your mind. It's back to neutrality . . . just like we agreed." He watched her suspiciously as he inserted the key in the lock and pushed the door open. "Right?"

She smiled back at him guilelessly. "Right."

"With your history of telling little white lies, you make me a bit uneasy," he admitted.

She smiled again and breezed past him without saying another word. After all, she had promised herself to reform. She had vowed *never* to tell another lie . . . if she could help it.

So, it was best to remain silent in this particular situation.

102

CHAPTER SIX

"Okay, kids. I'm taking names this time." Jillane walked into the kitchen and calmly picked up a pad and pencil. She began to write as grapefruits and apples haphazardly sailed around her head. For days she had overlooked minor skirmishes between the children, but the time had come for her to assert some authority.

Eben, Wong, and Joey were lobbing the fruit at each other and shouting at the top of their lungs. Apparently there were some differences of opinions concerning whose turn it was to take the trash out, and the dispute was being settled by brute—or more appropriately, "fruit"—force.

"It's *her* turn," Eben yelled as he pointed an accusing finger in Wong's direction.

"It is not! It's *his* turn," Wong denied, shifting all the blame on Joey.

Jillane noted that Joey didn't bother to deny the charge but merely stared his opponents down with a glacial glower.

Without taking sides Jillane walked over to the large poster board hanging on the wall and ran her finger down the daily list of chores Slater had carefully organized for the children. "Today is Friday. It's Eben's turn to take the trash out."

"What!" The persecuted boy disgustedly dropped the grapefruit he was about to hurl and stomped over to reaffirm his sentence. "Where does it say Eben has to take the trash out on Friday's! I'm kitchen duty on Friday's," he challenged.

"Not according to the new schedule," Jillane said patiently. "Congratulations. You've just been promoted to trash."

"Darn!"

"Are you going to tell Daddy?" Wong asked hopefully. Jillane had noticed that she was increasingly referring to Slater as "Daddy."

"No, I don't see any reason to bother your father. I'm perfectly capable of assigning extra dishwashing duties," she threatened.

The children disbanded amid grumbles of gosh-darn-its, I-told-you-sos, and shut-ups as Jillane walked to the door with them.

"Joey." Her gentle hand reached out to restrain the boy.

He paused and cast dark, aloof eyes in her direction. She was growing accustomed to those sad, distant eyes. For the past few days she had found time to slip away from Sue and come by to relieve Fay while she did the shopping and other household chores. She was pleased the way the children had taken to her so well; all except Joey.

"I just wanted to remind you that I'm going to be baking cookies in a while, and it's your turn to choose what kind."

"I don't want to bake cookies," he said curtly. "I don't like cookies."

"You don't? Well, I'm not crazy about them myself . . . except for snickerdoodles," she conceded.

He cocked his head and studied her suspiciously. "I've never eaten one of those kinds."

"They're pretty good," she encouraged. "They're a crisp, tasty cookie rolled in cinnamon and sugar."

"Sounds like a lot of trouble to me."

"Not really. Were you going to be busy doing something else this afternoon?" she asked pleasantly.

"No . . . I just don't want to bake no cookies."

"Well"—she took his arm and patiently led him over to view the new work schedule—"it says on here that you have kitchen duty this week, so I guess that leaves you and me to come up with some sort of cookie for dinner this evening whether we like it or not."

Once more those dark eyes turned on her defensively. "I suppose if I have to, I'll help, but working in the kitchen is girls' work."

She laughed and patted him on the head. "Not anymore, Joey. When you grow up and get married, chances are your wife will have to work just like you will. With two doing their share around the house, I can guarantee it will make for a much happier marriage."

"I ain't *ever* going to get married," was the sharp reply.

Ignoring his show of defiance, she walked over to the cabinets and took down a large bowl and measuring cups. "Would you rather cream and beat or sift and add?"

While they worked Jillane casually told him about her life as a child and how she had been raised in a large family. Joey obediently went about his chores but kept himself coldly detached from the conversation. On occasion she would pause for a moment, giving him time to add to the discussion if he wanted to, but he never did. When they were finished, he left the kitchen without a word or so much as a taste of one of the cookies cooling on the racks.

Jillane sat down at the table and thoughtfully munched on a handful of the warm cookies, trying to decide how to break through his cool veneer. He was going to be a tough one, but she'd made herself a promise to show him that trust and love could once again be his.

When Fay returned, Jillane helped her fold the wash, then hurried back to the apartment. She had left Sue alone that afternoon under the pretense of having a personal appointment, and she wanted to get back as soon as possible. The past few days had gone smoothly with not the slightest hint that all wasn't as it appeared. Slater had been a perfect angel about the whole thing, playing his part to the hilt. But that was only fair, Jillane reasoned. *She* had worked hard at keeping her end of the bargain too.

It was becoming increasingly hard to think of him as just another bed partner, she had to admit. They had continued to sleep in the same bed, and every night it had been taking longer for her to drop off to sleep with him lying beside her. Not

106

that he slept any better. She had smugly noted that he was having his own share of sleeping problems lately. But he continued to be the perfect gentleman, to her dismay. Other than the few kisses they had shared the other night, he had kept his distance. She'd caught him studying her at different times, though, and knew he wasn't completely immune to his counterfeit wife.

She had also noticed that Sue was a bit more moody than she had been when she first arrived. Jillane attributed it to the fact that she was missing her fiancé, since Arnie's name was the first and last thing that came out of her mouth each day. One thing was for certain: Jillane had the distinct impression that even if Arnold hadn't had a penny to his name, Sue still would have been in love with him. In a way that served to temper Jillane's feelings toward her. Even though Sue was a braggart and exceedingly money-hungry, at least she loved the poor guy she was trapping!

Tonight would be another test of her nerves, Jillane admitted as she stopped by the store for supplies. Since Sue would be leaving Sunday, Jillane had decided to go ahead with the small dinner party in her honor. She had carefully picked high-school friends with whom she rarely had any contact so there would be no chance of a slipup. By Sunday everyone would be gone, and she could breathe her first real sigh of relief.

"Hi, sorry I took so long." Jillane let herself in the apartment and dropped her shopping bags on the nearest chair.

Sue switched off the sweeper and smiled. "Hi! Get everything taken care of?"

"Yes, thank you . . . what are you doing?" Jillane eyed the sweeper.

"Oh, I just thought I'd help out by straightening up a bit. I hope you don't mind?"

"No, I don't mind, but you don't have to do that, Sue. You're company," Jillane protested.

"I really don't mind," she coaxed. "I suppose with the apartment being so small you don't have a maid right now?"

"A maid?" Jillane turned totally blank for a moment. "Goodness, no, I don't have a maid." She chuckled.

"I don't blame you," Sue comforted. "I've always told Arnie that even if I could afford to have one, I wouldn't. I'd much rather take care of my own house."

Picking up the discarded grocery sacks, Jillane started for the kitchen. "Afford one!" She laughed. "I'm sure a man of Arnold's wealth could afford as many maids as you liked. Besides, I'll bet with all the important people you'll be entertaining when you become his wife, you'll probably need several maids . . . you know, one to polish the silver, one to hang up your minks, one to bring you breakfast in bed, and one to help you blow your nose."

"Oh, yes. I just meant that I personally didn't care for one, but I suppose Arnie *will* insist."

"Yes, he probably will," Jillane agreed sympathetically. "I know Stanley will make sure I have a few when the new house is finished." Gads! Here she went again! She would simply have to change the subject as quickly as possible before she found herself telling more fibs.

"Speaking of minks . . . how many do you have?" Sue asked as she trailed behind her into the kitchen.

"I'm not sure. I hope I got enough chicken for this evening. Do you think three will be enough?"

"You're not sure? Why, Jillane. Surely you don't have so many furs that you've lost count!" Sue exclaimed.

Jillane bustled around the kitchen, putting the groceries away. "Oh, you know me, Sue. I never pay much attention to those kinds of things. I just go in and grab one off the hanger," she excused blithely. "I stopped by Meady's and picked up one of their German chocolate cakes."

Sue sank down in a chair and stared off almost wistfully into space. "Just imagine. Having so many mink coats you don't even know how many you have."

"Well, I don't really have that many. There are probably a few cloth coats thrown in here and there," she conceded lamely.

Sue's eyes grew brighter as she jumped up from her chair. "Let's go count them!"

"No! We can't!" Jillane pushed her back in place hurriedly. "They're all in storage right now!"

"Oh." Sue frowned. "Darn it. I know they must be lovely."

"They're really not anything special," Jillane murmured.

"I'm sure Stanley is just like Arnie, and he would buy you the very best. That Arnie and Stanley! Aren't they sweet? How did we ever get so lucky?" Sue's voice had grown tender at the mention of Arnie.

Shrugging her shoulders, Jillane grinned and tried to push down another smothering round of guilt. "I really don't know."

"Although I'd love Arnie even if he didn't have money," Sue pointed out again. "Money isn't everything, you know. I mean, there are many more important things to look for in a man other than money."

Jillane paused in her work and looked to see if those words had come out of Sue's mouth. "Yes, I agree . . . wholeheartedly."

"I mean, the *main* thing is to find a good, honest man who is kind and considerate. One who loves you and is concerned about being the right kind of husband and father. That's more important than having a lot of money, don't you think?"

"Absolutely. I want my husband to be exactly like that . . . and he is," she amended hurriedly. "I'd better get dinner started."

"You need any help?"

"No, you just go relax. I'll take care of the meal."

"Jillane . . ." Sue's eyes fastened on her hands. "I've noticed you aren't wearing any rings."

Glancing down at her barren fingers, Jillane grimaced. "Oh . . . they're at the jeweler's being cleaned and checked for loose stones. I'm supposed to pick them up in a few days."

"Gosh, I hope you get them back before I have to leave. I'm dying to see what a heart surgeon gives his wife in the way of diamonds."

"Oh, they're very nice," Jillane promised.

"Well, if you're sure you don't need any help, I think I'll go call Arnie."

Jillane had to laugh again. "Didn't you call him this morning?"

"Yes, but we didn't get to talk very long," she assured her with a blush.

While Sue went off to the bedroom to make her call, Jillane got dinner under way. Besides Sue, there would be three couples to prepare for.

As she was setting the table in the small dining area, the front door opened, and Slater walked in earlier than expected. The usual excited flutter in her stomach at the sight of him didn't fail her as she glanced up and smiled her hello. "You're early!"

"Yeah, I got away sooner than I'd thought."

"What do you have in your bags?" Jillane noticed that he was carrying several sacks from local department stores with him.

Slater glanced around apprehensively. "Where's Sue?"

"In the bedroom talking to Arnie."

"Again? This must be the tenth time she's called him since she got here!"

"I think she's very homesick," Jillane confessed. "What's in the sacks?"

"I stopped and bought a new shirt to wear tomorrow night," he explained, "but the rest is just more of my clean clothes. I figured if I brought them in a suitcase, that would look suspicious."

Jillane paused and tried to fight down an almost painful surge of disappointment. Apparently he had made other plans for tomorrow evening. Although they had not discussed it, she knew he was aware of the reunion dance on Saturday night, and she had been secretly hoping he would consent to accompany her.

"Oh? And what exciting plans have you made for tomorrow evening?" she inquired pleasantly, trying to keep her voice natural.

"Isn't that when your dance is?"

She kept her eyes glued to the table for fear he would see the elation beginning to fill them. "Yes, are you going to be able to take me?"

"Yeah. I traded shifts with one of the other men. I *was* supposed to take you, wasn't I?" he asked, uncertainty filling his voice now.

For a moment she wanted to shout with joy that he was actually going to take her! "Oh, yes! I just wasn't at all sure you'd be able to." She let out a sigh of relief and rushed over to help him with the sacks of clothing. "Here, let me put these away for you."

"No, I'll just throw them in on the bed and hang them up later."

Jillane smiled and carefully took them out of his hands. "Better let me do that. Petunia is taking her nap in the bedroom."

He grimaced. "Thanks."

While she was gone Slater walked over to the refrigerator and took out a cold beer. Snapping the top open, he took a long drink and looked around him. He had to hand it to Jillane. She sure knew how to make a home feel comfortable. This evening on the way over, he was actually looking forward to coming home to her. He quickly forced his thoughts in another direction before he really started thinking crazy things, and Jillane came back in the room.

"How was your day?" she inquired brightly as she went back to setting the table.

"Not bad. You want some help?"

She handed him the plates gratefully. "Thanks. I really need to start getting dressed."

"Go ahead. I'll finish here while you shower. It always takes you thirty minutes longer than it takes me."

"Can you handle it?" She watched in amazement as he expertly set the table without a moment's hesitation.

Glancing up at her, he grinned. "Of course I can handle it. You think you're the only one around here who can set a decent table?"

She grinned back at him, marveling again at how much she enjoyed his company. "You're really very nice, do you realize that?"

He shrugged philosophically. "You're not bad yourself."

"Glad you noticed." She winked at him coyly.

Leaving him to his chore, she hummed happily under her breath as she made her way to the bathroom. When he came in the bedroom to take his shower twenty minutes later, she was finished with hers and sitting at her dressing table.

"Where are my clean clothes?" He casually stripped off his shirt.

Jillane avoided looking at his bare chest. She knew by heart the blond mat of curly hair that spread enticingly across the broad width of his shoulders, then down his middle, to disappear at his waistline. It had been all she could do for the last couple of days to keep from touching him to see if the hair was as soft and silky as it looked. "I hung up your shirts and trousers, and your . . . underwear and socks are in the second drawer of my dresser."

"Thanks. I'll only be a minute." He disappeared into the adjoining bath as she continued to apply her makeup. When he returned a few minutes later, he was wearing a pair of clean trousers and smelled like fresh soap and shampoo.

"There's something about a shower that makes a person feel like new. . . ." His words faltered as he paused, and his eyes darkened to a misty gray as he quietly surveyed her new attire.

Jillane turned from the full-length mirror she had been standing before and whirled around prettily. "How do I look?"

"I think that's dirty pool," he scolded huskily as his eyes took in the blue dress he had mentioned a few nights earlier. It was made of a soft jersey material that clung to her hips and bottom in all the right places. She had been guilty of turning more than one man's eyes at work with that dress, Slater concluded.

"Isn't this the dress you liked so well?" she chided innocently, hoping it would have the same effect it always did on him.

"It is, but I wish you would wear something else tonight."

She turned back to the mirror for another look, callously ignoring his silent plea for mercy. "I thought I should try to look my best this evening. One of my old flames will be here, you know." She glanced over her shoulder to see if that little hand-selected piece of news had the desired results. She had no idea why she would expect him to be jealous, but she did.

"Oh?"

"Yes, Ty Hendricks . . . he's one of the men coming tonight. We went steady for two years in high school. He was captain of the football team, and all the girls were simply wild about him."

"I thought this was going to be couples-only tonight," he said absently, still trying to get his eyes off her delectable posterior.

"Oh, it's going to be. He's married to Retta Manley now."

"Tough luck. I suppose you're still carrying a torch for him." He finally got his eyes to move as he walked over to the dresser for a clean shirt.

"Nope. I have one for you now," she bantered.

"Sure you do."

"I do . . . really." She knew she was being daring again, but he always seemed to bring the adventurous spirit in her to the surface with just one glance from those beautiful gray eyes.

Pulling a light blue shirt from the drawer, he turned around to face her once more. "You know something? One of these days you're going to say something off the wall like that and I'm going to take you seriously."

"Would that be so awful?"

"Not for me, it wouldn't," he confessed, "but you might come out on the short end of the stick."

"Because you still don't want to get involved with me?"

"Because we don't want to get involved with each other," he corrected gently.

She showed unusual interest in one of her earrings. "I've been thinking about that lately. I have almost come to the conclusion that it wouldn't hurt to explore our feelings somewhat . . . you know, sort of let things take their natural course. I mean, I really don't see why we have to keep shying away from each other the way we have been. Surely we could enjoy each other's company without asking each other for any sort of permanent commitment," she reasoned. "Can you help me with this zipper?"

"How did you ever manage to get dressed before I came on the scene?" He strolled over to the mirror to stand behind her. She felt her knees growing weak with him so close. No doubt about it, there was something about Slater Holbrook that turned her insides to jelly.

The faint aroma of a floral perfume teased the air as his hands reached up to fasten the dress. Then he hesitated. Their eyes met in the mirror and held for a few moments, drinking in the image of each other. "You are making this deliberately hard on me, Ms. Simms," he accused, feeling familiar desires stirring within him. He knew he would be crazy to get mixed up with her. He knew that, but for some reason he was having to remind himself of that fact several times a day now.

"By wearing my blue dress and suggesting that we enjoy each other's company? Now, how could there be anything wrong in that?"

"You know what that dress does to me, and your talk about us getting involved makes me nervous. It's crazy and you know it." He unwillingly reached up to run his fingertips gently along her creamy shoulders. Their eyes continued to hold each

116

other captive in the mirror as the sexual tension now simmered unchecked between them.

"Why would it be so crazy?" she wondered softly, forgetting for the moment all obstacles that stood in their way. "We're both unattached and free to do what we want."

He leaned over and pressed his mouth tenderly to her bare skin. "Because we might not be able to keep it simple, and I don't want either one of us getting hurt."

"I know we would be taking certain chances, but don't you think we owe it to ourselves to at least explore the possibilities?" she ventured. His mouth was sending molten lava racing through her veins now. "Sometimes I have the distinct feeling that you're trying very hard to ignore the fact that I'm a woman."

He chuckled wickedly against her ear as he pulled her close to his body, allowing her to feel the full effect she was having on him. "I know you're a woman. Okay?" Deciding that he was losing the battle, he pulled her closer and playfully nipped at her ear. "You want me to make an indecent pass at you, Ms. Simms? Would that make you feel better?"

"Well, you have been a perfectly disgusting gentleman toward me from the moment we met." She drew in a soft gasp as he moved against her sensuously.

"And you want me to be otherwise?"

"No . . . well, maybe. At least you could have given me some indication that you were just a little uncomfortable sleeping with a woman every night and never so much as touching her."

"Jillane, my gosh, I've been trying my best to ignore the fact that you're a woman." He groaned, burying his face in the fragrance of her neck.

Her smile was almost devilish as she allowed him better access to the slender column. "Maybe I don't want you to ignore that fact."

"Look, do you want me to make love to you?" he challenged. "Maybe I'm being too stubborn. Maybe it wouldn't hurt to spend one night together. . . ."

"I don't know . . . maybe."

"Either you do or you don't," he pressed.

"I do . . . and I don't. I know what you say about us not getting involved would be the best, but I have to admit to you, Slater, I'm finding you more attractive every day." She might as well be totally frank with him. Maybe he could help her make some sense out of what she was feeling right now.

"Maybe it wouldn't hurt to give it some thought," he relented.

Again their eyes met and lingered in the mirror. "Funny, that's exactly what I was thinking," she agreed in a soft whisper.

Turning her around slowly, he drew her up against him, his mouth descending slowly to meet hers. "We could start with this. . . ."

There was a soft rap on the door, and they sprang apart guiltily.

"Hey, you two!" Sue's voice drifted from the hallway. "Nettie and Bob have just arrived."

"Be right there," Jillane called in an unsteady voice.

"Hey." Slater took hold of her arm and pulled

118

her back to him possessively. "I think we should continue this discussion later."

"Sure. You name the time and place. I'll be there."

"Tonight . . . in bed?"

"Tonight," she agreed, and leaned over to steal one more lingering kiss. "In bed."

CHAPTER SEVEN

When the couple returned to the living room, Sue noticed that Jillane's face was flushed and radiant after spending time alone with her husband. Once again she had to push away the lonely feeling for Arnie that had been with her all week. She would see him soon. Only a couple of days and they would be together. And if she had anything to say about it, they would never be parted again. She hugged that thought close to her heart and greeted Slater and Jillane warmly. "There are the two lovebirds!"

Nettie and Bob Lawrence were standing by Sue in the living room, waiting for the host and hostess to make their appearance.

Nettie was a bubbly, vivacious blonde. She didn't look a day older than she had when she'd graduated. Her husband, on the other hand, looked every day of his age and as dull as dishwater. About the same height as his petite wife, he wore wire-rimmed glasses and had light red hair that was combed in a wide sweep over his receding hairline. If Jillane remembered correctly, they would have to forcefully pull every word of conversation out of Bob Lawrence tonight.

"I'm sorry, we didn't hear the door bell." Jillane smiled an apology and took Slater's hand in hers. "Nettie, I don't believe you've met my husband, Stanley?"

"No, I haven't, but I'm simply dying to." She extended a friendly hand in Slater's direction. "Hi, I'm Nettie Lawrence, and this is my husband, Bob."

The men made the appropriate greetings and shook hands as the three women broke out in a flurry of happy chatter.

"Oh, I wish Arnie could be here!" Sue exclaimed disappointedly. "I just know all of you would simply love him."

"I know we would," Jillane consoled, trying to keep her patience at yet another mention of Arnie. "Did you have a nice phone conversation with him?"

"No, he wasn't there, and they didn't know when he would be back." She frowned. "Maybe I'll try him again in a few minutes."

"I'm sure he would like that," Jillane pacified. "After all, he hasn't heard from you in at least an hour," she teased. "Oh, there's the door again. It must be Ty and Retta."

Moments later the newest arrivals were being introduced to the other guests. Once more the comparison in the couple's looks were wide and varied. Retta Hendricks was shy and unassuming, worshiping her husband's every move and clinging to him as if she were afraid someone might try to bite her. In contrast, Ty was the hulking jock who had the world by the tail, and he knew it.

"Nettie, I don't know if you know Ty's wife,

Retta? She graduated a couple years after we did."
Jillane introduced the couples.

"I think I remember the face," Nettie said pleasantly. "And Ty, you devil! You're just as good-looking as you were when you were captain of the football team and every girl's dream at Garnet High!"

Ty Hendricks was still the muscular six-foot-three brute of a man who had always given the girls a thrill in high school. Time had certainly done nothing to destroy his macho image.

Ty proudly patted his muscled stomach and gave her an arrogant grin. "It's a good thing I keep myself in prime shape. Those stairs could kill a person!"

"That's exactly what Bob said when he was able to breathe again." Nettie giggled. Reaching over to her solemn-faced husband, she gave his slightly protruding stomach an affectionate love pat. "Wasn't it, dear?"

Bob smiled lamely.

"Well, I can tell you right now," Ty exclaimed, letting his eyes rove over Jillane and Nettie at will, "you and Jillane haven't let yourself go to pot, either!"

His gaze centered on Jillane, and he grinned at her exclusively. She *was* just as pretty or maybe prettier than she had ever been. Seeing her stand there before him took him back ten long years ago.

"That's sweet of you, Ty." Jillane hoped Slater was taking this all in. "I want you to meet my . . . husband, Stanley Marcus."

Ty towered over Slater and reached out to pump his hand, a big friendly grin spreading across his handsome features. "Stanley, my man. Don't believe I recognize the name. Did you go to Garnet High?"

"No. I graduated from high school and college in a town about two hundred miles from here." Slater studied the man who had held Jillane's interest at one time and wondered what all the fuss had been about.

He wasn't all that hot.

"Well, you men get acquainted while I put the chicken on the grill," Jillane suggested.

"We'll keep you company." Sue and Nettie left the men to their own pursuits as they followed her out to the kitchen.

"Well, well. So you're the lucky man who married Jill," Ty congratulated as all three men walked over to the sofa and seated themselves. "That's something." He sat down opposite Slater and looked him over with interest. "How long you two been married?"

Slater wasn't quite sure how to answer him, since Jillane hadn't mentioned how long they were supposed to have been married. "Just long enough to know that I am indeed a lucky man," he agreed coolly. "What about you, Bob? How long have you and Nettie been married?"

"Two years."

"Two years. That's great." Slater looked around uneasily. "Can I get you something to drink?"

"Thanks . . . a beer would be fine."

"Ty?"

"Yeah, beer would hit the spot," he acknowledged. "So, you and Jilly married." He made the remark as if he found it hard to believe. "Did she

123

tell you she and I used to have quite a thing going back when we were in high school?" He chuckled and crossed his legs comfortably. "Just one of those kid things you know . . . but still . . ." His face grew dreamy for a moment.

"Yes, I believe she did mention it. I'll get the beer." Slater left the room and returned momentarily with the drinks.

"Yessir," Ty continued pleasantly, "it was just one of those kid things, but I can tell you that we both thought it was going to be the start of something big."

Slater smiled pleasantly and nodded. "Tell me, Bob, what sort of business are you in?" This overgrown athlete was beginning to get on his nerves!

"Insurance."

"Insurance . . . well, that's interesting." He sat down and ripped the tab off his can. "Around here?"

"Yeah."

He smiled again. "That's nice. Nice town to live in."

"Yes, we like it."

"Jilly still crazy about butterscotch sundaes?" Ty persisted conversationally. "I'll tell you, I spent more money on butterscotch sundaes when I was dating her than I did on gas. Of course, in those days we didn't worry about gas that much." He guffawed. "Shoot, I remember we used to go out by the lake and park for hours under that big old full moon. . . ." His voice trailed off thoughtfully. "Boy, those were the good old days."

Slater smiled sourly and took a sip of his beer. "You in business for yourself, Bob?"

"No."

"What company you with?"

"Prudential."

"Nice company."

"I have my own chain of sporting goods stores," Ty volunteered. "Twelve of them now. Things are going pretty good financially. What's your line of business, Stanley?"

Slater took another drink of beer and sat the can down. "Excuse me a minute, I think I hear Jillane calling me."

"Sure, sure. Go right ahead," Ty urged happily. "Me and Bob will sit here and chew the fat while you're gone. I'd be interested to know if Jilly still loves those butterscotch sundaes."

"I'm sure she does," Slater said politely.

He entered the kitchen and pulled Jillane asided hurriedly.

"What's the matter?" Her eyes widened with worry. "Have you slipped up?"

"No, I haven't 'slipped up,' " he whispered peevishly. "But I'm about ready to bust your old boyfriend in the mouth if he doesn't stop talking about the good old days!"

"Who?"

"Ty!"

"Oh, him." Jillane drew a sigh of relief. At least he hadn't given their charade away yet. "Just ignore him. He always was a blowhard. What's he bragging about now?"

"How many butterscotch sundaes he'd bought 'Jilly' in his lifetime!"

"Butterscotch sundaes." She licked her lips at

125

the tempting thought. "Oh, gosh, I love those things!"

"So I've heard for the last fifteen minutes."

"Well, can't you just ignore him and talk to Bob?" she suggested, casting an apprehensive glance at Nettie and Retta, both of whom were sitting in the dining room talking. "Dinner will be ready in a few minutes."

"I'd love to! But Bob doesn't seem to be able to speak in anything but one-syllable words!"

"Oh, all right. You can stay out here and help me," she relented, too busy at the moment to try to analyze why Ty should be upsetting him so. "Find out how many want barbecue sauce on their chicken."

Obediently he trudged off to do his assigned chore, mumbling something under his breath about "a super jock with an over-inflated ego!"

He was back a few minutes later, still complaining. "They all want barbecue sauce."

"What about you?"

"None for me. I like mine plain."

"Oh, Slater! Why not? I have this simply delicious new brand I'm trying, and I know you'll like it!"

"I don't *like* barbecue sauce," he argued.

"Why? Is it too spicy for you?"

"No, I just don't like it. In the first place, it's downright nasty to eat," he griped. "It almost makes me sick watching people slurp the stuff off bones and ribs. Haven't you ever noticed how some people nearly get down and wallow in their food when they're eating something with barbecue sauce on it?"

"No. I happen to like it," she objected.

"Good, then you're welcome to my share," he returned stubbornly.

She shot him an exasperated look and turned back to cutting up the salad. "You are the pickiest man I've ever met," she grumbled. "You don't like barbecue sauce, you don't like oranges . . ." She hesitated, and her eyes narrowed suspiciously. "Have you been eating the fruit I've packed for you each day?"

Guilty eyes immediately sought the bottle of barbecue sauce. "Oh, all right. If it's going to upset you, I'll put some of the repulsive gook on my chicken." Reaching for the basting brush, he swaggered past her. Grinning exaggeratedly, he gave her a quick kiss and headed for the small terrace where the chicken was cooking before she could interrogate him about the fruit he had thrown away every day this week.

The phone rang as he slid the glass door open. "Want me to get it?"

"No, I want you to come over here and try that again."

"Try what again?"

She gave him a come-hither look. "That puny kiss."

He lifted an injurious brow. "What was wrong with it?"

"It was way too short," she said, flirting.

"Too short, huh?" He shut the door and walked back to her amid peals of the ringing phone. "Well, try this one on for size, 'Jilly,' " he challenged as he pulled her tight against him.

She giggled. "Your mustache tickles."

"You complaining?"

She wasn't. His mouth closed over hers and kissed her long and hungrily. Reluctant to part, he glared at the shrilling phone while they were still kissing.

"You'd better answer that," Jillane murmured against his mouth a few moments later when he showed no signs of releasing her. "Nettie and Sue are beginning to stare."

He gave her a sexy wink, then slowly released her and picked up the phone.

"Hello?"

"Slater?" Fay Holbrook's voice came over the wire.

"Mom?" Slater grimaced. He had no idea why she was calling here, and he had even less of an idea how he was going to explain his presence. "Is that you?"

"Yes, dear. I certainly never expected you to answer the phone. Where's Jillane?"

"Uh . . . right here. I just stopped by to discuss her . . . hours when she takes over next week. You want to speak to her?"

"Please. Tara is fussy tonight, and I can't find her teething lotion. I was hoping Jillane would know where it was since she was over here today."

"She probably does. I'll get her. Hold on." Slater put his hand over the receiver and motioned for Jillane.

Wiping her hands on her apron, she hurried over beside him. "Who is it?"

"It's Mom. How did she get this number?"

"I gave it to her the other day in case she should need me in an emergency." Her face paled slightly. "Is something wrong with one of the children?"

"Tara's fussy. Here, you talk to her."

Jillane took the phone. "Fay?"

"Hello, dear. I hope I'm not interrupting anything, but Tara is a little restless tonight. I think it's her teeth again. Do you know where her teething lotion is? I can't seem to find it anywhere."

"Oh, gosh, Fay. I used the last of it this afternoon. You want me to have Slater go to the drugstore?"

"Oh, no, that would be an extra trip for him. I can send Hubert."

"Is she running a fever?" Jillane inquired anxiously.

"She's a little warm, but I don't think it's anything to be concerned about," Fay comforted.

"I don't know, Fay. You never know about babies. Maybe we should call the pediatrician and see what he thinks."

"Well, whatever Slater thinks," Fay relented.

Jillane peered at Slater anxiously. "Don't you think she should call the doctor?"

"It probably wouldn't hurt. Tara gets sick real easy."

"He thinks you should," Jillane relayed quickly. "Do you want me to call him?"

"That's not necessary, dear. I have the number right here. You and Slater go right on with whatever you were doing. I'm sure Tara will be fine."

Slater took the receiver out of Jillane's hand once more. "Mom, you think I should come home?"

"No, not at all. I'm sorry I worried you. I'm sure

it's only her teeth that are bothering her, but in order to ease your worry, I'll call the doctor. Are you going to be gone all night again?"

"Yeah . . . that is, if you don't need me. I need to stick around work and keep an eye on things," he fabricated.

"I worry about you, dear. Are you getting any rest at all?"

"I'm fine, Mom. The lounge has a comfortable sofa I can sack out on. Listen, if you need anything tonight, get in touch with Jillane. She'll know where to reach me. I mean, I'll make sure she does."

"I will, and don't worry. Everything will be all right."

When they finally hung up, Jillane was still uneasy. "Maybe we should go over and check on the baby when everyone leaves?"

"When did you turn into such a worrywart?" he teased. "I'm sure she'll be fine."

"I know, but I would feel better if I could see for myself."

"Stop worrying. She'll be fine," he said soothingly. "Her teeth are always giving her trouble."

"Well, if you're sure she'll be all right." She relented against her better judgment. "But we are going to call again before we go to bed."

"Yes, Mother," he returned obediently.

She flipped her dish towel at him playfully. "You'd better see about the chicken," she told him, going back to her chores. "I'm sure our guests must be wondering what's taking so long."

Thirty minutes later the meal was progressing along without incident. Everyone seemed to be having a good time, even though most of the conversation was dominated by the four who had gone to school together. Jillane could tell that Ty was getting on Slater's nerves, and it was with smug satisfaction that it finally dawned on her why. He was just a tiny bit jealous! This discovery, and the thought of what was yet to come, elated her and sent butterflies tumbling around in her stomach. She had no idea if he actually had intentions of making love to her tonight, but the thought was enough to send her pulse racing feverishly.

Dessert was just being served when the door bell sounded. Jillane glanced up in the middle of telling a story and frowned. "Now, who in the world could that be?"

"I'll get it," Slater said. "You go on with your story, honey."

Shivers of delight unexpectedly ran through her at the casual way he had called her "honey." Some women would resent being called by that rather old-fashioned term of endearment, but she wasn't. And, for some reason she knew he wasn't doing it for the benefit of the guests this time but for her alone. "Thank you . . . darling." Their eyes met briefly and they smiled at each other.

Jillane went back to the story she had been relating as Slater walked through the living room to the front door. When he opened it, he found a casually dressed man carefully looking over a piece of paper he was holding in his hand. The man was of average height with no particularly distinguishing features. He had a slight potbelly and looked a bit confused.

"Excuse me, is this the Marcus residence?" the man asked hesitantly.

Slater frowned. "Marcus . . . no, you must . . . oh, wait. You mean, Stanley Marcus?"

The man glanced at the slip of paper he was holding in his hand. "Yes, Dr. Stanley Marcus, 22658 Willow Wood Drive?"

"Yeah. This is the place," Slater conceded, wondering who he was about to confront this time.

The newcomer let out a sigh of relief. "That's good to hear. I was almost sure I had the wrong place!"

Slater held the door open wider. "No, you've got the right one. Won't you come in?"

"Thanks. Boy, those stairs are a killer, aren't they?" He took a deep breath as he stepped into the living room and glanced around.

"They take some getting used to," Slater allowed. "I suppose you're here to see Jillane? I'm her husband," he added as a quick afterthought, just in case this was another one of her prior suitors.

"Yeah, I kind of figured that. You must be Stanley." The man offered his hand. "I'm Arnold Jones . . . Sue's fiancé?"

"Oh, sure, Arnold. How are you?" Slater took his hand and shook it politely. "This is a surprise. I didn't know Sue expected you."

"Oh, she doesn't," he admitted. "She's going to be surprised. I just decided to hop on a plane and get down here tonight so I could take her to the dance tomorrow evening. I've been having trouble finding someone to take over for me, but I finally got a college boy to help Henry look after things

132

while I'm gone. Hope I have a business when I get back." He chuckled.

"Well, she's in the dining room. Let's go in and let her know you're here," Slater suggested.

"Yeah, I can't wait to see the look on her face."

The men started for the dining area, exchanging idle pleasantries as they walked. Sue was just taking another drink of her iced tea when she glanced up to see the two men enter the room. For a moment her throat closed up and refused to swallow the liquid, then she began to choke and splutter, her eyes refusing to believe that Arnold was standing in the doorway with Stanley!

Jillane peered at her friend uneasily and finally got up to pound her on the back when she showed definite signs of strangling to death.

"Honey, are you all right?" Arnold was immediately at her side, trying to administer help along with Jillane.

"Arn-i-i-ee," she managed to squeak, fighting her huge gulps of air. "What are *you* doing here?"

Arnold knelt down beside her and patted her on the back until she began to regain some of her composure, his eyes lighting in a special smile for her. "Are you surprised?"

"Yes," she responded weakly. "How . . . what . . ." She had to keep from panicking, but it wasn't going to be easy. Arnold was here in Jillane and Stanley's apartment! It was going to be close to impossible to keep them from finding out that she'd been lying all along about Arnold's position in life!

"I just got to thinking after I talked to you this morning that life's too short to not spend it like we'd like to, so I got busy and found a college student to help Henry, and I took the next plane out," he explained lovingly.

"Oh, Arnie . . . you shouldn't have," she protested lamely. He *really* shouldn't have!

"But I wanted to. I would have been miserable thinking about you at that dance tomorrow night and me not there by your side."

Her hand went out to tenderly caress his cheek, and her gaze grew warm and affectionate. "Oh, you . . . what am I going to do with you?" she scolded.

"You wouldn't honestly want me to tell you right here in front of all your friends, now would you?" he said, teasing. Leaning forward, he pulled her to him and proceeded to kiss her hungrily.

The forgotten guests in the room laughed, breaking the silence and bringing them back to the present. Breaking apart in embarrassment, Sue wiped at the happy tears in her eyes. "For heaven's sake . . ." She gave up and threw her arms around him adoringly again. "Everyone, I want you to meet my Arnie!" Sue declared happily.

Jillane glanced at Slater apprehensively and took a deep breath. Oh, brother! One more clog in the ever-growing chain! Now, not only would they have to keep Sue convinced that they were Mr. and Mrs. Stanley Marcus, they would also now have to satisfy the great and powerful Arnold Jones.

Slater strolled over to stand behind her chair, draping his arm around her shoulders protectively. "Arnold, I don't think you've met my wife, Jillane."

Arnold stood up and reached for Jillane's hand.

"No, but I've heard enough about her to feel I already know her."

Resignedly accepting this new twist of fate, Jillane took his hand and laughingly acknowledged that she felt the same way. The proper introductions were made to the other guests as Arnold pulled a chair up to the table and Sue disappeared into the kitchen to fix him a plate of food.

The rest of the evening was spoiled for Sue and Slater and Jillane. All three were on edge while they tried their very best to keep the subject away from professions and private lives.

When the final guest left a little after midnight, Jillane closed the front door and leaned against it wearily. Arnold and Sue were still sitting in the dining room talking and drinking coffee, allowing her a few moments to plan her next maneuver with Slater.

"Well, what are we going to do now?" Jillane fretted. "Arnold will probably want to stay here with Sue."

"So?" Slater said without concern. "You worry too much. Things are going fine, and I don't see any reason for anything to change. Just keep away from any personal topics that are likely to arouse suspicion and we'll be okay."

She closed her eyes and sighed. "Sometimes I wish I had just been honest to begin with. It would have been a lot less trouble."

"That's all water over the dam," he pointed out as he held out his arms. "Come here."

Without hesitation she did, and they kissed a warm hello. "I don't know about you, but I'm ready to go to bed," he breathed huskily in her ear as they parted a few moments later. The suggestive tone in his voice made her knees go weak as she wrapped her arms around his neck and pulled his mouth down for another encounter with hers.

His hands cupped her bottom tightly and moved her up against him as their tongues met and caressed each other lingeringly.

"Let's say good night to our guests," he prompted in a ragged whisper as their ardor threatened to carry them away.

"Ummmm." Her mouth was reluctant to leave his. "I guess we should. Oh . . . we need to call about the baby," she reminded him softly.

Another long, heated kiss followed before he reluctantly set her aside. "You go say good night for us and I'll check on Tara."

They kissed once more, finding it very easy to procrastinate. "Okay, but, hurry," she said, tempting him.

While he went to the phone Jillane joined Arnold and Sue.

"Well, I know you two must be tired. I know Stanley and I are, so we think we'll go on to bed." She yawned convincingly. "Just make yourselves at home."

The sofa was big enough for two, so they should be comfortable, although she was sure Arnold was used to much finer accommodations. But maybe he had missed Sue enough this past week to overlook the inconvenience.

Sue glanced up and cleared her throat uneasily. "Uh . . . could I speak to you in private a moment?"

"Sure." They walked into the kitchen, and Jillane began to stack the remaining dishes in the dishwasher. "There's an extra pillow in the linen closet," she offered. "I hope you and Arnold will be comfortable. . . ."

"Listen. I know this sounds rather strange, but Arnold and I aren't sleeping together," Sue revealed hesitantly. "He's very moral and wants to wait until we're married."

Jillane paused in her work and frowned. "Oh? Well, that's admirable." Jillane could feel a great deal of respect for his decision. Slater was the first man who had ever made her want to throw caution to the wind, and she could understand Arnold's feelings completely, but it *was* going to present a new problem. She had only two beds in the apartment.

"I suppose he could go to a motel," Sue offered, "but it's getting very late, and he doesn't know his way around. . . ."

"I don't think that will be necessary," Jillane said, dismissing this idea halfheartedly. She could see her rendezvous with Slater swiftly going down the drain. "I have a couple of sleeping bags. The men can bunk down in the living room, and you can share my bed."

"Thanks, I really would like for him to stay here tonight," Sue accepted gratefully. "I've missed him more than I ever thought I could."

Slater walked into the kitchen just as they put the last dish in the washer. "Hi. You about ready to turn in?" He smiled suggestively at Jillane.

"I'll go get the sleeping bags," Sue said. "Where are they?"

"In my closet," Jillane instructed feebly.

The moment she left the room, Slater took her in his arms and stole a hurried kiss before he asked. "What sleeping bags?"

"Uh . . . how was the baby?"

"Mom said she was resting better now. If she still has a fever in the morning, we're supposed to take her in and let the doctor check her."

"Don't you think we should run over and check on her now?" she fretted.

"No, I don't think we should go over and check on her," he mimicked in amusement. "For someone who doesn't particularly like children, you sure worry a lot about mine."

She had to admit that she *was* becoming attached to the children, and that worried her. All she needed was for them to work their way into her heart while Slater was working his way into her bed, and she would be doomed! "I didn't say I didn't like children," she protested as his mouth toyed with hers once more. "I just said I didn't want any of my own . . . for a while, at least. And this is a perfect example of why I don't. With children there is always something new to worry about."

Slater shrugged. "That's life. Anyway, Tara will be fine, worrywart." He kissed her again, long and ardently. "Let's go find some privacy."

"I'm afraid there's been a slight change in plans," she said lamely.

Slater groaned. "What is it this time?" He grimaced and held her away from him so he could study her face. "Don't tell me the sleeping bag is for me!"

She tilted her head and frowned at him apologetically. "Afraid so. Arnie and Sue aren't sleeping together, so—"

"Oh, brother!"

"I know," she comforted, smothering his frustrated groans with sympathetic kisses. "I'm disappointed, too, but I don't know what else to do. I hate to send poor Arnold to a motel since he doesn't know his way around town."

"We can go to one," he suggested hurriedly. "I know my way around!"

"Now, that would look rather ridiculous, don't you think?"

"Come on, Jillane! Have a heart," he pleaded.

"For someone who fought so hard not to become involved, you certainly have weakened," she chided, but she knew she was just as eager to begin a relationship with him.

Conversation was put aside for the moment as they once again exchanged another series of heated kisses, parting only when Sue popped her head back through the doorway to inform them that the men's beds were ready.

Assuring her that they would be right in, Slater switched off the light and stood in the darkness, snatching a few more minutes with her.

"Still think I'm too young for you?" she goaded playfully when his breathing had become ragged and heavy and his caresses breathtakingly bold.

"Maybe."

"What will it take to prove otherwise?"

"About four hours of complete privacy."

"But, at your age . . . do you *really* think you should?" she murmured innocently, winding her fingers through the thick mass of blond curls on his head.

For his answer he pushed her up tightly against the wall and proceeded to make it abundantly clear that he could . . . without any trouble at all.

CHAPTER EIGHT

A series of feathery kisses caused Slater to open his eyes the next morning. He moved and groaned as his sore muscles reacted to his abrupt movement.

"Morning," a soft voice whispered brightly.

Cautiously opening one eye, Slater found the source of bubbling sunshine and groaned once more. "What time is it?"

"A little after seven." Another brushing kiss teased along his bristly jawline. "Did you sleep well?"

"Are you serious?" He moaned again as he tried to straighten out his stiff joints. The night had seemed like a torturous fifteen hours long. He hadn't closed his eyes until the sun had been streaking across the eastern horizon.

"My, my! I really *do* think you must be getting old, Mr. Holbrook."

"Oh, yeah. Well, you try sleeping on this floor all night long and see how well you fare," he said, grunting.

She laughed and rumpled his tousled hair. "I'm sorry you were uncomfortable. Maybe we can make other arrangements tonight," she whispered.

Slater grumbled some sort of garbled reply and pulled her into the sleeping bag with him.

"You'd better be careful," Jillane cautioned as he buried his face in the fragrance of her hair and snuggled down contentedly. "We don't want to disturb Arnold. He's still sleeping." She cast an uneasy glance across the room to the lumpy form lying on the floor by the sofa.

"I should hope so. He didn't go to bed until four or so. He and Sue sat in the dining room and talked—or whatever—half the night."

"I imagine it was the 'or whatever' that detained them," she agreed solemnly.

"I imagine. If we'd known they were going to kill all that time, we could have used it to our advantage," he murmured suggestively against her ear as his hands began to forage where they shouldn't. "What are you doing up so early?"

"I couldn't sleep," she confessed. "I've been worrying about the baby. I think I'll go over and take her by the doctor's first thing this morning . . . just to make sure it's her teeth. Do you have to go to work?"

"Yeah. The guy I traded shifts with is scheduled to work till six tonight. I'll just have time to rush home and clean up before we have to leave for the dance."

"Slater?"

"Hmmmm?"

"Thank you for being so nice about everything."

"You're welcome, but I haven't been any nicer than you have," he allowed graciously. "I think we've both lived up to our end of the bargain."

"No, you've done more," she argued. And he

had. He had been the model husband in front of her friends all week long, and she was beginning to feel confident that the scheme would be pulled off without a hitch. All they had to do was make it through another twenty-four hours, and Arnold and Sue would be on their way home. Then they could both relax. For a moment she tried unsuccessfully to fight down the surge of disappointment she experienced at the sudden realization that after tomorrow there would no longer be any reason for Slater to spend so much time with her, and after a few more weeks, there would be no reason at all. . . .

"I guess after tomorrow we can both relax," she mused.

"Mmmmmm."

"Then you can get back to your normal routine, and I can take over running the house for your mother until you find someone permanent."

"Yeah, I suppose. That reminds me, I guess I'd better run another ad in the paper Monday." He sighed. "If they settle this strike anytime soon, you'll have your hands full."

"Oh, I can manage," she assured quickly. "You don't have to worry about that. You take your time and find a good housekeeper . . . one who will stay around for a while and love the children like her own."

Slater chuckled. "What do you think I've been trying to do for the last six months?"

"Well, I just meant that you don't have to be in any big hurry to find someone. I will be available for as long as you need me. Besides, I've been getting bored lately. It will help break the monotony."

His hold on her tightened affectionately. "I'll keep that in mind. We certainly wouldn't want you to get bored."

"You be sure you do," she whispered, turning over to face him. "I want Joey to have someone he can place his trust in once more."

Slater's mouth touched hers exploringly. "That doesn't sound like a job for a housekeeper," he noted in a sexy whisper. "That sounds like a job for a mother . . . don't you think?"

They kissed a lazy good morning while Jillane tried to control her erratic pulse at his suggestive words. Were his words meant to feel her out on the subject now that they had both let down their initial objections and decided to enjoy each other's company? Her heart thumped loudly against his chest. Surely not. Even though they were undeniably attracted to each other, she was reasonably sure he didn't have any intentions of their impending relationship developing into anything permanent . . . and she knew she didn't. But if that were so, why was she suddenly so afraid to answer him? The answer came to her, clear and simple. It was because she didn't know her own feelings at the moment.

"I should be going," she evaded, reluctant to leave his arms. "Tara will probably be up by now. . . ."

She was silenced by the heady sensation of his lips claiming hers once more and the feel of his aroused body molding her tightly to him. It was all she could do to break the embrace a few moments

144

later and slide out of the sleeping blanket. "I really must be going or you'll be late for work."

He had not missed her reluctance to answer his question, but since he wasn't at all sure himself what he was feeling at this stage of the game, he decided it was best not to pursue the discussion. "Okay. I'll see you tonight," he relented with one last kiss.

She leaned back over and wrapped her arms around his neck, closing her eyes and savoring his feel for another brief second. "Would you care to play host to Arnold until Sue gets up?"

"Sure. I'll make coffee and entertain him with my quick wit," he teased.

Once more she let him go, and her gaze drank in the sensuality of his broad chest. "Thank you. I'll be looking forward to tonight."

"I will too." He reached up and touched her face gently. "Kiss Tara for me."

One last kiss was stolen before she forced herself to her feet and walked to the door.

As she slipped out the apartment door Arnold finally stirred and stuck his head out from beneath the sleeping bag. "Good morning," Arnold greeted as Slater sprang to his feet and began to roll up the sleeping bag.

"Morning. I was just about to put a pot of coffee on."

"Sounds good," Arnold accepted gratefully. "I don't know about you, but that was one of the most miserable nights I have ever spent!"

While Sue still slept the two men settled down at the kitchen table and began an easy conversation while they waited for the coffee to perk.

145

"Well," Arnold began. "So, you're a heart surgeon. That must be a very rewarding line of work."

Slater fidgeted uneasily with his spoon and tried to keep from looking directly at the man who sat across from him. He hated this misconception he was laboring under and couldn't wait until the day it was over.

"Yes, I've always thought that being a doctor would be a noble and gratifying profession," Slater managed discreetly.

"Yes, I agree. Any reason you happened to choose your particular field?"

"No, it just happened that way." Slater got up to pour the coffee. "You take anything in yours?"

"Nope. This will be fine. I guess the girls are still asleep."

"Sue is, but Jillane had an errand to run. She'll be back shortly."

Arnold yawned and ran a hand through his thinning hair. "I hope Sue and I didn't disturb you last night, but we hadn't seen each other in a week, and you know how that is." He grinned sheepishly.

"No, you didn't disturb me at all," Slater assured. He took a sip of the hot liquid and leaned back in his chair to light a cigarette. "You smoke?" He belatedly offered the rumpled pack to his guest.

"Nope, I kicked the habit a couple of years ago."

"That's smart. I've tried several times and have never been successful."

"It's tough."

The silence hung heavy for a few minutes as they devoted their full attention to the coffee. Searching for a way to ease the lull, Slater decided to approach Arnold's occupation, even though he felt very ill equipped to converse intelligently with a multimillionaire. Although he had always prided himself with making a good living, he was still a long way from being rich.

"Sue tells me you're in oil," he broached hesitantly. "That's interesting."

Arnold glanced up from the rim of his cup thoughtfully. "She did? Well, I suppose you could say that. At least, I feel like I wallow around in it all day." He chuckled.

Wallow in it? Taking another sip out of his cup, Slater tried to ignore the braggadocio. If there was one thing he detested, it was a braggart, and apparently Arnold was going to be as bad as Sue in that area. "Yeah, well it must be tiresome," he returned calmly.

"It sure can be. I thought I would never find someone I could trust to take over for me so I could fly up here and be with Sue this weekend."

"You don't have a reliable staff?"

"Oh, I wouldn't say that. No, Mac and Henry are good men, but Mac had to have a hernia operation, so he's in the hospital. Of course, the business is too big for Henry to handle alone, so that's why I had to scout up that college boy."

"You have only two men to help you run your business?" That was surprising. He would have thought with the kind of empire Arnold had built, he would need many times that number.

"Shoot, yes. There's times when we don't even need that many," Arnold confessed. "One to take care of customers and one to count the money at night. That's about all it takes. But Henry's been

147

around ever since the business first started, and since he's just about to retire, I thought I'd keep him on the payroll until he does."

"That's nice of you."

"Well, I look at it this way. Someone might have to do me a favor someday. I figure it don't hurt anything to let him hang around, and it sure makes him happy, so what the heck?"

"How did you happen to get into oil?" In all honesty Slater didn't really care, but since they had nothing in common to discuss, it might as well be Arnold's wealth.

Arnold looked at him blankly. "Well, I step in it if I'm not careful, then sometimes it drips off the pans of the cars while I have them up on the rack." He smiled engagingly. "You know . . . just the usual ways."

It was Slater's turn to look blank now. "Oh?"

"Yeah . . . say, listen." Arnold leaned up closer to the table. "I know the chances of you and Jillane getting up our way are slim, but if you ever do, drop by and I'll give you a free lube job."

Grinning lamely, Slater nodded and took another sip of his coffee, trying to figure out why the hell Arnold was making these peculiar jokes.

"Now, just because I've offered to grease your car doesn't mean I'm trying to get free surgery out of you," Arnold bantered.

"Grease my car?" He had to admit that he didn't understand why the man was offering such a thing.

"Yeah, if you're ever in my neighborhood, bring your car by my station and I'll grease it for you," Arnold offered sincerely. "I know it's not much,

148

but I'd like to repay you for the hospitality you've shown Sue all week."

A bulb suddenly popped on in Slater's head. "You own a service station?"

Arnold looked puzzled. "Sure. Didn't Sue tell you?"

Suddenly the whole situation became crystal-clear. Both Jillane and Sue had been lying their pretty little heads off to each other! Slater started to chuckle, then broke out in an outright fit of laughter.

Arnold watched him warily, wondering if all doctors were as strange as this one seemed to be. "Did I say something funny?" he prompted. Maybe owning a gas station wasn't as glorious as being a heart surgeon, but it was a good, honest job. He stiffened as Stanley's merriment increased. Funny, he hadn't seemed to be this snobbish earlier.

"Arnold." Slater chortled. "Let me get this straight. You own a service station?"

Ready to take offense, Arnold looked him straight in the eye. "That's right, Doctor. I may not bring in as much money a week as you do, but I make a respectable living," he returned coolly.

"You're not a millionaire oil executive?" Slater crowed.

"A millionaire! Good Lord, no. What ever gave you that idea?"

Once more Slater burst out laughing. When he was finally able to regain control of himself, he wiped at the corners of his eyes, then extended a friendly hand across the table. "Arnold Jones, I'd like to introduce myself. I'm Slater Holbrook, Operations Manager for the local branch of AT&T."

"Who?" He looked at him as if he had gone completely berserk.

Between spasms of glee Slater managed to relay what Jillane and Sue had been doing to each other the past few years and how he happened to find himself involved in their deceitful plans.

At the end of the story Arnold didn't appear to find it as amusing as Slater did. "I think that's sick! Why in the world would two grown adults do such a childish thing?" It hurt his pride to think that Sue would be ashamed of what he was.

"I think they would both welcome a way out of the hole they've dug for themselves," Slater speculated. "And, if you'll back me up, I think it's about time we force them to come clean with each other. And I'd like to teach two little girls a long-overdue lesson about telling lies, wouldn't you?"

Arnold leaned closer to the table, his eyes narrowing in conspiracy. "I certainly do. Have you got a plan?"

Slater gave him a cocky grin. "No, but I think between the two of us we might be able to come up with something, don't you?"

Nice, mild Arnold Jones's grin was bordering on the sinister as he picked up his coffee cup and lifted it in a mock salute toward Slater Holbrook. "I'm with you all the way, friend. *All the way!*"

"Okay," he said, plotting. "Now, I think we ought to let the girls have their fun impressing each other tonight, and I think we should do all within our power to support them," he observed slyly. "But then . . ."

150

The door bell rang that night as Jillane was putting the finishing touches to her attire. The reunion committee had decided that the participating alumni would wear the original gown or tuxedo they had worn to the senior prom ten years ago. For some the request would be impossible, since the years had not only mounted up quickly but the unwanted pounds had also. But in Sue's and Jillane's cases, they were both able to squeeze into their dresses with only the minimal amount of sucking and grunting.

The frothy emerald-green chiffon swirled in a delicate mist around Jillane's feet as she hurried to answer the persistent bell.

When she opened the door, she was greeted by a man wearing a florist's cap and holding two large boxes in his hand.

"Flowers for Mrs. Jillane Marcus and Ms. Sue Talbot," he announced blandly.

"Oh, really!" Her eyes eagerly surveyed his packages, thrilled that Slater would have been so thoughtful.

"If you'll just sign here, ma'am." He waited patiently while she scribbled her name on the receipt and reached into her pocket for a tip.

After she shut the door a few moments later Jillane eagerly tore into the box with her name on it. Her eyes widened as she withdrew an *enormous* arrangement of orchids . . . twelve of them, all different colors, all ridiculously large. She turned the arrangement around in her hand, studying it for a moment. Ye Gads! Surely there was some mistake. Slater had better taste than to send this ostentatious arrangement! Slowly she brought it up to her shoulder and stared at it in the hall mirror. Mercy! She looked like an orchid bush . . . if there was such a thing.

Sue entered the room, grumbling under her breath. "Can you help me with these pearls? I can't seem to find the clasp. . . ." Her voice trailed off as her gaze fastened on the clump of flowers on Jillane's shoulder. She began to giggle. "Good grief! What's that?"

Jillane smiled lamely. "Stanley sent me a corsage."

"Boy, did he ever," Sue sympathized. They both stared at the floral arrangement. For all its many colors not one of them complimented the dress Jillane wore.

"I was sort of thinking that the florist had made a mistake?" Jillane offered hopefully. She rummaged around in the box and came up with a card. Her heart sank when she saw "Stanley"'s name signed on it. "No, I guess not . . . well, maybe they put the wrong card in the box?" She tried again. "I'll just give them a quick call and check." She didn't want to hurt Slater's feelings by not wearing his gift, but she prayed there had been some mistake. Obviously this creation was meant as a casket spray. . . .

"Oh, by the way." She picked up the second box and handed it to Sue. "Arnold must have sent you a corsage too."

"He's such a dear. I knew he wouldn't forget." Sue tore happily into her box. Seconds later she wrinkled her nose. Inside the box was an equally outrageous corsage with at least twenty blooms of

152

an exotic flower. "Oh, my," she said weakly. "I think you're right. The florist *must* have made a mistake."

But a few minutes later the florist confirmed that there was no mistake. The corsages had been ordered by none other than Mr. Stanley Marcus and Mr. Arnold Jones.

As Jillane hung up the phone the two women looked at each other frantically. "Why do you suppose they ordered them so . . . large?" Sue pleaded.

"Ladies!" Slater emerged from the kitchen, followed closely by Arnold. Both of them looked breathtakingly handsome in their black tuxedos and ties. "I see your flowers have arrived."

Jillane glanced up and gave him a stupefied grin.

"I must say"—Slater turned to Arnold—"they look as lovely as we thought they would."

"My, my!" Arnold surveyed Sue affectionately. "They certainly do. Here, dear. Let me help you put them on." He took the flowers out of her hand and proceeded to pin them on her dress, using all five pins the florist had thoughtfully inserted in the box to keep it firmly secured.

"Arnie, these must have cost you a fortune," Sue protested in a hushed whisper.

"Nonsense, darling," he said, soothing her in a voice loud enough for all to hear. "Where you're concerned, money is no object. How many times do I have to tell you that?"

Sue looked at him in disbelief. He hadn't *ever* told her that!

"Brotherrrr," Jillane groused under her breath as Slater politely helped her secure her outlandish

153

corsage. "Was this Arnold's idea? No doubt it was. The millionaire wanting to show off!"

"No, it wasn't his idea," Slater denied in a hurt tone. "I thought a heart surgeon's wife ought to stand out in the crowd, so I told the florist to spare no expense. There." He patted his work proudly. "And, believe me, dear, you *are* going to stand out tonight."

Jillane's heart sank. That was what she was afraid of!

Slater's gaze softened as he noticed for the first time how very pretty she looked in her old prom gown. "May I say you look extremely lovely tonight?" he murmured.

She smiled at him despite her dismay and curtsied primly. "Why, thank you, sir. And may I say how handsome you look tonight?"

"You may." He leaned over to kiss her lightly.

"Don't smudge my lipstick!"

"I wouldn't think of it," he promised, but proceeded to smudge it, anyway. "Well, if my beautiful wife is ready to go, your carriage awaits." Slater bowed in a courtly manner and extended his arm to her.

It took some maneuvering to get the full dresses and petticoats down the narrow flight of stairs, but they eventually managed. As they walked out on the street, Jillane looked around expectantly. "Where's the car?"

"Oh, Arnold wants us to be his guest," he told her nonchalantly.

Sue stiffened with apprehension. Oh, no! How would she explain to Jillane and Stanley that her millionaire husband was driving a car seven years old? And how had he gotten the car here, anyway, when he'd flown into town?

But instead of Arnold's old blue Chevrolet sitting at the curb, there was a long, black limousine, reeking of luxury. A uniformed chauffeur was waiting to drive them to the dance.

Before either of the women could say anything, the men had helped them into the backseat and climbed in behind them. Sue looked around her, mystified. Turning to Arnold, she opened her mouth to speak, but he closed it with a quick tap of his forefinger.

Jillane's eyes were as round as silver dollars as she took in the splendor that surrounded her. The car had a bar, a television, and even a microwave oven!

"Impressive, huh?" Slater prompted enthusiastically.

"I'll say!"

"Arnold must really have the bucks," Slater agreed, taking out a cigar that was at least twelve inches long and casually lighting it.

The glowing tip of the cigar nearly touched the seat in front of them. Jillane's eyes opened wide with amazement. She didn't know they made cigars that long!

"I say, Stanley, old man. Where *did* you find a cigar that length?" Arnold inquired enviously. "That is quite impressive!"

"Oh, sorry, old man. Would you care for one?" Slater dug around in his coat pocket and came up with another cigar as long as the one in his mouth. "All successful doctors smoke them."

Jillane gasped at his snobbish remark and gave

155

him a warning nudge. She didn't know what had gotten into him tonight, but he was carrying his part a little too far!

He glanced over at her expectantly. "Did you want one, dear?"

"No, thank you." She looked at him crossly. She wasn't quite *that* urbane! "I just don't think you should talk about work tonight."

The car was soon filled with a gray, stifling smoke as Slater and Arnold puffed away, striking up a lengthy conversation on tax shelters. Jillane and Sue rode in silence, trying their best to figure out what was going on. By the time they got to the school gym Slater had professed to owning fourteen apartment complexes, two dairy farms, and a thoroughbred racing stable. But even as obnoxious as he was being, Arnold was even more overbearing as he had bragged about his vast holdings. It occurred to Jillane that instead of envying Sue, she actually felt sorry for her. She would feel sorry for *anyone* who had to spend their life with Arnold Jones. If *all* millionaires were this unbearable, then she would be more than happy to settle for one very average man!

The school auditorium was already teeming with people when the two couples arrived. The chauffeur let them out, promising to be back by midnight.

Jillane and Stanley walked ahead as Sue and Arnold hung back.

"Can you believe that guy?" Jillane fumed under her breath. "I was about ready to tell him to take his money and shove it . . . and you too!"

"Me? What did I do?"

"You're *over*doing it," she accused. She slapped irritably at her corsage, feeling like it was about to shut off her air supply. "Why don't you just act normal, instead of like some rich lunatic!"

"But, I thought that was what this was all about. I thought you wanted to impress Sue with how well you're doing in life. . . ."

"Maybe I did at first, but I don't anymore! If I were married to a pompous ass who went around talking about how wealthy and successful he was, I wouldn't think I was doing all that well! I think I'd have to reevaluate my goals in life!"

Slater grinned and took another puff off his ridiculous cigar. "Are you trying to tell me in your own subtle way that all this lying and pretending was a complete, asinine waste of time and that being married to a rich man is not what it's cracked up to be?"

She felt her face flood with color when she realized how easy he had trapped her into confessing what she had felt all along. "Just because Arnold is the pits doesn't mean that a man can't have money and be nice at the same time," she defended lamely.

"I realize that, but I think a woman would look for other more redeeming qualities in a man than the size of his bank account. Now admit it. You do too."

He was deliberately goading her and she knew it, but she wasn't about to make a scene in front of Arnold and Sue. She still had her pride even if she was wrong! Snatching the cigar from his mouth, Jillane angrily stomped it out on the floor, taking

157

out all her pent-up frustrations on the glowing butt.

"I take that to be yes?" he inquired calmly.

"Arnold Jones! What is going on?" Sue demanded under her breath as they followed Jillane and Stanley down the long hallway filled with green lockers.

"Going on?" He looked at her innocently. "What do you mean?"

"You know what I mean!" she hissed. "Where did that limousine come from?"

"You mean that limousine we just rode in?"

"Yes, of course I mean *that* limousine!" she snapped. "What in the world do you think you're doing? You don't have that kind of money to throw away!"

He peered at her angelically. "Why, isn't that what any respectable oil barren would drive?" he asked innocently.

A cold chill ran down her spine as the awful truth began to dawn on her. He knew! He knew about the lies she had told Jillane! And now he was going to make her suffer for them. *When* and *how* had he found out? It must have been sometime today, because he had been perfectly all right last night. Her mind raced frantically as her face turned a sickly gray. Exactly *how* far would he go to protect her? Would he continue to play the part of a millionaire in front of Jillane and Stanley? Or would he be the typical Arnold Jones she knew and tell them the truth and apologize for her despicable actions?

"A-Arnie . . ." she stammered helplessly. For

one brief moment she had seen the hurt in his face and she knew what he was thinking. That she wasn't proud of him, not in the way she would be if he were actually the filthy-rich oil executive she made him out to be. And he couldn't have been more wrong! She loved him for what he was, and she was willing to spend the rest of her life proving that to him, if only he would be willing to let her after this disastrous weekend.

Taking her hand tightly in his, he pulled her toward the gym door where Jillane and Stanley were waiting. No more could be said for the time being.

All Sue wanted to do was dig a hole and bury herself in it, but she took a deep breath and pasted a fake smile on her face for the benefit of Jillane and Stanley . . . and, for the life of her, she didn't know why she continued to bother.

CHAPTER NINE

As she waited outside the gym, Jillane started to think that if they were wise, she and Sue would refuse to go to the dance with Slater and Arnold the way they were acting. Obviously Slater was up to something, but she couldn't figure out why he had picked this time to try to teach her a lesson. After all, he had bent over backward all week to help her carry out the charade. Perhaps he had gotten caught up in the lie himself and was simply amusing himself by trying to outdo Arnold? She could hope the two men would cease their despicable bragging before they were introduced to her old schoolmates, but somehow that seemed like an awfully big chance to take.

Grabbing Sue's arm, she pulled her aside for a few moments' privacy. "Uh . . . listen. Do you really want to go in that hot gym and mill around with people we haven't seen in years?" she whispered anxiously. "I mean, we've already visited with the ones we were really close with several times this week," she argued.

Sue looked at her blankly. "Are you serious?"

"Perfectly," she returned between clenched teeth.

Since the night was already ruined for Sue, she was more than eager for a quick reprieve and the chance to speak with Arnold in private. "Well, I don't mind, but how are we going to explain it to the men? They have gone to an awful lot of trouble. . . ."

Jillane glanced over at Slater and Arnold. "I know they have, and I don't want to hurt your feelings, Sue. But don't you think they're both being a little obnoxious about their money?"

Sue cast her eyes down guiltily. The men had annoyed her too. But she knew Arnold was only trying to impress Stanley and Jillane for her benefit, so how could she criticize him? "Well, I did notice that Stanley was going on a bit about his wealth tonight. . . ."

"Stanley!" Jillane's eyes snapped wide-open. "Don't blame it all on Stanley! I thought I was going to fall asleep with all of Arnold's talk about his precious stocks and bonds!"

Sue gasped indignantly. "He wasn't one bit worse than Stanley Blowhard was when he was boasting about all the time-deposit certificates he's got molding away in the *four* banks!"

"Stanley Blowhard . . . well, I *never!*"

"Now, come on, Jillane! Don't you think Stanley was overdoing it just a teeny bit when he lit Arnold's cigar with a rolled-up dollar bill?" Sue cornered.

Slater glanced up at the mention of his name and frowned as the women's voices began to rise above the noise of the crowded hallway.

"All right," Jillane said. "I'll admit they're *both* acting like perfect jackasses, and I don't want to take the chance that they'll embarrass us at the dance. So you'd better get busy and help me think of something else we can do!"

A glance at their fancy attire proved to Sue that there wasn't a whole lot of choice. "I don't know what we *can* do with all four of us dressed to the gills," she complained.

The sound of Arnold's and Slater's robust laughter reached them as Slater slapped his companion on the back, then lit another of the gigantic cigars and began to puff away.

"We'd better hurry," Jillane warned. "I'll bet he's just told another big one."

"What do you mean, 'another big one'?" Sue countered suspiciously.

"I mean, we'd better hurry and get them out of here before they ruin us!"

Hurrying over to the men, they spun them around and headed them down the hall as fast as they could.

"What's going on?" Slater demanded indignantly as Jillane hustled him down the hall through the thronging crowd.

In truth he knew what was going through her mind. Undoubtedly she was thinking that he and Arnold would embarrass her and Sue in front of their friends tonight, which was far from the truth. Both Slater and Arnold had agreed that their performance would be solely for the ladies' benefit alone. But, of course, Jillane and Sue would have no way of knowing that. Having watched Jillane's discomfort grow and balloon from the moment they had left the apartment, Slater was still determined to carry through with the plans he and Arnold had made that morning. He knew how ridiculous and overbearing they were being. But they wanted to prove the valuable point that what the two women had bragged about all those years to one another was not what they really wanted out of life at all.

Slater's conscience had nagged him once or twice since they'd come up with the plan. In all fairness he had to admit that Jillane did regret her rash actions of the past few years and had been miserable all week because of them. Sue, too, must have been on pins and needles, in fear that her sins would be found out. But Arnold was adamant that the two women needed the episode to leave a strong and lasting impression on them—which it no doubt would before the evening was over.

Smiling brightly at several new arrivals walking in the door, Jillane pushed Slater ahead of her and out into the balmy night air. "We've changed our minds. We aren't going to the dance," she explained as Arnold came stumbling through the doorway with Sue right behind him.

"Not going to the dance!" Both men chorused at the same time. "Why not?"

"Like I just said," Jillane snapped. "We've changed our minds!"

"Well, this is a fine time to change your mind!" Slater grumbled as he fell in step with her. She had turned and flounced off down the street at a rapid pace, leaving him little time for argument. "I thought this was the *big* night."

"It's not so big," she insisted, glancing around the street and trying to figure out what to do next.

"Do you mind telling us where in the devil we're

going?" he demanded. "We don't even have a car
. . . and we won't have one until midnight."

Her eyes fastened on the bus coming down the
road, and she took the only way out she could
think of. "Let's ride the bus!"

"The bus!" Three voices echoed in disbelief as
Jillane motioned for the driver to pull over.

All four climbed aboard, and the women went to
the back of the bus and took their seats, trying to
look as inconspicuous as possible—a very difficult
task indeed, as they were dressed in chiffon!

Trying to steady themselves as the bus's doors
swooshed shut and the vehicle lurched forward,
the men made their way down the aisle and took
the seat across from the two women.

Biting her lower lip pensively, Sue was close to
tears. "I don't want you to think badly of Arnold,"
she whispered. "I've never seen him act this way
before."

"Don't worry about it," Jillane said, trying to
soothe Sue absently, and thinking that none of this
was Sue's fault. Actually Slater was the culprit!
Why he had picked this time to make her miserable
she didn't know. Especially since the week was
about over and his part in the scheme nearly finished. Maybe he was trying to get rid of her!

Hazarding a glance across the aisle, Jillane felt
her heart miss a beat at the thought that maybe
he'd decided he didn't want to become involved
with her after all, and this was his way of getting off
the hook. For some reason that speculation frightened her. Though she had tried to guard against it,
her feelings for him had grown . . . to the point
where she was beginning to wonder if, despite all

her good intentions, she was actually falling in love with the man.

The bus jostled along as Jillane blindly turned her attention to the passing scenery, trying to decide what they should do. It seemed to her that the air had become stifling, and she was finding it hard to breathe.

"I'm going to have to get off this bus," she warned, reaching up to jerk the cord above her head.

"But where are we?" Sue protested as she fell into step behind her.

"I have no idea. I only know I'm going to be sick if I don't get out of here."

"Hey, wait a minute!" Slater called. "Is this where we're getting off?"

Jillane shot him a scathing glare. "This is where *I'm* getting off," she corrected.

But when the bus pulled away from the curb, Slater and Arnold were standing on the street corner with them. They smiled angelically. "Now what?" Slater asked in a pleasant voice.

Jillane and Sue began to walk. By now they had run out of patience and had decided to completely ignore the two men in hopes that they would soon take the hint and leave.

"Come on, ladies. We can't just wander around the streets all night," Slater coaxed.

"Do you have any other suggestions?" Jillane barked.

"Yeah. Let's go buy a paper and see how the stock market closed," he proposed.

"Good idea!" Arnold said, supporting Slater enthusiastically.

Jillane paused and glanced up to read the large sign they were standing under: CITY ZOO. It was open late that night.

"I have a better idea. Let's go visit some of your relatives." Reaching for Sue's hand, she gathered up her gown and stepped up to the ticket office, waiting while the men purchased tickets.

One hour later Arnold and Slater was standing in front of the monkey cage, pitching peanuts as the women sat on a park bench miserably munching on popcorn.

For much of the evening Jillane had been toying with the idea of confessing to Sue that she had been lying all along. Then they could get this fiasco over with, let Sue and Arnold have their laugh, and then all go home. But, somehow, every time she opened her mouth to speak, the words became lodged in her throat.

"This has been the most miserable night of my life," Jillane admitted wearily, watching the monkey house with a defeated gaze. Since the monkeys in the City Zoo were known for their disgraceful manners, Jillane wasn't at all surprised to see one of the smaller animals scoop up a handful of feces and hurl it at Slater and Arnold, making them stumble all over each other in a frantic scramble for safety. Turning to Sue, Jillane observed dryly, "Get that monkey's name, and the next time we come out here, we'll bring him an extra banana."

"I wish he'd hit them both," Sue said heartlessly. "It would serve them right. They've been throwing enough of their own around tonight—it would only seem like poetic justice."

Jillane sighed. "Sue, I think we need to have a long talk."

Sue let out her own fatalistic sigh. "That's a good idea. I have something I've been putting off telling you, but I think the time has come to—"

The sound of a high-pitched scream interrupted her. They glanced up to find a young girl kneeling on the ground beside an elderly man who had been feeding the monkeys only moments earlier.

"Help me, someone!"

Jillane and Sue jumped to their feet and rushed over to join Slater and Arnold, who were already kneeling at the young girl's side.

"Please help me," she cried in dismay. "I don't know what's happened to him!"

Slater unbuttoned the old man's collar as Arnold hurriedly felt for a pulse. "I'm not getting anything," Arnold warned sharply.

"Does he have heart trouble?" Slater demanded.

"No . . . at least, he never has before. Do you think that's what it is?" she pleaded.

"I don't know, but I'll go get a doctor." Slater was on his feet and entering a phone booth as the last words left his mouth.

"But, you *are* a doctor!" Sue shouted after him in a puzzled voice.

"Oh, no!" the girl wailed. "Is my grandpa dead? He just can't be! We were just standing there feeding the monkeys when he had some sort of a fit and just fell over. . . ." She started to cry.

"Just take it easy." Arnold spoke softly and tried to calm her fears. "We'll get some help. . . ."

Sue turned to Jillane helplessly. "Why isn't

167

Stanley doing something instead of calling a *doctor?*"

"Wellll . . ."

Not waiting for an answer, Sue turned to the fear-stricken girl. "If it is your grandfather's heart, I'm sure he'll be fine, dear. That man over there is a famous heart surgeon, and he will take care of him," Sue said, trying to comfort the girl, and peering at Stanley anxiously as he inserted coins in the pay phone. "Won't you, Stanley?"

Jillane cringed. She busied herself with removing the man's jacket and propping it under his head of snow-white hair. This was the moment she had been dreading. And what a horrible time for it to happen!

Glancing at Jillane helplessly, Slater shrugged a weak apology. "I'm sorry, Sue, but no, I'm not a doctor," he confessed, then picked up the phone to dial the emergency number.

"You're not?" Sue looked at him as if he had picked this time to make a bad joke.

"No, he isn't," Arnold intervened calmly. "No more than I'm a filthy-rich oil executive."

Jillane's head snapped up. "You're not?"

Both girls looked at each other, their eyes narrowing suspiciously. Then they spoke at the same time, as it dawned on them: *"You've been lying to me!"*

At the sound of loud voices the old man's eyes opened, and he looked around in confusion. "What . . . what happened?"

"Oh, please lie still, Grandpa! We think you've had a heart attack," his granddaughter said nervously, trying to soothe the old man.

"Heart attack! Balderdash!" He sat up and rubbed his head painfully. "I just tripped over my own feet! That fool monkey was throwing **#!# at me, and I was trying to get out of the way!" he said indignantly.

Jillane and Sue blushed at his colorfully descriptive words, then burst out laughing. Slater and Arnold joined in, and before long, they were all laughing at the top of their lungs.

Suddenly Jillane and Sue stopped and looked at each other sternly.

"Stanley isn't a heart surgeon?"

"No. He works for the telephone company, and his name isn't even Stanley," Jillane admitted. "And Arnold isn't an oil executive?"

"No. He owns a service station . . . a very prosperous one, though," Sue said defensively.

"You don't drive a Jaguar?"

"No, and if you're not really married to a wealthy heart surgeon, you don't have a Porsche, aren't building a new home, don't have diamond rings at the jeweler's, or so many fur coats in storage you can't even count them!"

"Heavens no . . . not even one."

"That's wonderful!" Sue exclaimed.

"Then it's true . . . you're just as ordinary as I am?"

Sue grinned lamely. "Probably more so."

"You dirty rat! I can't tell you how happy I am to hear that!" Jillane's face broke out into a wreath of grins as they fell into each other's arms and laughed until their sides hurt.

The men helped the elderly gentleman to his

feet and assured them that he was all right before Slater went to cancel the emergency call.

By that time, the girls had managed to get themselves under control and were happily babbling away to each other, all tension of the past week broken.

"You were in on this all the time, weren't you?" Sue accused, looping her arm through Arnold's lovingly. "When did you find out how awful I really am?"

"At breakfast this morning," he revealed, then made his face turn stern. "I hope you've learned your lesson. Honesty is *always* the best policy."

"I've learned, believe me, I've learned. I'll never tell another lie as long as I live!" she vowed adamantly.

"That goes double for me!" Jillane joined in.

Slater pulled her to him and kissed her long and hard before he released her. "I hope you're not mad at me."

"Let's just say I was rooting for the monkey all the way," she scolded. "But I suppose I deserved everything I got."

Both couples caused heads to turn as they exchanged long, forgiving kisses.

"Well, look, if no one minds, I think Sue and I have a lot to talk about," Arnold said. "We'll see you back at the apartment later."

"I think that's a great idea," Slater agreed. "And I think Jillane and I might go by the house and check on the kids."

"What kids?" Sue exclaimed.

"Oh, I'm sorry. Sue, I want you to meet Slater Holbrook," Jillane said with a laugh.

Slater and Sue grinned and shook hands.

"He has six children."

The grin dropped off Sue's face instantly.

"Six what?" she repeated sickly,

"Six children, and they're every one precious!" Entwining her arm through Slater's, she smiled up at him adoringly. "Let's go see *our* children."

The entire household was sleeping when they arrived by taxi thirty minutes later.

Tiptoeing up the carpeted stairway, Slater paused at his parents' doorway and tapped on the door softly.

"Who is it?" Fay's sleepy voice answered.

"It's me, Mom. I just wanted to let you know that Jillane and I have stopped by for a few minutes."

"Oh, do you want me to get up?"

"No, no, you stay where you are. I'll talk to you in the morning."

"There's a fresh-baked cake in the pantry. Help yourself."

"Thanks, we will."

Deciding to check on the children, the couple sneaked in and out of the row of children's rooms, pausing only long enough to admire each sleeping child.

The last room was Tara's, and they stood at her crib, looking down at her in awe. She was sleeping on her stomach, her knees pushing her chubby bottom straight up in the air. Damp tendrils of dark hair framed her face, and she looked like an angel to Jillane. She smiled tenderly and read-justed the light blanket around her to make her cooler and more comfortable.

"She really is beautiful, isn't she?" Slater whispered reverently.

"Yes, she certainly is," Jillane agreed in a voice that held much more pride than it should have.

Slater's arm came around her and pulled her close as they stood staring down at one of God's most perfect creations.

"You'd make a nice mommy," he whispered against her ear, his warm breath sending tingles along her skin.

Instead of resenting his words, she thought about them seriously for a moment. Would she make a good mother?

Apparently he didn't expect an answer, because he was soon guiding her out of the baby's room and back downstairs where he made coffee while she sliced the cake.

When they had finished eating, they wandered out on the deserted patio. The mellow lights and floating candles illuminated the shimmering turquoise water in the pool, making the area a seductive and inviting haven for lovers.

Reaching over to flip a switch discreetly hidden by a curtain, the soft strains of music immediately filled the air as Slater closed the patio door, affording them complete privacy.

The air was warm and smelled of fragrant honeysuckle as he took her in his arms and began to glide her around the pool to the melody of a dreamy love song.

"Did I happen to mention that you were the prettiest girl at the prom tonight?" Slater murmured in a low, sensuous voice.

"How would you know?" she bantered flirtatiously, suddenly feeling as if time had taken her back ten years and she was once again dancing with a high-school sweetheart. "We didn't even make it into the gym where you could survey the candidates."

A warm shiver raced through Jillane as his eyes ran lazily over her lovely features. She was wearing her hair down tonight, and that pleased him. Somehow he thought it made her look older. The soft brunette hair fell over her shoulders in a luxurious mass, framing her oval face and making her eyes a dark, smoky green. "I don't have to look at the others," he said softly. "I know who the prettiest is."

Drawing closer to him, she buried her face in the warmth of his neck, and they whirled around the edge of the pool under a sky filled with a million tiny lights.

"Would it scare you if I told you that I think I'm falling in love with you, pretty Jillane Simms?" he whispered softly in her ear.

"Yes. But it scares me more to know that I feel the same way," she confessed.

"I'm still too old for you," he argued as he nuzzled her neck gently.

"No, you're not."

"I'll be forty years old in a few more weeks. I was starting junior high when you were born."

"Twelve years. That isn't so very much time. When two people love each other, age shouldn't matter. Age is only a state of mind, anyway," she sustained. "Besides, that isn't the real problem."

"No, I realize that. It's the children."

"The children are wonderful," she defended.

173

"It's me I'm concerned about. I'm not at all sure I'm what you need Slater." But in his arms she found herself forgetting all the years she had vowed that she didn't want a family. All the work and disorganization, illnesses, noise, and confusion . . . all that didn't seem to matter one whit at the moment, only the feel of him pressed against her and his familiar, pleasant smell filling her senses to the point where she could no longer think straight. Maybe she had been wrong. Maybe a family was exactly what she needed, if they would have her. "I think I would be lucky to have such a fine man and lovely children to call my own," she finished lovingly.

He pulled back, startled, yet hopeful that he had heard her correctly. "Are you serious?"

She could only nod weakly—even she could scarcely believe the words she was saying.

"You mean, you might reconsider your feelings and marry me?" he said, prodding hesitantly. His feelings right now were completely foreign to him. For so long he had dismissed the idea of remarrying. He had honestly thought he could be happy spending the rest of his life playing the field, but this last week had turned his world upside down.

Wagging her head more eagerly, Jillane's face fairly glowed with anticipation. "If you'd ask me."

"If I'd ask you . . ." His voice turned husky with emotion, and his eyes searched hers hungrily, seeking the truth of her words. "Oh, lady, I have a feeling I'd ask you much more than that if you'd let me."

"Then you've changed your mind about marriage?"

"No. You've changed it for me."

Parting her lips to receive his kiss, she raised up on tiptoe as he gathered her tightly to him, his mouth capturing hers.

A surge of hot desire passed between them as the kiss grew deeper and more passionate. Slater was slightly heady from the feel of her breasts molding against his chest as his hands explored her soft lines and gentle curves. If anyone had told him one short week ago that he would fall so quickly and overwhelmingly in love with this woman, he would have doubted their sanity, but it had happened, and now he felt completely intoxicated by her presence.

Brushing her lips against his as she spoke, Jillane sought to slow down his ardor until she could think a bit more clearly. There was no doubt she loved him, but this was all happening so fast. "We don't have to get married right away, do we?" she asked softly, her voice anxious.

"Whenever you say. Why? Would you rather wait awhile?"

"I think that would be the wisest thing to do," she offered hopefully. "That way, we can get to really know each other, and the children can become used to the idea." She felt the thrilling sensation of his mouth as it moved along her neck in sensuous kisses as she spoke. "I mean . . . this *has* been sudden, and I wouldn't want either one of us to make a mistake. Don't you agree?"

"If that's what you want," he acquiesced, kissing the pulsing hollow of her throat.

"You don't sound very convinced," she murmured.

"No, I can't say I'm adamant about it," he confided. "I guess that's one of the few benefits to being forty years old. By that time, a person pretty well knows what he wants out of life and is ready to go for it. But if you want to wait for a while, I'll try to be patient."

At that moment it was important to Slater that she know her mind, and he was willing to wait until she was absolutely sure.

"It isn't because I question whether I love you or not," she assured him quickly. "Even though it's been sudden, there isn't a doubt in my mind that I love you."

"I know, and I understand. Right now, all I can think about is getting you alone somewhere and, as you say, 'really getting to know you,' " he urged.

"Ummm . . . me too," she agreed dreamily. "It won't be long. Arnold and Sue should be leaving first thing in the morning, and then we'll be totally alone."

"Have a heart, lady. Why don't we find a little place of our own to spend the night together?" he pleaded in a low voice.

"That would be terrible," she chided.

"Oh, no, it wouldn't," he corrected suggestively.

"It would be nice?" she amended impishly.

"I'd try my best to make it that way," he promised.

Looping her arms around his neck, she gazed at him solemnly. "Slater, you *do* understand why I want to wait for a little while before we get married?"

Slipping his hands up her arms, he drew her

176

closer, his mouth gently touching her lips with tantalizing persuasion. "When you're ready, I'll be waiting."

Once more they became lost in a smoldering kiss, caught up in desire and the magical night surrounding them.

Only once—and ever so slightly—did she feel a slight tug of uneasiness over what she had just committed herself to. But she soon forgot all doubts as he danced her into the dark cabana and proceeded to kiss away all her apprehensions.

Mrs. Slater Holbrook. Mother of six.

Now, that really didn't sound all that bad . . . did it?

CHAPTER TEN

"You're going to *what!*" Both Slater and Jillane nearly dropped their cups of coffee as they sat at the table the next morning having breakfast with Sue and Arnold.

"Don't look so surprised," Sue told them calmly. "After all, Arnie and I *have* been engaged for six months. We've just decided to go ahead and get married while we're here. That way, you and Slater can stand up with us. Isn't that great?"

"Well . . . yes, I suppose so," Jillane conceded weakly, "But, isn't this sort of sudden? I mean, I had no idea you were thinking about getting married . . . here."

"Oh, we weren't," Arnold admitted. "But I've checked with Henry and he says everything is going great at the station, so I've decided this might be the best time for me to take off a few extra days." He smiled at Sue affectionately. "We'd talked about coming up here on our honeymoon, so we figure now is as good a time as any to tie the knot."

"It'll take awhile to get a license and blood tests, unless you drive to Reno," Slater pointed out, trying to keep the disappointment from his voice. If

Arnold and Sue stayed a few more days, what would that do to his need for privacy with Jillane?

Now that the air had been cleared and Sue and Arnold knew he wasn't Jillane's husband, it was going to be harder to be alone with her. He supposed he could continue to share her bedroom, but knowing Arnold's highly moralistic view on the subject, he would feel downright guilty if he did.

"That's exactly what we were thinking of doing. Driving to Reno and getting married tonight," Sue supplied eagerly. "That way, we can leave Monday and have a short honeymoon on the way back."

"Oh . . ." Slater looked at Jillane hopefully. "Well, that's great. You say you want to go tonight?"

"Yes, if possible," Arnold confirmed. "Sue and I thought we might rent a car and drive up to Reno this afternoon by ourselves. Then you and Jillane can join us this evening."

"Are you sure you'll have the money to rent a car?" Sue chided. "I'll bet those flowers and that chauffeured limousine you rented last night set you back a pretty penny."

Arnold grinned. "It did, but it was worth every cent of what I spent to see the looks on your faces."

"Renting a car sounds great," Slater intervened with an uneasy chuckle, noting the looks the two women *still* had on their faces at the mention of the evening before. "But I'm not at all sure I can get off long enough to accompany you."

"Oh, Slater, no! This is Sunday," Jillane protested.

"I know, but with the strike going on, there's no such thing as Sunday," he reminded her.

"Don't you think you might find someone to work for you?" Jillane prompted softly. It had been past three when they had finally parted last night, she to her shared bedroom with Sue and he to his sleeping blanket made even more uncomfortable by thoughts of where he could have been and what he could have been doing if it weren't for Arnold and Sue.

Her mouth still tingled at the memory of his possessive kisses and ardent murmurs of love when they had been alone in the dark cabana. She had hoped he would seek her out this morning for a more personal good morning, but just as he had walked in the kitchen, Sue had followed right behind.

"I don't know, honey. Everyone down there is already pulling double shifts," he cautioned. "But I'll see what I can do." He turned to Arnold. "What time do you want us to meet you if I can pull it off?"

Arnold shot Sue a special smile, one that passed only between those thoroughly in love. "I thought we might make the ceremony early so I could take us all out to dinner and celebrate."

"Oh, that sounds like fun," Jillane exclaimed, beginning to get caught up in the unexpected plans. "And we would *have* to celebrate such a happy event," she reasoned, turning back to Slater excitedly. "What do you think the chances are of being able to find someone to take your place?"

"Slim to zero, but I'll try. Even if I do find someone, I'm sure I won't be able to get more than a few hours off," he cautioned. "We'd have to be back by morning."

Jillane could have sworn she saw the faint beginnings of an embarrassed blush tinge Arnold's receding hairline. "Oh, my. I'd planned on being back long before then," he assured, casting a sheepish glance in Sue's direction. "I'm looking forward to a good night's sleep on a real bed again . . . among other things."

All four laughed, knowing full well what the "other things" were that he was looking forward to.

"Well"—Slater picked up his cup and hurriedly drained it—"I'd better get down to the office and see what I can come up with." Leaning over to Jillane, he kissed her warmly, his gaze locking briefly with hers in a silent exchange of "I love you."

"I'll give you a call and let you know what I've come up with."

"I'll keep my fingers crossed."

Snatching one last kiss from her, he left for work as Arnold sat his cup down and pushed away from the table. "If you ladies will excuse me, I need to see about getting a ring for my bride before we get this shebang under way. I want to say good morning to Petunia too. I like that little rascal."

Jillane had to laugh. She would give anything if Slater and Petunia got along half as well as Arnold and the dog did. Even Sue had grown fond of the little terrier while she had been here.

As he made his exit Sue pulled her chair closer to Jillane expectantly. "I'm glad we're finally alone. Now, tell me what's *really* going on between you and Slater Holbrook!"

Other than the brief explanation they had given each other at the zoo the night before, the girls had not had an opportunity to discuss the unexpected turn of events.

"What's there to tell? I'm crazy in love with the big buffoon!" Jillane confessed happily.

"Who could blame you? He's such a doll and he has a marvelous personality!" Sue said, complimenting enthusiastically. "How long have you known him?"

"I've worked with him for quite a while, but I've only actually known him personally about a week," she acknowledged.

"You've only known him a week?" Sue let out a low whistle. "Then it's been rather a whirlwind romance?"

"Yes, I guess you could say that. We both tried to avoid becoming involved, but that turned out to be a big joke." Jillane's smile tugged at the corners of her mouth, just thinking about their ridiculous agreement. "Actually you're the one responsible for us being together. I guess I should thank you for showing up on my doorstep at precisely the time Slater was there to fix my phone and mistaking him for Stanley Marcus. That's what started our relationship."

"Who else would I have thought was standing in the doorway of your apartment half dressed?" she teased. "Mercy, what a chest that man has on him!"

"It is rather nice, isn't it?" Jillane accepted the compliment proudly, because he most certainly *did* have a marvelous chest, and she planned to explore it more fully the first chance she got! "Oh, and by the way, I still have the lovely silver tea service you and Arnold sent me and my fictional husband as a wedding gift. I'll give it back to you before you leave. I was too ashamed to use it."

"Please keep it. That way, when you actually *do* get married, I won't have to go to all the bother sending you a gift again. But back to the original discussion. Why would you and Slater even attempt to stay away from each other?" Sue said, bantering. "I would think two healthy adults would find that rather hard to do sleeping in the same bed together . . . and you *have* been sleeping together, haven't you?"

"Not the way you're thinking. We've been in the same bed, but he's been disgustingly civil about this whole thing," she complained. "I didn't want to get involved because I was afraid I'd do just what I've done—fall in love with the guy. And with his children and all, I wasn't sure that would be wise. I have been fascinated by Slater Holbrook from the first day he walked past my desk and glanced in my direction with those heavenly gray eyes." She paused and let the familiar shivers race along her spine, the shivers that unfailingly appeared every time she thought about him. Moments later she cleared her throat and continued. "He didn't want to get involved because he has this crazy idea that he's too old for me."

"Too old? How old is he?"

"Almost forty."

"And he thinks *he's* too old for *you*?" Sue

laughed. "Arnie's forty-five! By the way, what do you think of my Arnie?"

"I think he's everything and more than you said he was," Jillane returned sincerely. "Oh, Sue, I think the two of you are going to be so happy together!" No matter what they had been doing to each other over the years, Jillane was honestly happy to see her friend end up with such a good, solid man in her life.

"I know we are!" Sue bubbled. "But what about you and Slater? Are you actually thinking of making your relationship permanent?"

She was aware of Jillane's feelings concerning children after all these years. Sue knew it wasn't anything personal, but Jillane had always been surrounded with younger brothers and sisters and had developed an unusual need for a little breathing space all her own. That's why Sue was finding it difficult to believe her friend would actually be considering marriage to a man with a ready-made family, no matter how nice the guy was.

"We've talked about it," Jillane confirmed hesitantly.

"I know it isn't any of my business," Sue said, "but am I talking to the same Jillane Simms who, one night at a bunking party, took an oath in blood that *she* would never be caught with a houseful of children after she married? I mean, is this really *the* Jillane Simms, whose idea of a perfect wedding gift for the happy couple is a certificate for a vasectomy for the groom?"

"One and the same." Jillane grinned guiltily.

"What happened?"

"I fell in love with a man who had six kids, that's what happened!"

"Oh, dear. That does complicate matters, doesn't it?" Sue sympathized.

"A little," Jillane admitted, "but, surprisingly I'm already beginning to grow attached to the children in just the short time I've been around them. They're polite and well behaved. And except for the baby, they've had so many upheavals in their life, I'd like to try to make things easier for them if I could. Who knows, maybe I might make a wonderful mother," she suggested, more to convince herself than for the benefit of the woman sitting opposite her.

"I'm sure you would, but since your feelings against having children have been so strong all these years, are you sure you know what you're doing?"

"Yes, I think I do."

"You're afraid you're letting your emotions override your common sense? I think you really have to think about this, Jillane," she cautioned softly, having only her friend's welfare at heart. "After the honeymoon glow wears off, you'll still have six children to look after."

"I know. . . ." That thought alone had cost Jillane several hours' sleep last night. Was she being foolish to even consider such a relationship? But then the niggardly thought would always return to haunt her; she *loved* Slater Holbrook. Could she callously cast aside the only man whom she had ever fallen hopelessly in love with because of a set of unusual circumstances fate had dealt to him,

185

merely because they were not particularly to her liking?

A lot could be said for a man who unselfishly devoted his life to raising another man's children, and she couldn't see herself penalizing him for that. Wouldn't she want that very same sort of man to raise her own child if the occasion ever arose? "Slater and I have discussed this at great length," Jillane said, defending herself. "Neither one of us plans to rush into anything until we see that it's going to work."

Sue let out an audible sigh of relief. "I'm glad to hear you say that. At least give yourself some time to be sure. You two seem so right for each other, it would be a shame to throw it all away with one hasty decision."

Jillane reached over and touched Sue's hand affectionately. "Thanks for caring. We'll be careful, and in the meantime, you and Arnold have a happy life."

"Oh, I intend to see that we do. Unlike you, we want children just as soon as we can have them," she confided. "Arnold says he isn't getting any younger, and I would sort of like to have at least one before I turn thirty."

"Well"—Jillane grinned impishly—"if you can ever get that rascal into bed, you can get started!"

"That rascal only has a few more hours to savor his celibacy," Sue said matter-of-factly. "Then it's curtains."

They giggled at the impending doom of Arnold Jones while they lingered over their coffee a few moments more. Finally Sue announced that she had to do her hair and nails and went off toward the bathroom, happily humming under her breath.

Jillane picked up the phone and called Fay to check on the children. A sleepy Fleur answered on the fifth ring.

"Did I wake you?" Jillane apologized.

"Uhmmmm . . . what time is it?"

"A little after ten."

A low groan was audible as Fleur burrowed back under the covers.

"Hey!" Jillane prompted. "May I talk to Fay?"

"They've all gone to church," Fleur managed groggily.

"I bet you were out late last night," Jillane guessed.

"Very."

"Don't you have a curfew?"

"Yes. . . ."

"What is it?"

"Midnight."

"And what time did you get in?"

"Two . . . or three, I didn't look at the clock." Her voice suddenly became more alert. "Don't tell Slater. He's a real beast about that curfew time."

"He should be since he's responsible for you," Jillane pointed out gently.

"For heaven's sakes!" Fleur moaned. "I'm going to be married in a few weeks!" Fleur had begun to realize that even though Jillane was only ten years older than her, she would not give her any slack when it came to obeying Slater's orders. Consequently they had already had a couple of minor run-ins with Fleur informing the youthful housekeeper that she was not her boss!

187

"And when you are married, you'll be able to stay out as long as you want," Jillane reasoned. "Until then I think you are obligated to obey Slater's rules."

She didn't like having to play the heavy any more than Fleur enjoyed having her do it, but after all, since Slater couldn't be there lately as often as he would have liked, it was one of her jobs as housekeeper to see that his household was run according to his wishes.

"Grandma didn't say anything about me getting in late!" she challenged.

"I don't want to argue, Fleur. Just take care that it doesn't happen again," Jillane warned kindly.

The resounding sound of the receiver being slammed down was a clear-cut reminder that Fleur had no intentions of following Jillane's orders.

The altercation put a damper on Jillane's spirits the rest of the day. The last thing she wanted to do was have Fleur upset with her, but she still felt she had a job to perform and would perform it the best way she knew how.

Slater called around two to let her know that he had performed a miracle and found someone to take over for him. He said he would be home around four, and they could leave as soon as he showered and changed clothes.

Confessing that she and Fleur had just had a small disagreement, she apologized to him for upsetting her but explained why she felt she had to do what she did.

"Don't worry about it. You were right and she was wrong," he upheld matter-of-factly. "She knows what time she's supposed to be in, and

188

she also knows she'll have her tail in hot water if she isn't."

"I hate to have her mad at me," Jillane said fretfully.

"She'll get over it. I have to run," he urged. "I'll see you around four."

When she replaced the receiver, she still wasn't convinced she had done the right thing by making Fleur angry. But there was nothing she could do about it now.

Making a mental note to do something extra nice for her next week, she went to take her bath and get ready for the coming evening.

The drive to Reno was a pleasant one. Slater looked exceptionally handsome in his dark suit and tie as he helped Jillane into his old station wagon.

"I thought you might bring your B.K. car," she speculated, glancing around the messy interior of the old car.

There were discarded soda cans and candy-bar and gum wrappers littering the floorboards.

"I wanted to, but I loaned it to Fleur and John for the evening." Slater grimaced as his eyes took in the evidence of the children's earlier presence. "I was going to run by and have this car cleaned up, but I didn't have time. I know this isn't very fancy, but it will get us there and back."

"It's fine," she dismissed, caring not in the least what she rode in. As long as she was with him, nothing seemed to matter.

She had selected a dress of soft, pale yellow to wear for the occasion. Slater had thoughtfully

189

stopped at the florist again and bought her a bouquet of summer flowers to carry and a spray of miniature roses and baby's breath to pin in her hair.

Unlike the night before, these floral offerings were dainty and lovely and completely befitting the lovely creature who wore them.

Pulling her over next to him, Slater put his arm around her and snuggled her close to him.

"You look good enough to eat," he murmured suggestively, "and you smell good enough to attack."

"You like my perfume? It's called, Take Me."

"Okay. You have any preference where?"

She gave a seductive laugh and nibbled on his neck. "No, surprise me."

"How about right here in the middle of the highway?" he bargained.

"No, I think I would rather pick somewhere a little more private."

"All right," he persisted. "How about your place . . . tonight."

"Uhmmm . . . I think if Sue and Arnold are planning on staying with us tonight, we should be nice and give them our bed," she decided.

"You think they're really planning on staying at your apartment tonight?" he inquired.

"I'm sure they must be . . . at least they didn't indicate any differently." She sighed.

"They're nuts. I wouldn't want to spend my wedding night in someone else's house," he grumbled.

"Oh . . . any particular reason why not?" she parried.

190

"Let's just say I work better alone." He grinned and stole another kiss. "Okay, if our bed is going to be occupied, how about the sleeping bags?" he suggested, undaunted in his plight. "We can share one of those bed of nails tonight."

"No, I hate to sleep on the floor, and I hate beds of nails even more."

His hand came over to gently mold to one of her breasts. "Then I guess we're back to the highway, because in another few minutes you're going to have me in a situation that is going to have to be taken care of in some way before the evening's over."

Their mouths met for a lingering kiss as he tried to keep his eyes on the road and his hands off her. Taking pity on his overworked libido, she sighed and lay her head down on his chest.

"I made time to call Fleur this afternoon," he informed quietly.

"Oh, I hope she wasn't still mad at me?"

"She'll get over it," he reiterated. "I told her that when I wasn't around, you had the final word and she wasn't to give you any trouble."

"Maybe you shouldn't have. That will only make her resent me more, and I'd like to be able to get along with her."

"She needs to know who's boss when I'm not around," he argued. "And as far as getting along with her, you're doing a great job with all the children. Caleb told me yesterday that he thought you were a pretty foxy lady," Slater teased.

"He does! And what did you say?"

He shrugged indifferently. "I said you were all right as far as housekeepers go."

"Housekeepers!" She pulled his mouth back over for a renewed assault. When she had him where she wanted him moments later, she giggled and laid her head back down on his chest. "I think running off and getting married is romantic, don't you?" For a moment he didn't answer, causing her to repeat the question. "Don't you?"

"Yes, I think it is. In fact, I've been wishing all day that it was our wedding we were going to," he confessed in a voice that had suddenly grown husky.

Glancing up, her heart melted at the wistful tone of his voice. "Oh, Slater . . . that's a sweet thing for you to say."

"You can take it as sweet if you want to, but I didn't mean it that way."

"Oh . . . then how did you mean it?"

Careful, Jillane. If he's getting serious, it's much too soon, she warned herself.

"I think I might have meant it as a proposal," he admitted, squeezing her lovingly. "Oh, honey, I know you want to wait for a while, but I haven't been able to think about anything else all day, Jillane. Why don't we make it a double wedding and get married along with Sue and Arnold tonight."

She closed her eyes, feeling as if she were being caught up in a whirlwind. "Slater, how could you? We just had that long talk about marriage last night and how we were going to wait . . . don't you remember? We decided to get to know each other better before we actually took that kind of step. . . ."

"I remember, but I also remember how you feel

192

and taste and smell, and I guess I go a little crazy. I'd like to show the world that you're mine and take you home with me," he defended. "The more I think about it, the more sure I am about my feelings, and I just don't see any point in waiting."

"But it's too soon. What about our age difference?" she pleaded, searching for any excuse to postpone a decision. "Have you forgotten about that?"

"No, but you said it doesn't matter." He glanced at her worriedly. "Does it?"

There was no way she could be anything less than honest at this point. "No, of course not."

"Well, I know, no matter what you say, that it's the children who worry you, and I've been giving that some thought too. In a few years they'll be up and gone and we'll have the rest of our lives together," he challenged. "They're really good kids, Jillane, and even if there are a lot more of them than you ever dreamed about having, I think you would grow to love them just like your own if you would allow yourself. I mean, surely you weren't thinking of waiting until all the children are grown before you would consent to marry me, were you?" he asked in the most pitiful voice she had ever heard.

Actually, that thought *had* crossed her mind once or twice.

"Oh, Slater." She didn't know what to say. He was making it sound so reasonable . . . so tempting. "I just don't know. We barely know each other."

"Don't you think I've thought about that too? But I'm in love with you and I think you're in love with me," he argued. "I'm going to be forty years old before too much longer. I've wasted a lot of time looking for you, lady, so at least give me a chance to offer you a few good years before I get old and feeble."

"Old and feeble . . . Slater, you're getting paranoid! You're not going to shrivel up and drop off the end of the earth the day you turn forty," she objected. "Why, some people even say that life begins at forty."

"*Those* people are only trying to make forty-year-old people feel better!"

"You are worrying entirely too much about your age," she scolded, then began to giggle at his unfounded fear. "I read somewhere that you know you're forty when your back goes out more than you do, and your little black book contains only names ending in M.D. Is that really the truth?"

"Hell, yes! When you go to a fortune-teller and she offers to read your face, it begins to hurt your feelings," he noted sourly.

She patted his hand in mock reassurance. "It must be rough."

"Now that I've found you, Jillane, I want to get on with my life. I don't want to wait around to marry you," he implored huskily.

Her mind whirled with confusion, love, anger, complete frustration, and, yes, resentment. Resentment that she would find herself in such a confusing situation and not know what she should do about it.

Laying his hand over hers, he gazed at her with those dark pools of smoldering ash. "I love you. Marry me, Jillane . . . tonight."

"What if it's all wrong?" she whispered.

"It won't be. It's right, and if you'll give me the chance, I'll prove it without a shadow of a doubt." There was such love radiating from his eyes that she was powerless to resist his tender urgings, and in the end, her good common sense flew right out the window, and she allowed love to win out.

Sighing hopelessly, she lay her head back on his chest and closed her eyes in defeat. "All right. I'll marry you, Slater Holbrook, and I hope to goodness you know what we're doing!"

The ceremony took less than ten minutes, and when the final legalities were out of the way, the new Mr. and Mrs. Slater Holbrook and Mr. and Mrs. Arnold Jones left the small chapel and found a nice restaurant not far down the road to eat their celebration dinner.

An hour later all four plates were barely touched, and they soon gave up all pretense of being interested in the meal.

"I'm sorry Jillane and I have to start back so soon and drag you with us, but I have to be at work first thing in the morning," Slater apologized as they left the restaurant and got in the car for the return trip home. "It would have been nice if we all could have stayed up here tonight."

Assuring him that nobody minded, they made the drive back to town in record time. Unlike the drive up, Slater kept his wife close to him but discreetly refrained from touching her. The front seat of the car was not conducive to making love to his new bride, which he feared he would do once he touched her.

Jillane seemed to understand his need without being told, and she sat quietly lost in her own world of thought. She wasn't sorry she had married him. Deep within her heart she knew she would never regret for a moment becoming his wife, but there were other concerns she couldn't keep dormant, no matter how much she willed herself to try.

Concerns such as, how in the world would she react to having six children? Could she handle her new responsibilities and what would the children think when they had yet another new mother brought into their life?

Noting her unusual silence, Slater pulled her closer to him and picked up her hand to kiss it tenderly. "I'm sorry we had to use my class ring for your wedding ring. I intend to replace it with a diamond and gold one just as soon as I can get a chance to go to the jeweler's."

"I don't mind," she assured him, snuggling against him with a contented sigh. "I have everything in the world I want right now."

As their car came into the city limits Slater glanced at her and smiled. "I think I could go to work from a motel just as easily as I could from our apartment," he noted. "That way, no one would have to sleep on the floor." He pulled the car into the drive of a Ramada Inn. Kissing Jillane briefly, he glanced into the rearview mirror to see if Arnold had followed him into the parking lot. "I'll just check with the Joneses to see if that would be all right with them."

A few minutes later Slater returned and grinned. "It's fine."

As the two men entered the registration office to secure the rooms, Sue got out of the car and came over to join Jillane.

"Jillane . . . I . . . I wanted to wish you all the happiness in the world, but I can hardly believe you actually married Slater tonight. I mean, not after what you said this morning," she blurted.

"I know what I said this morning, but I changed my mind," Jillane said curtly. "Slater and I discussed it on the drive up to Reno, and we decided there was really no reason for us to wait."

"Oh . . . well, I just hope you know what you're doing," her friend said meekly.

"I do. I love Slater very, very much . . . just like you love Arnold," she said in an effort to convince herself that she had been right as much as to convince Sue. "I can see no difference in our cases."

"There are *six* differences I can think of right off hand—"

"Not in my opinion, there aren't," she said, cutting Sue off irritably. "Not only do I love Slater, but I'm sure in time that I will learn to love the children as well. It will just take a small period of adjustment, that's all."

"Okay." Sue relented, determined to let the subject drop. Jillane was a grown woman who should know her own mind, and Sue wasn't going to worry about her any longer. "I only wanted to be sure you knew what you had let yourself in for."

Now that she had done her duty and warned Jillane of what she could be facing, she was now going to devote her full attention to her husband, and Jillane could worry about her own problems.

"I know what! Let's make a pact. Let's meet at this very same motel ten years from tonight and celebrate our anniversaries together," Sue proposed brightly. "By then, Arnold and I will probably have at least three children of our own, and we can compare notes!"

"That sounds like fun," Jillane agreed. "Slater and I will be here . . . with however many children we happen to have at that time."

"It *will* be fun." Sue giggled. "You know Slater is going to want sons and daughters of his own. Maybe by then you'll have eight or nine kids!"

"Yeah." Jillane's eyes turned slightly glassy. "Maybe we will. . . ."

CHAPTER ELEVEN

"Sorry, honey. This was the best I could come up with on such short notice," Slater apologized as he handed her the meager toilet articles he had been able to buy from a machine in the motel hallway. "I think it will get us through until tomorrow morning."

Jillane smiled and gratefully accepted the toothbrushes and toothpaste from him. "I'm sure they will be fine."

"I told Arnold we would give them a call in the morning when we got up. I hate to ruin the honeymoon, but . . ."

"I'm sure they understand," she said, trying to soothe him.

They looked at each other for a moment, a sudden shyness stealing over them. "Well . . ." Slater laughed nervously. "You're welcome to use the bathroom first."

"Thanks. It shouldn't take me long," she murmured.

Switching on the television, Slater went over to the bed and sat down as she disappeared into the bathroom.

He needed to have a little talk with himself. All

of a sudden he was as nervous as a high-school kid about to have his first encounter with sex.

His new wife was twenty-eight years old. He wouldn't be surprised if this wasn't her first time to make love, so why should he be so apprehensive? To his dismay he found he was answering himself, something he had been doing more and more the older he got, long before he finished the question. It all just seemed so darn perfunctory! It would be so much nicer if the first time they made love it could be a natural thing: highly combustible and completely spontaneous. Somehow, sitting here waiting to be plucked like a Christmas goose was unnerving.

Did he need a shave yet? His hand reached up to explore the smooth jaw that had seen a razor only a few hours ago. No, he was all right. At least he wouldn't leave skid marks on her tender skin when he kissed her.

Underwear! Had he put on a good pair instead of reaching in the drawer and grabbing whatever his hand happened to land on? It seemed like he was always in such a hurry, and he wouldn't be a bit surprised if he had put on a pair of briefs that needed a road map to get into. Standing up for a moment, he took a cautious peek and discovered that luck was with him.

Sinking back down on the bed, he closed his eyes and leaned back on the pillow, deciding to just relax and quit thinking about it. After all, he was forty years old, and if he didn't know how to make love to a woman by now and have her enjoy it, he probably wasn't ever going to learn.

Married. He was married again! Heaving a sigh,

he ran his fingers through his hair nervously. It would be all right. They might have a few more problems facing them than the average couple starting a marriage, but he loved Jillane more than he had ever loved anyone or anything in his whole life. Even though he felt she still had some reservations about their hasty decision, it would work out all right. He would make it. This time he wasn't that impetuous teenager who had been carrying his brains in his pants. This time he knew what he wanted, and it went far beyond the natural physical attraction he felt for her.

For a moment he let his mind linger on his new wife, and he found himself growing aroused at the mere thought of her.

Maybe he'd better make a flexible game plan so he wouldn't do anything wrong. Let's see . . . When she came out of the bathroom, they would lie on the bed and talk, maybe neck a little, watch television. . . . His eyes focused on the set before him. Maybe there would be a good movie on. His mouth dropped open at the picture of the nude man and woman making guttural noises on the screen, and he scrambled guiltily off the bed and ran to the set.

Those people were sick! He peered down to see what channel the set was on for possible future reference as Jillane emerged from the bath. Turning the picture off quickly, he grinned lamely at her. "That was fast."

"It's amazing how quick I am with a toothbrush," she bantered. "What were you watching?"

"I don't know . . . whatever was on," he excused, his face growing a bit red.

"Well, the bathroom's all yours," she offered.

It took even less time in the bathroom for him, and he was back five minutes later, helping her turn down the bed.

"Was there a good movie on?" she asked conversationally, wondering why they should all of a sudden be so tense around each other.

"I really didn't check," he admitted, climbing in on his side and settling the blankets around him. She noticed in his haste that he had forgotten to take his trousers off.

"Do you think we should put in for a wake-up call? I'm a pretty sound sleeper."

"Yeah, and you'd better make it plenty early. I'll have to run by the apartment and change clothes before I go to work."

Taking care of the chore efficiently, Jillane switched out the light and lay down beside him a few minutes later.

They lay in silence for a few minutes, listening to the heavy traffic roar up and down in front of the motel. Suddenly Jillane broke out in a fit of giggles.

Slater propped up on his elbow and stared at her. "What's the matter with you?"

"I thought you *always* slept in the buff," she taunted.

"I do. . . ." He paused, and it dawned on him what she was referring to. With an embarrassed chuckle he reached under the cover and removed the pants she was laughing at, along with her skimpy underwear while he was gaining courage. Pulling her over on his bare chest, they snuggled against each other's warm, bare bodies as he kissed

202

her between spurts of laughter. "Is that what you were wanting?" he coaxed.

"No . . . not exactly, but you're close." Their laughter ceased gradually as he put his hands on either side of her face and drew her mouth back down slowly to his. "Hello, Mrs. Holbrook."

"Hello, Mr. Holbrook."

"Is my beautiful wife trying to tell me she wants me to make love to her?" he coaxed lovingly.

"I think she is a bit eager to discover her new husband. Does he mind?"

All shyness and uncertainty had fled, and it now became a natural and spontaneous act of love as Slater murmured her name and kissed her long and passionately.

When his hands cupped her breasts, she felt her body tighten and respond to his intimate touch. Giving a soft, contented sigh, she wrapped her fingers through the thickness of his hair and let her tongue tease with his until her lips parted willingly under the probing command of his.

She could feel the strength of his body next to hers. It was so strong and powerful, easily capable of overpowering hers, but his touch was gentle, almost reverent, as his probing hands sent a hot flame of longing racing through her.

His mouth continued to open over hers, his sensuous caresses taking her higher and higher to elevating planes of desires as he rolled over with her. Then he was lying on top of her, his fingers buried in her hair, kissing her with a passion he had held in check far too long.

"We're going too fast," he murmured against her ear, letting her feel his urgent need against the bareness of her thigh. "Do you want me to slow down, or should we just let nature take its course this first time?"

She could feel the desperate thump of his heart mingling with hers. She wanted to tell him he could not go fast enough for her, but words failed her as she shook her head and whimpered softly, burying her face in the carpet of silken hairs on his chest.

"Do you want me half as badly as I want you?" he urged, needing to hear that she was as on fire for him as he was for her.

"Oh, Slater . . . from the first day I saw you I've always wanted you, in every way."

His arms tightened in command, and she was willingly lifted up to receive him as his mouth smothered her moan of desire.

"Well, lady, you can rest assured, I'm yours for as long as you ever want me," he murmured just before his words were smothered by her lips and they both became lost on a sea of passion.

And then all was lost as they both raced toward a desire that wanted not only to please but also to totally consume.

His mouth claimed hers with a demanding mastery. Their passion grew and grew until it became a white-hot volcano and completely swept them along in its molten tide.

Several hours later the cool draft of the room's air conditioner made Jillane reluctantly stir and pull a light blanket over them. They had dropped off to sleep almost instantly after making love, and she was still drowsy from passion.

Moving only slightly, Slater gathered her back in

his arms, his mouth searching hungrily for hers, but he fell back asleep before the kiss was completed.

It was right! her heart sang contentedly as she dropped off to sleep. Their marriage was right, and everything else would work out.

Jillane was still half asleep the next morning in the car when Slater handed her a cup of coffee and glanced over at Sue and Arnold's car. "Are you sure you two wouldn't like to have breakfast before we go?" he called to them from out his car window.

Sue was cuddled in Arnold's arms, still half asleep. She yawned and murmured something unintelligible.

"Thanks, but we'll wait until we get back to the apartment. We don't want to be the cause of your being late for work," Arnold refused in a sleepy voice.

Slater looked down at his wife, who was innocently sipping on her coffee. "It won't be their fault," he noted with a sexy wink at his wife. "I'm afraid we didn't get up as early as we had thought we would."

The wake-up call had come on time, but they had forgotten to allow for certain distractions that were unforeseen, consequently causing them to be running about forty-five minutes behind schedule.

She smiled, and her eyes assured him that she had enjoyed every minute of the delay.

Resting her head on his shoulder, she savored the feel of him next to her. It was still hard to believe that she was now Mrs. Slater Holbrook as they made the short drive back to the apartment.

Refusing an offer for breakfast again, Arnold and Sue went off to the bedroom to pack for their return trip home that afternoon, while Slater showered and shaved. Jillane busied herself with fixing their first breakfast as man and wife. As they sat down to eat the majority of the food went untouched as they kept finding excuses to kiss one another.

Walking to the door with him, Jillane reached up and straightened Slater's collar affectionately as the two lingered.

"What a way to spend a honeymoon," he lamented. "I'm on my way to work, while the little phone company peon gets to stay home and do nothing all day except think up more clauses you want put in the contract. See, if you'd only hustle up there and get your fellow workers to sign the contract the company is offering, I could probably play hooky today, and no telling what we could come up with to keep us entertained."

"Yes, that is sad," she sympathized wistfully. "It's a nice, rainy day. We could probably think of lots of things to do if only you didn't have to go to work." She made work sound like a dirty four-letter word. "Granted, our honeymoon was rather brief, but I still thought it was wonderful. Are you insinuating that you didn't care for last night . . . and this morning . . . and what's to come this evening . . . and in the morning . . . and tomorrow night . . . and—"

"Whoa! You're not talking to Superman, you know." But his kiss gave her the impression that if he weren't, at least he was close. "I'll make it up to you, honey. As soon as the strike's settled, we'll get away for a week or so. How does Hawaii sound to you?"

"Hawaii!" She squealed and threw her arms around his neck in excitement. "Are you serious?"

"Of course I'm serious." He chuckled, closing his eyes and holding her tightly against him. "If you get a chance, stop by a travel service and pick up some brochures. We'll start making plans."

"What about the children?"

"You just make the plans and let me take care of the rest."

"Speaking of taking care of things." Her voice grew very shy. "I think we got a little carried away last night, but I don't think there has been any harm done . . . yet."

"Oh . . . yeah, I thought about that . . . after it was too late. You want me to take care of the birth control?"

"If you wouldn't mind. At least for a while." She tilted her head thoughtfully. "I think the Simms family has several sets of triplets in it. I must remember to ask mother when I call her today."

Slater's face paled visibly. "Triplets! I'll get something today."

"You're sure you don't mind?"

"Believe me, I don't mind." He picked up the sack lunch she had prepared for him. "Oranges again today?"

"No, I put a banana in this morning," she related absently, trying to remember exactly who in the family had the triplets.

"I hate—"

"I know, I know. You *hate* bananas!" she finished resignedly. "I can't say that I'm surprised to hear that. Eat it, anyway."

Leaning over to kiss her good-bye, he patted her fanny adoringly. "I'll get away just as soon as possible today. We'll pick up where we left off this morning."

Jillane grinned and shook her head in disbelief. "How old did you say you'd be on your next birthday?"

He grinned. "I warned you I was still in prime shape," he boasted with mock arrogance.

"Go to work." She laughed.

"I guess I don't really have a choice. Oh, you mentioned calling your parents today. Why don't you meet me over at my house around six or so. I'll take a dinner break, and we'll break the news to my family, then we can call yours. I'm sure if they can't meet me personally, they'd at least like to hear the voice of the man who married their daughter."

"They'll love you, just like I do," she promised.

"And be sure the kids are all there. I want to introduce them to their new mother personally," he said proudly.

When he was finally on his way, she shut the door and leaned against it, her lips still tingling from his last kiss.

Mrs. Slater Holbrook. She still couldn't believe it!

The moment she stepped in the Holbrook house late that afternoon, a wall of new apprehension sprang up around her. No matter how hard she tried to pass it off as jittery nerves, she couldn't shake the slight feeling of uneasiness that prevailed upon her.

Hercules was chasing the family cat through the living room as she let herself in the front door, nearly knocking her off her feet as he barreled by her like a whirlwind.

Grabbing for a vase that wobbled precariously on the hall table, she sucked in her breath and caught it moments before it reached the floor.

Fleur was descending the staircase as Jillane set the vase back on the table and dared to breathe again.

"Oh. It's *you,*" the nineteen-year-old said, greeting less than enthusiastically.

Jillane tried to make her smile much brighter than she felt. "Hi. Where is everyone?"

"Grandma and Grandpa had to take the baby back to the doctor, so I'm stuck baby-sitting."

"Is Tara ill again?" Jillane asked apprehensively.

"Something was sure wrong with her," she informed Jillane irritably. "She woke up several times last night and bawled her head off. Grandma isn't sure what's the matter this time, so they took her back to the doctor."

Setting her purse down on the sofa, Jillane glanced around at the unusually messy interior of the room. "What's happened to the house?"

Fleur looked at her blankly. "What's wrong with it?"

There were three sets of muddy boots discarded in the hallway, dripping-wet raingear draped around chairs, a sack of discarded cookies in the middle of the floor, not to mention the path of potato-chip crumbs that would rival the Oregon

Trail leading into the kitchen. "It looks like some-one has been eating in here."

"Oh, yeah. I guess they have," she agreed. "Since it's raining, the kids are playing inside to-day. Wong has several friends with her. They're in the kitchen making peanut butter and jelly sand-wiches. Joey and Eben are up in their room making a Play-Dō city. Gad, Grandma's going to have a heart attack when she sees what they've done to the carpet! Say, are you going to stick around here for a while?" Fleur cocked her head and looked at Jillane expectantly.

"Yes, Slater's supposed to meet me here at six. . . ."

"Oh, great! Can you look after the kids until Grandma gets back? I promised John I would meet him for a hamburger before he goes to work."

"Well, I—"

"Gee, thanks." She turned and bounded back up the stairs before Jillane could protest.

"Hey! Slater wants all you children to be here when he gets home this evening," she shouted to Fleur's fast-disappearing back.

"Oh, good grief! What time will he be here?"

"Six o'clock. Can you be back by then?"

She let out a snort of aggravation. "I suppose I'll have to be!"

Heaving a tried sigh, Jillane began to pick up the wet boots and carry them to the utility room. As she walked through the kitchen she tried to ignore the four little girls sitting at the table smearing gobs of peanut butter on a gigantic loaf of french bread.

"Hi, Jillane," Wong greeted her warmly. "We're making sandwiches. Want one?"

"No, thanks." She peered at the long loaf of bread oozing with brown peanut butter and sticky jelly. "Why aren't you using regular bread?"

"We were awful hungry," she explained. "We wanted a fat sandwich." Tumbling out of her chair, she went over to the refrigerator to retrieve the milk, her hands leaving sticky imprints wherever she touched. Graciously she proceeded to pour milk into four of the largest glasses she could find.

Apparently the girls hadn't eaten in weeks, Jillane thought as she sat the boots in the utility room on newspapers. She dismally surveyed the overflowing hamper of dirty clothes and decided Fay had been too busy with the baby to start the wash today. Fifteen minutes later she had sorted out the laundry and started a load of towels.

The girls were just finishing their snack, and it looked as if they had more on their clothes than had reached their mouths.

"We're going up to my room to play paper dolls," Wong announced with a strawberry grin. A large plop of jam fell off her dress and hit the floor in a plop.

"Not until all of you wash your hands, you're not." Jillane killed that theory quickly. "There are towels and soap in the bath off the utility room."

A herd of trampling feet passed her as the children rushed to obey her orders. After a lot of giggling and the sound of faucets being turned on full force, they came back to the kitchen, the front of their dresses sopping wet. "We're through."

"Yes, I can see that. Why don't you run along

and play at the other girls' houses for a while?" Jillane suggested tactfully. By the time she cleaned the kitchen, living room, and the bathroom they had just destroyed, it would be time for Slater to come home. She was trying not to think about what Joey and Eben were doing with the Play-Dō.

"Unh-uh. We can't," Wong said with a solemn shake of her dark curls. "All their mommies already told us to come over here and play."

"Naturally," Jillane muttered. "Well, go to your room and play, but try to be neat. Okay?"

"Okay!"

"And when Slater gets home, he wants to talk to all you children. Will you give Joey and Eben the message?"

"Sure!" Wong wasn't hard to get along with. They pushed their way out of the kitchen and left the swinging door flapping like a branch in a high wind.

After they left Jillane automatically went about cleaning up the kitchen, trying to force down the frightening thought that this could very well be the story of her life from now on!

She had just finished mopping the last remains of jam off the floor when the back door slammed and Caleb came tracking across the clean floor in his hiking boots.

"Caleb! Those darn shoes are dripping mud all over the floor," Jillane scolded.

Glancing down at his feet, Caleb failed to understand what she was complaining about this time. "I wiped my feet!" he defended.

"It sure looks like it."

Huge gobs of mud and grass now adorned the

floor as he shrugged and picked up an apple from the bowl on the table. "What's for supper?"

He was saved from hell's fury by the back door opening once more. In walked Fay, Hubert, and Slater, who was carrying the baby.

Forgetting the mud, Jillane peered at the baby anxiously. "How is she?"

Slater walked over and kissed her hello. "Hi, honey. Mom says the doctor isn't sure what it is. We're supposed to watch her closely and keep him informed."

"Does he think it's serious?"

"No, I don't believe he does," Fay comforted. "It may be as simple as her coming down with one of the childhood diseases. We'll just have to wait and see." She sat her purse down on the table and turned around to face Jillane, her face breaking out in a joyous smile. "Now, what's this I hear about congratulations being in order?"

Slater grinned guiltily as Jillane shot him a puzzled glance. "Mom and Dad drove up just as I did. I'm sorry, but I have been so darn excited all day, I found myself telling them before they could even get out of the car," he confessed.

"My dear ones, you don't know how happy this makes us," Fay said in praise, reaching out to take her son and his new wife's hand. "Hubert and I couldn't be happier!"

"We certainly couldn't," Hubert supplied with a wry chuckle. "So, you and this lovely little thing have decided to get together. My, my, who would have ever thought it?" He winked at his son knowingly, both of them recalling Slater's adamant protestation of such an event a few days before.

213

Once again Slater could only grin repentantly. "Can you blame me?"

"Can't say that I do." He beamed. And to prove their words, the elder Holbrooks hugged them both and welcomed Jillane into the family with open arms.

Caleb was watching the strange series of hugs and pats with a puzzled look on his face. "What's going on?"

"Caleb, change those boots and go get the other children," Slater prompted, shifting the sleeping baby around in his arms more comfortably. "I'm going to put Tara to bed, honey, then I'll be right back."

"Do you want me to take her?" Jillane offered.

"No, you just help Caleb get the others rounded up."

As he started up the stairway the front door flew open and then was slammed with a resounding bang throughout the house, announcing the arrival of a slightly miffed Fleur.

By the time Slater had returned to the kitchen, the whole family was assembled, wondering what all the fuss was about.

"What is going on?" Fleur demanded petulantly. "I had to cut my date short with John to get back here on time!"

"That isn't going to kill you," Fay said reproachfully, her mild voice sounding sterner than Jillane had ever heard her when she addressed one of the children. "Now just sit down and be quiet! Slater has an important announcement he wants to make."

Giving her grandmother an impatient look,

Fleur quietly took a seat at the table and waited along with the rest for the mysterious announcement.

"Somebody in trouble again?" Eben speculated disinterestedly as he tried to pick the sticky gobs of Play-Dō from under his fingernails. "If it's about the broken window in the garage, I didn't do it this time."

"What broken window? Did one of you guys break another window?" Slater groaned. That would be the fifth one this month!

Eben immediately sank back against his grandmother for protection. "I don't know *who* did it," he vowed innocently. "I think it might have been some stranger passing by the house who did it this time."

"Come on, Eben. A stranger?" Slater raised a highly skeptical brow.

"Slater, dear, we can talk about the window later on," Fay coaxed eagerly. "Don't you have something more important to say right now?"

Turning his attention back to Jillane, her son glanced down adoringly at his new wife. "Yes, I do. Children, the reason I've called you together is to let you know that I got married last night . . . and I want to introduce you to my new wife."

Ten eyes searched the room for an additional female, but they failed to come up with anyone new. Only their grandmother and Jillane were standing there watching them carefully.

"Where is she?" Wong asked warily.

"She's standing right here next to me!" Slater grinned.

"Jillane's standing next to you," Caleb scoffed.

215

"That's right. Jillane and I were married last night in Reno."

"You're kidding!" Fleur grimaced distastefully and stood up. "Why would you do something crazy like that?"

"Because I happen to love her," Slater said curtly, defending himself and not at all pleased by Fleur's reaction to his news.

Feeling a slight twinge of jealousy, Fleur walked over to the swinging door and prepared to leave. "If this is all you wanted, can I be excused now?"

Slater's arm tightened around Jillane protectively. "As soon as you offer Jillane your congratulations."

"Congratulations. I hope you'll be *very* happy!" she replied flippantly, then pushed the door open and ran out of the room.

"Now don't let Fleur upset you," Fay said, speaking up quickly. "I think she's always had a girlish crush on Slater, and she wouldn't want to see *anyone* marry him."

Wong stepped over and tugged on Jillane's shirt, peering up at her with wide eyes. "Are you going to be my new mommy?"

Leaning down, Jillane took her chubby hands in hers. "Yes . . . do you mind?"

"No," she returned promptly. "I have new mommies all the time. Well, I think I'll go back to my room and play paper dolls." She skipped off happily.

"It really could have been a stranger that broke out that window, Dad," Eben pointed out once more, not the least disturbed by the unexpected news.

"We'll talk about it later." Slater tousled his hair affectionately.

"What time are we going to eat?" Caleb grumbled, reaching for another apple.

"I'll have dinner in about an hour," Fay promised. "Aren't you going to say anything about Slater's new wife?"

Caleb studied Jillane. "She's pretty foxy."

Jillane smiled, realizing that he meant it as a compliment. "Thanks, Caleb. You've made my day."

Joey started to leave the kitchen undetected when Jillane stepped over and blocked his way. For some reason it was his opinion that interested her most. "Joey . . . how do you feel about all of this?"

Black, brooding eyes turned on her, and she knelt down in front of him, holding her breath as she waited for his answer. It was slow in coming but more encouraging than she had expected it to be.

"I don't care . . . one way or the other."

"I want you to care," she challenged softly. She reached out to hesitantly touch his face, making him draw back a fraction. "I'll try very hard to be a good mother to you," she whispered secretly, her openness taking him completely by surprise.

"I don't want a mother," he vowed defensively.

"You don't? Why? I thought everyone wanted a mother."

"Because . . . mothers always leave you," he confessed in a rare show of vulnerability.

"Not all of them," she said, trying to soothe him.

His gaze came to meet hers directly, and for the

217

first time, she noted a hesitant spark of interest somewhere in their dark, hidden depths. "Mine always have."

Her heart broke at the sadness of his words. "Well, maybe this time things will be different."

"Maybe." He didn't sound at all convinced, but at least he hadn't closed the door on her permanently.

As Joey left the kitchen Slater strolled over and took her in his arms, drawing her against him for strength. "We're going to make it, honey. Don't worry. There'll just have to be a small period of adjustment."

She smiled weakly and accepted his mouth in a kiss, forgetting for the moment that, like Joey, her doubts still persisted.

"Now, let's call your parents and tell them the good news," he suggested a few moments later. "And please stop worrying. Everything is going to work out all right."

CHAPTER TWELVE

Heaven.

The dictionary defines the word as not only the dwelling place of God, the angels, and the spirits of the righteous after death, but also as a place or state of supreme happiness.

Hell.

The same dictionary interprets the word as a place or state of punishment of the wicked after death, or any place or state of torment or misery.

As far as Jillane was concerned, for the last three weeks she could have thrown out all other words in the English vocabulary, and those two words would have described her life to a tee.

In Slater's arms her nights were heaven with his kisses of uncontrolled passion and tender avowals of love. But in the cold light of morning when she faced the endless duties that awaited her in order to keep a household of eight running smoothly, her life could be described as nothing less than hell.

And, she had to admit dismally, she wasn't doing well at all.

She had always prided herself on being organized and in control, but that had all flown out the window the moment she had taken complete control of Fort Holbrook. Even though the children did their share of the work, she could never seem to get caught up. The house had become messy, the meals were invariably late, and she knew Slater must cringe at the helter-skelter atmosphere that awaited him every time he walked in the front door.

Then guilt would assail her in full force, knowing he was used to an organized household, and she would become even more distressed. Never once had he made mention of the fact that things seemed to have fallen apart since his mother left, and she was grateful for his patience. But the disturbing question was always with her. Was she going to be able to handle her new duties as a mother and wife . . . or much more to the point, did she even want to?

She was trying, but it just wasn't working.

Days earlier, Arnold and Sue had left for their slow, romantic drive home. And now that Fay and Hubert were gone, she was on her own, and the ever-growing feeling of doom hung over her head like an ominous, black cloud.

The only thing she knew for certain these days was that she was falling more in love with Slater every hour. He was all she had ever hoped for in a lover and a husband. And in all honesty the children had not really been any more trouble than six children would naturally be. Fleur was still cool to her, but she was slowly beginning to accept the marriage as a fact she couldn't change. Slater would have a life of his own, and Jillane would be a part of it.

It was the constant noise and lack of privacy that seemed to be the crux of the problem. At times she felt she was still at her childhood home, and then all of the old resentments would begin to grow and fester inside her until she would have to forcefully shove them aside. She loved Slater, and she would do anything to be with him. It was just that she had always envisioned her life as being so different from the way it had turned out.

At times she blamed her growing animosity on the fact that she and Slater were finding it hard to find even a few brief moments together since their marriage. His job kept him away for long hours, and sometimes she would barely get to spend a few minutes with him before his weary body would seek his bed. She was dismayed to hear herself being irritable and cranky, complaining about petty incidents the few times they did manage to slip away together. Slater had been understanding, blaming her irritability on the lack of sleep and her new, awesome responsibilities.

The baby had come down with chicken pox last week, finally revealing the cause of her recent fussiness, and Jillane had had to sit up with her a few nights.

Like Slater had said, it was a hell of a way to spend a honeymoon, but there was no other choice.

After a particularly trying day she had picked up the phone and called her mother, just to have her reassurance that she wasn't losing her mind.

"I really don't know how you did it, Mom," she praised. "I have only six children and you had ten!

Weren't there times when you thought you'd go off the deep end?"

"Oh many." Her mother laughed. "But then there would be other days when I'd stop and count my blessings."

"Mom, didn't you ever resent . . . I mean, just a little bit, the fact that you didn't have a life of your own anymore after the children came along?" she asked hesitantly. "I know Daddy helped, but he wasn't there most of the time. You had all the responsibilities and headaches of running the family."

"What's the matter, dear? Your new family about to get you down?" She chuckled.

"Oh, Mom. I really am trying, but I just seem to be spinning my wheels," she said dismally.

"You're not having doubts about your feelings for Slater, are you?" Her mother's voice lost its former merriment.

"No, but that's the only thing I am sure of at the moment. I love Slater dearly. It's just everything else that's piling in on me."

"Well, I'd be less than honest to say that there weren't a few days when I longed to run off by myself somewhere," she admitted. "But then I'd get to thinking about how lucky I was to have children who were normal and healthy and a husband who loved me. Then I'd stop feeling sorry for myself, put a little more starch in my backbone and a smile on my face, and give them all a big hug. It's simply a matter of getting your priorities in order. Those precious children will be grown before you know it. Then you and Slater will have all the time in the world together."

222

"Yes, I suppose . . . if he doesn't want children of his own," she mused. "Mom, are Aunt Bev's and Aunt Jane's triplets the only ones in the family?"

"Uhmmm, it seems to me that there are more somewhere further down the line. Why?"

"Oh," she replied weakly. "I was just wondering."

Replacing the receiver absent-mindedly, she mulled over her mother's advice. Less sympathy and more starch?

Well, she'd give it a try.

They had been married close to three weeks when Jillane was sitting at the kitchen table with her portable sewing machine in front of her, trying to make a costume for Slater. Wong's dancing class was having their annual father-daughter rehearsal tonight, and Slater was cast as a large, purple grape . . . one of many in a dance where the participants were a giant bowl of fruit salad. Wong was a banana. Since Wong's costume had been furnished, that left only Slater's to contend with.

Her nagging headache wasn't helping the matter any, nor was her lack of expertise in sewing. And one of the children was trying to play some sort of an instrument upstairs; the noise was almost intolerable.

Some progress was beginning to be made on the costume when Eben came dragging a brass instrument into the room, exhibiting a toothless grin. "You want to hear me play 'The Star-Spangled Banner'?"

Actually she didn't. "On a tuba?"

"Yeah. I'm gittin' real good," he boasted proudly, hoisting the shiny monster up on his shoulder. The bulky weight nearly took him to his knees, but he managed to regain control of his teetering limbs and took a couple of practice toots.

"Is that *your* tuba?" she asked in disbelief. She found it hard to imagine that Slater would buy a child Eben's age such a large instrument.

"Nope, it's Caleb's, but he don't want it no more. Slater says I can take lessons on it when I get big enough."

"Oh, then you really don't know how to play it," she noted with relief.

"Sure I do! I learned it all by myself. Watch!"

Her head fairly throbbed as he began to puff and wheeze, sending an undistinguishable and colorfully off-key rendition of "The Star-Spangled Banner," Eben-style, reverberating off the walls. The salt and pepper shakers sitting on the table began to get up and dance as he continued to regale her with his newfound talent.

After what seemed like an eternity he ran out of wind and finally lowered the instrument, reached up to take a hug wad of bubble gum out of his mouth and beam at her expectantly. "There! What did you think of that?"

Shaking her head to try to clear the ringing sound, she was forced to agree with his glowing critique. "Well, it certainly was . . . interesting."

Anyone who could play the thing at all with that many pieces of gum in their mouth had to be given a little credit!

"Hercules is about to eat Petunia!" Wong burst through the swinging door, her eyes wide with fright.

Jillane immediately dropped what she was doing, and all three of them ran to the backyard to quickly separate the animals. This wasn't the first time the two dogs had gotten into a fight, but it was becoming a serious problem. Shouting for Eben to turn on the water faucet, she liberally doused the two feuding dogs with cold water.

Petunia was whimpering painfully as Jillane picked up the quivering bundle of fur and angrily ordered Hercules back to his doghouse. The St. Bernard paused only long enough to shake the water off his heavy coat and issue one final authoritative growl to his opponent, before he slunk off.

Jillane took the little dog into the house and examined her injuries, which luckily proved to be minor this time. With sickening realization she knew that she was going to have to give up her pet. The little dog still failed to get along with Slater, and she was afraid that someday Hercules might actually kill Petunia.

Since Sue and Arnold had seemed to take such a liking to Petunia while they had been here, she decided that if she had to give her up, the dog could find no better home than with the Joneses, if they would have her. Before she changed her mind, she picked up the receiver and dialed their new number.

Sue was delighted to hear from Jillane and readily accepted the unexpected gift. "We would love to have Petunia, but are you sure you want to give her up?" she asked incredulously, knowing how attached her friend was to the pet she had had for years.

"No, but I really don't have any other choice," she had conceded with a shaky laugh. "I'll get

Fleur to watch the baby, and I'll send her to you by air express this afternoon."

It was all she could do to push her resentment aside and lovingly prepare the dog for the trip. As she stood at the airport later that day and watched the plane take off she couldn't help but think that once again she was having to give up another part of her life that had been important to her.

It was late when she arrived back at the house. The costume was still only half finished, and Slater was due home at any time. Because of the unexpected trip to the airport, she hadn't even thought about what to have for dinner.

"I don't suppose you could start dinner for me," she hinted, a little more crossly than she had intended to as Fleur came in the kitchen to get a soft drink.

"No, I can't! I'm meeting John and we're going to the movies."

"Sorry!" Jillane snapped. "I just thought I'd ask for a miracle while I was at it!" She went over to the freezer and started pulling out packages of frozen hamburger.

Caleb came in the back door, leaving oily streaks across the clean floor. He and several other boys had been working on an old car in the garage all afternoon, and he had made countless trips into the house for cold drinks and snacks.

"Hi, when's supper?"

Once more it seemed to Jillane that the boy had a depressingly limited vocabulary, not to mention a one-track mind!

"I have no idea!" she nearly shouted.

"Whew! What's the matter with her?" Caleb looked at Fleur expectantly.

Shrugging her shoulders indifferently, his sister exited the kitchen without another word as Jillane sat back down at the sewing machine.

"You care if I fix me a sandwich?" Caleb inquired reluctantly.

"No, you can't ruin your supper! You'll just have to wait and eat with the rest of us!" she barked.

Reaching for a banana lying on the counter, Caleb headed for the garage once more, deciding not to push the issue.

As the patio door closed behind him Jillane covered her face with her hands and burst out crying. How could she have been so sharp with him? She had been sharp with everyone lately! Caleb was merely a growing boy with a healthy appetite, and it wouldn't have hurt her to let him fix a sandwich.

Wiping at the wet rivulets cascading down her cheeks, she tried to focus her attention on the costume. The baby would be awake and hungry in another half an hour, and she had to have the suit finished by then.

An hour later Slater walked in as she was trying to feed vegetable soup to the baby, put the finishing touches on the grape costume, and keep an eye on the hamburgers that were shooting a black plume of smoke in the air and popping grease all over the stove.

Absently dropping a kiss on her mouth, Slater walked past her, whistling cheerfully. Turning the flame down on the stove, he picked up the spatula to flip the now repulsive-looking meat over. "Hi, honey. I have two good pieces of news for you!

Number one, the union and company finally managed to come up with a new contract this afternoon. They're going to ask the employees to vote on it Friday. That means your boredom will be over and you'll be going back to work soon!" he informed cheerfully.

Her mouth dropped open. Back to work! What in the devil did he think she had been doing for the last three weeks!

Sunning in Acapulco?

Slamming the baby's spoon down on her tray, Jillane's face puckered helplessly as she burst out in tears once more and ran toward the bedroom. The baby broke into a rash of delighted giggles and picked up her bowl of soup and dumped it over her head. Letters of the alphabet dripped off her dark curls and down her ears as her chubby hands gleefully smeared the spilled soup all over the tray. "Look at me!" she squealed.

"Honey, what's the matter? Did I say something wrong? I thought you'd be delighted!" Slater dropped the spatula and started after his wife, then paused indecisively as Tara decided the fun was over and set up a loud wail.

"Come on, Tara, do you have to make such a mess when you eat?" He viewed the sticky conglomeration smeared all over her and shuddered.

It was at least twenty minutes before he was able to get things in the kichen under control, and by that time Jillane had regained her composure and returned.

"Are you all right?" Glancing up from the salad he had been washing, he worriedly studied her red eyes and blotched face.

"Yes, I'm sorry about the outburst. I'm all right now."

"You're sure?" His face revealed his growing concern as he walked over to give her a tender kiss. "I was coming up to find you just as soon as I had the children settled."

"I'm fine, really. What needs to be done?"

Joey came through the doorway, his eyes searching Jillane's tear-streaked face. Walking over to her, he patted her hand and spoke quietly. "Don't cry, Jillane. I'm going to set the table for you."

She looked down at his solemn features, and her heart melted. "Why, thank you, Joey. I really appreciate that." This was the first time she could remember that he had ever voluntarily offered his services to anyone in the family.

"I could even make some of those cookies you like," he offered. "You know . . . those ones with the funny name—snickerdoodles. I remember how."

"No, I don't think that's necessary, Joey, but thank you, anyway."

He went over to the cabinet and took down the plates, then disappeared into the dining room.

Snatching a cracker away from Tara before she ground it into the tray, Slater smiled at her encouragingly. "Why don't you sit down and rest for a few minutes before we eat?"

"I can't," she refused curtly. "I still have to sew the buttons on your costume."

Instead of arguing with her he quietly returned to fixing dinner as she sat back down at the sewing machine.

As usual the house was cluttered, dinner was

late, and it was all she could do to keep from crying again as she angrily picked up a needle and threaded it. How he must rue the day he had married her! she thought dispiritedly. Instead of enhancing his life, she had only succeeded in making it worse.

But if he were having such thoughts, he kept them carefully hidden as he called the children to dinner and got them settled.

Jillane looked up a few minutes later to see him setting a plate full of food down before her. Pulling up a kitchen chair, he picked up his own plate and sat down beside her.

"Why aren't you eating in the dining room with the children?" she scolded softly, deeply ashamed of the way she had been acting.

"Because I would rather eat with my girl," he stated simply.

"Your 'girl' has been acting like a big baby," Jillane snapped, biting back a fresh round of tears.

Setting his untouched plate aside, he rose and walked over to the coffeepot. Moments later he handed her a cup, their gazes meeting briefly. "I wish I could help you with what you're going through right now, Jillane, but I can't," he offered gently. He knew what a hard time she was having adjusting, and he was powerless to help her. "I know it isn't easy, but I want you to know I love you and I'll do anything I can to help you through this rough adjustment period."

"You can't do anything, Slater," she confessed sadly. "You've been wonderful. It's just something I have to work out for myself." Avoiding his penetrating gaze, she wiped at a tear that had slipped out. "You said you had two good pieces of news. Other than the strike being settled, what was the other one?"

"I've found a permanent housekeeper."

"A housekeeper?" His announcement took her by complete surprise. She had assumed *she* was the permanent housekeeper now.

"Yes, I had a chance to interview her today, and I think she's just what we've been looking for." His voice took on an excited pitch. "I think you're going to love Mrs. Steele. She reminds me of Alice on *The Brady Bunch.*"

"What's the matter? Don't you think I can handle my responsibilities?" Jillane challenged defensively. Obviously she couldn't, nor did she even want to, but it smarted to think she was being fired so soon!

"Oh, honey . . ." He sat his cup down and came over to kneel down in front of her, his eyes growing soft and adoring. "Of course I think you can handle your responsibilities. But your main responsibility is to be my wife. I didn't marry you to gain a housekeeper!"

"You don't think I've been a good wife to you?" she returned irrationally. She knew she was being unreasonable, and it made her that much madder. "Well, I've tried, Slater! How am I going to be a good wife if you're never home!"

"Jillane! I know I'm never home," he apologized curtly, beginning to grow short with her unjustified reasoning. "But that's all going to change just as soon as the strike's settled. And with the new housekeeper coming in, we'll have a chance to get things running smoothly again. . . ."

"I knew it!" She jabbed the needle through the buttonhole one final time and angrily bit the thread in two. "I knew you thought this household had gone to pot since I've been running it!"

He sighed heavily. "I didn't say that!"

"You've thought it!" she accused. "Admit it. You think I'm a miserable wife and a pitiful excuse for a housekeeper!"

"I have *never* thought that," he denied. "I have always intended to hire a housekeeper, you know that! I wouldn't expect you to try to keep up with eight people all by yourself. I know I couldn't do it," he offered hopefully, trying to make her feel better.

Granted, she hadn't quite gotten the knack of running such a large household, but he knew she had been trying her darnedest.

Bounding out of her chair, she drew herself up to her full height and glowered at him. "Well, I can . . . if you'll just give me a little time!"

"Jillane, be sensible. You cannot run this entire household and hold down your job at the phone company," he stated firmly. "Those are two full-time jobs, and I won't have you killing yourself. I can afford to hire a housekeeper, and if you want to continue your job at the phone company, you'll be free to."

"There are millions of women who work and keep their own house everyday," she said, disputing him. Her eyes darkened with growing suspicion. "You're upset because my dog chewed the sleeves off your new dress shirt again, aren't you?"

"No! I'm not upset about . . . oh, hell, Jillane! Did that damn dog do that again?" he asked incredulously. "That's the third time this week! I'm telling you, that dog hates me!"

"Well, you can rest assured that she won't bother you again. She's gone!"

"Gone?" Slater glared at her skeptically. "What do you mean, gone? Did she run away?"

"No, I gave her to Arnold and Sue," she blurted, nearing tears again at the thought of having to give up her pet.

"What are you talking about? Why would you give your dog to Arnold and Sue!" he demanded.

"Because Hercules nearly ate her alive today, and I decided that since you and she didn't get along, I would just have to give her away—" Her voice broke with renewed emotion.

"Oh, honey. . . ." Reaching out to console her, he drew her off her chair and cradled her against his chest, murmuring her name softly. "You didn't have to give up Petunia for my sake. Why didn't you wait and talk this over with me first?"

"Because there wasn't any way you could change things," Jillane said, sobbing.

"Maybe I could have," he said, trying to soothe her. "We could keep Hercules chained instead of letting him have the run of the house. And as far as the dress shirts go, I'll stick them away in the closet and wear a long-sleeved sweater with them this winter."

"No, Arnold and Sue love Petunia and will give her a good home." Jillane sniffed. "That way, I don't have to worry about her too!"

"Well, if you change your mind, I'm sure they'll be happy to return her to you."

"I don't want her back," she said stubbornly.

"Okay," he relented quickly in an effort to pacify her. "Petunia can stay with the Joneses, and I'll call Mrs. Steele first thing in the morning and tell her we won't be needing her."

"And make *me* do all the work around here! You *will not!*"

He threw his hands up in complete exasperation. "Jillane, honey, I don't think you're thinking straight at the moment. Why don't you go take a nice hot bath and I'll clean up the kitchen, then we'll all go to the rehearsal," he suggested, setting her firmly on her feet.

"I am not going anywhere," she replied. "I have a splitting headache and I feel horrible. I'm going to take a hot bath and go to bed!" It was as if someone had pushed a nasty button somewhere deep inside her and it was working overtime.

"Fine!" Slater finally lost his temper. "Stay right here and pout, then!" Snatching his grape costume out of her hand, he shot her an irritable scowl and left the kitchen in a mad huff.

"All right! I will!" she shouted, dismayed to realize that they were having their first real fight.

After Wong and Slater left the older children disappeared to their rooms as soon as the dishes were done, and Jillane put the baby to bed early. All night long she vacillated between anger and remorse and the sickening realization that due to her childish behavior, her brief marriage might be falling apart.

She had been lying in bed, listening to the rain patter on the roof when she heard Slater coming down the hallway later that evening. Casting aside the magazine she had been reading, she pretended

234

to be asleep, determined to avoid another confrontation with him when she was in such a rotten mood.

Slamming into the bedroom none too quietly, her eyes popped open as he roared her name. "Jillane!"

"What do you want!"

"Oh . . . there you are." He stood before her in the doorway, a big, dripping purple grape that looked mad enough to spit nails.

She bit back a giggle at his comical appearance. "What are you shouting about?" she finally managed to say.

"Didn't I ask you to put gas in the station wagon today?" he asked calmly.

She grimaced. He had, and she had completely forgotten when she took Petunia to the airport. "Yes, but in all the confusion, I forgot."

"Because of your carelessness, Wong and I have been standing out in the rain for the last hour trying to flag down a cab," he said, exploding, "because *you* forgot to put gas in the car! I asked you to do one simple thing, and you can't seem to handle it," he accused. "Do you know how impossible it is for a grape and a banana to hail a taxi at ten o'clock at night?"

Under ordinary circumstances he would never have raised his voice to her, but in addition to having his nerves worn thin by thirty-five giggling little girls all evening, he had been worried sick about the earlier fight with her, and all he wanted to do was get home and right whatever wrong he had done.

"Where is Wong . . . is she all right?"

"She's in the bathroom soaking in a hot tub so she won't come down with pneumonia!" he bellowed.

"Stop yelling at me!" she ordered hotly.

His face suddenly lost its former anger as he began to realize that this wasn't just a matter of them having their first argument. With chilling apprehension he began to sense that it went much further than that. "What in heaven's name has come over you, Jillane? You have never been this hard to get along with." He looked hurt and puzzled at her sudden change of personality as his temper cooled. He stepped in the room and closed the door.

"Nothing has come over me," she snapped. "I just don't like you yelling at me! *You* should have checked the gas tank before you left," she pointed out sharply. "Why does everyone expect *me* to do everything around here!"

"I am going to yell at you until you listen to me," he warned, taking a menacing step forward. "I have been going out of my mind all evening worrying about you. What is making you so damned unhappy all of a sudden? From the moment we got married you have been brooding about something, and I want to know what it is."

"Leave me alone, Slater!" She bounded out of bed and angrily jerked on her robe. "I told you, it has nothing to do with you."

"Nothing to do with me! I'm your husband, Jillane. Remember me? I'm the guy who's crazy in love with you?"

"Well, you shouldn't be," she cried out. "I'm not worth loving!"

And she wasn't. She had made a complete mess out of everything. He and the children deserved so much more in a wife and a mother.

Heaving a resigned sigh, he ran his fingers wearily through his wet hair and sat down on the bed. "It's our marriage, isn't it? You're regretting that you married me, and all this arguing is your way of looking for a way out."

The room suddenly went deathly still as her hands paused in buttoning the robe, his words stunning her into silence.

"No . . ." she denied hastily.

But was that what she was doing? Was she so ashamed of the way she had botched things up in his life that she was seeking an easy way out?

"I mean, I don't think so," she said, correcting herself in a small, frightened voice. "I don't seem to know anything anymore."

The pain that instantly flashed across his pensive features tore at her heart. "You're not sure if you love me?"

"Oh, Slater . . . of course I love you," she cried softly. "Very, very much. It's just that I don't know if I can handle all of this . . . and what's more, I'm not even sure that I want to anymore."

"Handle what? The children? Me? What is it that's making you so unhappy?"

"I don't know," she agonized. "I just don't seem to have a life of my own any longer, and I'm ruining yours."

"You're not ruining mine," he objected. "You *are* my life."

"You can't be happy with the way things have been going the last couple of weeks," she challenged. "Your house is a pigsty, I'm snappish with your children, and I *hate* your wife! How could that make you happy? Are you aware that I can't even complete a normal sentence anymore without sounding like a babbling idiot?"

It seemed she was forever yelling at the kids and having to run the complete gauntlet of the alphabet to come up with the proper name of the one she was after.

"Have you heard me complaining? I know you're having a hard time adjusting, but it will all work out in time," he promised. "I had a hard time getting used to having children myself in the beginning, but it begins to grow on you. And as far as your not putting gas in the car, that's understandable with all you've had on your mind lately. I was just in a rotten mood when I came in, and I unthinkingly took it out on you."

She backed away as he moved off the bed to take her in his arms. Once more, hurt and rejection crossed his face as his arms fell limply back to his sides. "Okay, Jillane. What do you want me to do, have the marriage annulled?"

"Annuled!" The words sliced through her like a razor.

"Yes, annuled. If you're this unhappy with the situation you find yourself in, then I love you too much to watch you suffer."

"Annuled," she repeated numbly. Never once had she thought about that possibility. Was *he* the one sorry about their hasty marriage and looking for a way out? "I . . . I don't really know what I want," she whimpered, feeling sick at the thought of losing him. "It isn't that I don't love you or that

238

I'm not fond of the children. It just seems as if all of a sudden Jillane Simms doesn't exist anymore, at least not the way I've always thought of her."

"I know . . . and I wish I could help you," he reiterated. "But before we jump in with both feet and make another mistake, will you at least allow me to make a suggestion?" he prompted.

She looked at him through a gathering veil of tears. He had been so good to her; so patient and so loving. How could they even be considering hurting each other this way? If nothing else, she owed him this one consideration. "Yes, what is it?"

"Why don't you go and spend some time with Sue? We're both too close to the situation right now, and we need time to think before we do anything drastic," he said softly. "I'll put you on a plane tomorrow, and you can spend some time without me and the kids . . . allow yourself to carefully think this situation through."

"But what about the children . . . my job with the phone company?"

"I'll have Mrs. Steele start tomorrow morning, and if the employees ratify the contract before you come to any decision, then you can turn in for a few days' vacation."

"I just don't know. Are you having your own second thoughts about the marriage too?" she plied hesitantly.

"I want you to be happy, Jillane," he conceded gently. "Let's give ourselves some breathing space before we discuss it anymore."

"All right, if you think that's what we should do," she agreed sadly. At this point she was totally at his mercy because she could no longer discern right from wrong.

"I'm not at all sure I'm right, but it's the only thing I know to do," he confessed in a tired voice. "In the meantime I'll see what it will involve to annul the marriage . . . if that's what you choose." A muscle quivered in his jaw as he fought to keep his voice steady. "I'm sorry, Jillane. I blame myself for putting you through this. I should have allowed you more time. I should have never pressured you into marrying me as quickly as I did. At the time I thought it was so right, but maybe I was wrong," he conceded huskily.

"No, Slater. It was all my fault," she consoled. "I thought I was ready to be the person you needed, but maybe I was only fooling myself."

"Do you want me to sleep in the guest room tonight?" he offered.

He looked lost and very much alone as he stood before her, and she wanted so badly to ease the hurt and frustration she was causing him.

"No, I want to be with you tonight," she whispered tearfully.

"I guess I should get out of this wet costume and take a hot shower."

"Yes, you should, but hurry. . . ." There was only one thing she was sure of at the moment, and that was the undeniable fact that she desperately needed to be in his arms.

It took only a few minutes for him to complete his task, and then he climbed in bed next to her,

"Slater . . ." Her hand reached over to touch him. "I'm . . . scared."

"I know. I am too."

With a sob she rolled over in his arms and they held each other tightly until dawn filtered its rosy light through their bedroom window.

CHAPTER THIRTEEN

Miserable.

A new and even more frightening word now entered Jillane's life. Wretchedly unhappy, the dictionary defines, but that seemed like a puny explanation for the torment she was now going through.

It had been difficult, to say the least, when Slater had taken her to the plane the next morning. They had left the children sitting quietly at the breakfast table, their bowls of cereal untouched. Their solemn faces remained impassive as Slater explained that a Mrs. Steele would be coming in that day. She would be taking over the household duties while Jillane was visiting a friend.

They could not help but overhear Jillane and Slater arguing the night before, so they were not surprised by the morning's announcement.

Joey's puzzled eyes sought to capture Jillane's, but for fear of breaking down in front of the children, she carefully avoided his gaze. Instead she leaned over and placed a lingering kiss on the baby's forehead.

"Be sure Tara gets two pieces of fruit today," she reminded Fleur with a gentle smile. "And try to keep her from scratching her scabs. Wong, you and Eben behave yourselves, and Caleb . . . please wipe your feet for Mrs. Steele before you come in the house. We don't want to scare her away the first day."

"Okay. Will she be fixing supper tonight?"

"Yes, Caleb, I'm sure she will." She picked up her suitcase, feeling the large lump painfully rising to her throat. "Joey, perhaps Mrs. Steele will have time to help you put that new horn on your bicycle today—" Her voice broke as she thought of the way she was failing him . . . just like all the others. "Good-bye."

Slater opened the back door, and they walked out to the car and got in. The drive to the airport was made in silence, and he made only one effort to touch her before she boarded the plane.

Breaking down for one brief moment, he had pulled her into his arms and buried his face in her hair, finding it harder than he ever thought possible to let her go.

"You're going to make me cry again," she cautioned, closing her eyes and wrapping her arms around his waist to hold him tightly.

They held each other, trying to draw from one another's strength until the loudspeaker gave the last boarding call.

"I have to go now," she said brokenly. "Will you call me sometime this week?"

"I don't know . . . I'll try," he promised in a voice that was very close to tears.

He was still standing at the gate, his eyes riveted on the plane as it lifted off the runway and soared high into the blue of the heavens. Feeling as if someone had just cut out half his heart, he slumped against the railings and watched as the silver jet disappeared in a fleecy bank of clouds. The scent of her perfume still lingered where she had laid her head on his shoulder, and he felt his eyes welling with unshed tears.

She would be back, he told himself, trying helplessly to fight off the overwhelming sense of desolation and loneliness that had settled over him like a heavy mantel. As soon as she was alone, she would realize everything she wanted in life was waiting back home for her.

He just had to be patient.

"But it's been over a week!" Jillane complained, rising from her bed to pace the floor in front of Sue. "He surely could have found time to call before now!"

"He's probably busy," Sue reasoned. "And sit down! The doctor told you not to overdo."

Scratching gingerly at her blotched skin, Jillane grimaced. "Drat these chicken pox, anyway!" She had promptly broken out with the childhood disease the minute she had stepped off the plane. "You're sure you've had these miserable things?" she questioned for the tenth time since she had arrived. "I couldn't believe it when Mom told me I hadn't had them!"

"I'm positive. Now get back in bed and I'll bring you some juice."

Crawling beneath the sheets, Jillane still couldn't get over the fact that Slater had not called her once since she had been here. True to his word, he was giving her plenty of time by herself, and she had found she wasn't so crazy about having it!

Swallowing her pride, she had called home every day to check on the children, but each time Slater had been gone. She had spoken with a different child each time, and they had informed her that all was going well, but Wong and Eben had admitted to missing her. Caleb had even gone so far as to ask her when she thought she would be coming back. It seemed Mrs. Steele's spaghetti and meatballs couldn't hold a candle to Jillane's, and he was hoping she would cut her visit short and return early.

Even Joey had said a few carefully chosen words into the receiver, asking her if she was having a nice time and discreetly informing her that the cookie jar was full of cookies, awaiting her return.

Hearing their familiar voices brought a wave of homesickness to her, and she realized how much she was missing them too.

"I hope you like pineapple juice. That's all we have left," Sue announced as she came back in the room and sat a glass down on the bedside table. "I need to go to the store."

"I don't care what he said." Jillane continued to fret. "He could have called. Maybe he's decided that things are running so much better without me around that he's proceeded with the annulment without waiting for my decision," she said, groaning helplessly.

Sue shook her head and laughed. "Why don't you just admit you're missing your husband and children and call and tell them you're coming home. You know that's what you're going to end up doing," she informed her.

"Well, maybe they don't want me to come home," Jillane returned anxiously. "From what the children tell me, Mrs. Steele has that house running like a well-oiled piece of machinery. They don't need me to come back and throw a clog in the motor," she confessed glumly.

"So maybe you're not up for the Homemaker of the Year award." She shrugged. "Maybe, just maybe, the Holbrook family needs you in a much different way."

"You don't think they're sick to death of me?" she asked hopefully. "You can't imagine what a beast I was before I left . . . why Slater practically *sent* me up here."

"You were getting sick, trying to adjust to having a new husband and a ready-made family. I'm sure they understand and forgive you," she coaxed.

Yes, all that was true, but would the children and Slater really want her back? This last week had taught her the painful lesson that she wanted *them* back.

"Well, I think I'll run on to the market before my hungry bear comes home," Sue decided. "How does stuffed pork chops sound to you?"

"Fine. Do you think Slater might have called and we just didn't hear the phone?"

"No. I think if you want to talk to him, you'll have to track *him* down."

"Gee, thanks. You could have at least let me hang on to my one last shred of hope," Jillane grumbled. "I really can't understand it. The employees have ratified the contract, so the strike's over. He's undoubtedly back to his regular routine and has time to call me. Come to think of it, though, I really don't know what his regular routine is."

Sue left Jillane to go through all the possible reasons her errant husband had been true to his word and not contacted her. She picked up her purse and left the room.

"Pork chops, asparagus, baking powder, milk . . ." Sue recited her grocery list under her breath as she jerked open the front door and stopped abruptly.

Slater Holbrook was standing before her, just about to knock on the door.

"Well, for heaven's sake, hi there!" she greeted enthusiastically.

"Hi, Sue. Is Jillane around?"

"She certainly is," Sue grinned. Oh, happy day! Here he was, and Jillane was in there missing him like the devil, and Sue was on her way out . . . there was going to be a hot time in the old town tonight!

"Could I talk to her?"

"Sure, she's in the bedroom. Just go on in," she invited. "I'm on my way to the store. I'll probably be gone . . . oh, at least two or *three* hours," she emphasized helpfully. "You and Jillane just make yourselves at home. Arnold won't be home for at least *four* hours, and if I decided to stop by the service station on my way home from the market, why, we might not be home for at least *five* hours."

"Oh?" Slater eyed her warily. "Well, I'll just go on in . . ."

"Yes, please do. And lock the door behind you."

247

"Sure." He obediently did as he had been instructed but didn't have the slightest idea why he was doing it.

Making his way through the unfamiliar house, he found the hallway leading to the bedrooms, unconsciously following the sounds of an afternoon soap opera on television.

Locating the room where the sound was coming from, he pushed open the door slightly and grinned as he spied Jillane lying on the bed propped up on several pillows, absently scratching behind Petunia's ears.

"Is this a private party?" he bantered lightly. "Or can your husband get in on the act?"

Jillane glanced up, her mouth dropping open in surprise at seeing him standing in the doorway. "Slater!" In a split second she was off the bed and into his arms, covering his face with a shower of adoring kisses.

"Holy Moses, lady," he exclaimed laughingly as the force of her jumping on him made them tumble back on the bed together. "And here I worried all the way up here you wouldn't want to see me—" His words were cut short by her mouth eagerly capturing his for a long and ardent kiss.

Their mouths moved together passionately, trying to make up for the time they had been apart.

"After I make love to you remind me to tell you how mad I am!" she reminded with gruff affection.

"Yes, ma'am," he returned with a lazy grin, docilely letting her remove every stitch of clothing he was wearing in what had to be a new record. "But I . . ." He started to warn her that this wasn't going to help her case any if she decided to seek an annulment in the future, but he quickly discarded the idea.

"Will you kindly be quiet and just let me make a complete fool out of myself?" she scolded, pitching his socks away in wild abandonment. She paused, and her green eyes peered at him expectantly. "The children . . . you're not here because something is wrong with one of the children?"

"No, the children were doing fine when I left them this morning," he said, trying to console her.

Tumbling back on top of him, she drew his mouth to hers in a renewed surge of eagerness. "Oh, have I ever missed you, Slater Holbrook!" she breathed into his parted lips.

"Show me just exactly how much," he urged in a husky voice.

Soft, small hands began to shape out the feel and texture of him as her mouth trailed lingering kisses along his warm skin. From the moment she had left his arms an agonizingly long week ago, she had thought of nothing else but being back in his embrace. She wanted to taste him once more, to touch him, to whisper his name and to cry out how very much she loved him. Her body knew a sense of urgency that cried out for fulfillment, yet she wanted this to be a special time, a time when her mouth and her tongue and her touch would say all the things she had such a need to tell him but found impossible to put into words.

The soft feel of his mustache against her heated skin as he pulled up her gown and let his mouth touch and tease the swelling fullness of her breasts sent her passion spiraling. Their kisses were hot

249

and insatiable as his hands moved over her body with smooth and practiced expertise. In just the short time they had known each other, they had instinctively found each other's pleasure points and knew how to please with breathtaking assurance.

"Have you missed me?" she encouraged.

"Yeah, a little," he bantered, then unexpected emotion took over and he buried his face in her hair and groaned softly. "Of course I missed you. I haven't had a decent night's sleep since you left and took that stupid fan with you."

She giggled and squirmed against him suggestively. "Missed my fan, huh?"

"Among other things," he granted, outlining the tip of her nose with his forefinger. "I really couldn't decide if it was the fan, the lemons, Johnny Carson, or Petunia trying to take my hide off, but something sure in hell has been making me lose sleep. Hey! What are all those red blotches on your face?"

She felt her cheeks tinging a bright pink. He would never let her live this down! "I . . . I have Tara's chicken pox."

"Chicken pox . . . you have chicken pox?" A deep chuckle rumbled in his chest.

"The doctor said it's only a light case," she protested, failing to see what was so darn funny! "And you'd better make sure you've had them before you lay an egg cackling."

"I had them when I was ten years old," he scoffed. "See, I told you, you're nothing but a kid!" Stripping her gown off, he let his gaze tenderly run over every square inch of her body, his eyes growing dark and desirous. "You really do, don't you?" He kissed her stomach lovingly. "The little girl has the nasty old chicken pox . . . cluckkkk, cluckkk, cluckkkk!"

"Yes, she really does, but surprise! She isn't a little girl anymore!" His laughter knew an instant death as she smothered his taunts with a series of smoldering kisses.

When she was convinced that he regretted his rash assessment, she propped herself up on her elbow and grinned at him. "Do you think it's possible you could have missed me for any other possible reason than those you've just ticked off?" she quipped, wishing that he would clear the air and demand that she come back home to him.

But he had firmly promised himself that he would never pressure her again. He had done that once before with disastrous results. If she came back to him, it would be of her own accord, but he had been powerless to resist his urge to fly up here and see her today.

"Possibly, but I can't even imagine what they would be," he said innocently, letting his hand tantalizingly explore the insides of her silken thigh.

Burying her face in the thick, silken carpet of his chest, she closed her eyes and whimpered his name, savoring the familiar smell of his musky skin melting into hers as her hands traced lovingly over the flatness of his taut stomach and rib cage, and then on to more intimately explore her husband's aroused body. He was all sinewy muscle and inherent strength, totally male and completely captivating.

She snuggled against him as their legs intertwined. Kisses that started out languorous began to grow more aggressive and demanding as he rolled over to claim her as his once more.

Moments later, with a sharp intake of breath, his arms tightened around her waist and the white-hot fire that had been threatening to engulf them now consumed them wholly and sent their senses shattering into a million fragmented embers.

It was a long time before either one of them wanted to move as the languid feeling of bliss lingered with them. Finally summoning up enough strength to ease gently off her, he kept her cradled firmly in the crook of his arm as he sighed and lay back on his pillow. "In case I forgot to mention it, you're one terrific lady, Mrs. Holbrook," he complimented in a drowsy voice.

"Umm . . . Slater, why haven't you called me this week?" she confronted.

"I've . . . been busy," he defended lamely.

"That busy? I thought you would at least call to check how things were going."

"I knew how things were going. The kids said you called every day."

She felt a blush flooding her cheeks once more. "I did. I bet they wondered why I was being such a mother hen all of a sudden."

"No, on the contrary, I heard them flipping coins one night to see who got to talk to you the next day," he murmured.

"Even Fleur?"

"She's the one who came up with the idea," he acknowledged.

"Obviously, *you* didn't want a turn," she accused.

"I can think of ways I'd rather spend my time with you other than talking," he said dryly.

"Oh?" She leaned up on her elbow again. "How?"

His hand trailed down the side of her hip teasingly. "Just ways," he said evading her question with a wicked twinkle in his eye.

Her face puckered with disappointment. She had been hoping he had come to take her home, but he seemed to be avoiding all mention of the subject.

"How have you been, babe?" His gaze softened as he pulled her mouth back to his for a nibbling kiss.

"A little cranky . . . and a lot lonely," she confessed. "Have . . . have you talked to a lawyer yet?"

The gray of his slumberous eyes met hers. "No. I've been too busy, but I will." He tweaked her nose playfully. "I've really missed you. All of us have."

"Honest? I'd certainly like to feel someone has," she blurted, feeling a little put out that he wasn't exactly begging for her return.

"I don't remember anyone ever implying that they didn't want you around," he reminded stubbornly.

"*You* did. You practically sent me away, I was so horrible."

"Only because I could see you were about ready to break. But I don't want to get into the subject right now," he warned, kissing her into silence.

253

When their lips finally parted, she settled back on her pillow and irritably scratched at her arms. Obviously he was content for the moment to let their precarious marriage just drift aimlessly along.

Admitting that she had been a bit too eager to see him, she belatedly allowed that she should have made him sweat just a little before she literally attacked him! "Then if you didn't come up here to talk, what are you here for?"

Gently pulling her hands away from her arms, he scolded in a voice she had heard him use with the kids. "Stop that! You're not supposed to be scratching those things."

"They itch!"

"Well, don't scratch!"

They settled back down on their pillows, and she nestled in his arms comfortably. "Why are you here?"

"I don't know. I got up this morning and realized that today I was forty years old . . . forty years old!" he mused. "It's funny how when you're young, you never think about actually getting to be forty years old, but before you can get turned around, you are, and suddenly out of nowhere you've got all these nagging aches and pains and you notice new wrinkles that you're positive weren't there the day before. I think I even found a gray hair this morning," he mourned, tipping his head over for her to examine. "Look, do you see that . . . right there in the crown of my head?"

Peering at the spot he was jabbing his finger at, she studied the evidence solemnly. "No, I don't see a gray hair. It's only your imagination."

"I tell you, it was there this morning," he complained. "Anyway, I poured myself a cup of coffee and stepped out on the patio, and I could see you everywhere I looked. I even imagined that I could smell that perfume you wear, and it was such a physical pain, I thought, 'What the hell!' I'm going to hop a plane and come up here and spend the day with my wife . . . and that's exactly what I did." He rubbed her bare arms absently as he spoke. "I just wanted to be with you today, Jillane. I don't want to complicate our problem, and I'm not demanding that you make a decision about our marriage right away. Let's just enjoy being together."

"Oh, Slater, today's your birthday, and I didn't even know it!" she apologized. He had dreaded this particular birthday with a passion. If he hadn't taken the initiative and flown up here, she wouldn't have known his doomsday had arrived.

"Oh, that's all right," he said, soothing her in a shy voice. "I don't know yours, either. I guess we sort of jumped the gun and fell in love before we actually knew anything about each other," he noted with a chuckle.

She rolled on top of him again, cradling his face in her hands protectively. "Well, maybe I don't have the usual sort of birthday gift for a forty-year-old . . . you know, corrective shoes, crutches, hair tonic, denture cream . . . laxatives . . ."

"Very funny. You wait until *your* fortieth birthday," he groused, not able to find one thing amusing about his age.

Her eyes devoured him hungrily. "You planning on being around to help me celebrate?"

"It depends entirely on whether you give up the corny forties jokes," he grumbled.

"Okay. I repent. But, I do want to give you something very special from me alone," she whispered. "Happy birthday, Methuselah. . . ."

And she proceeded to give him a gift that would be cherished and carried warmly in his heart for the rest of his life.

It was growing late in the afternoon when their second round of lovemaking ended. They had taken their time and made it a celebration of love, one neither one of them would ever forget.

"Sue should have been back a long time ago," Jillane observed as they both toweled off from the hot shower they had just taken.

"She and Arnold might be gone four, maybe even *five*, hours," Slater joked, realizing now what Sue had done for them.

"It takes that long to buy pork chops?"

"No. I think the Joneses are allowing us some time together."

Draping her arms around his neck, she rubbed the tip of her nose against his affectionately. "Do you really have to go back tonight?"

"Yeah, I'm afraid I do. I have a nine o'clock flight." Their mouths brushed teasingly. "And I've been away from the kids much more than I should have been lately."

"I'm glad you came," she whispered.

"I'm glad I did too. It's been the nicest birthday I can ever remember having."

Tilting her head back, she surveyed him with an

impish grin and coined a popular phrase: "You're not getting older, baby, you're just getting better."

"I wasn't bad, was I?" He wiggled his eyebrows suggestively.

"No, not at all. But now that you're . . . forty" —she made a dramatic pretense of covering her brow and swooning—"I'll never really know if the gleam in your eye is from desire or from the sun glancing off your bifocals."

"I thought we were giving up the corny forty jokes," he reminded.

"We lie, remember?"

Scooping her up in his arms, he carried her back in to the bed and unceremoniously dumped her in the middle, then proceeded to tickle the meanness out of her. That led to another round of kisses, which led to another round of lovemaking.

"If I don't hurry up and get out of here, there's a strong possibility I may never make it to my forty-first birthday," he complained good-naturedly as they both stepped back in the shower again. But she knew he didn't mean it. He didn't want to leave any more than she wanted him to. She longed for him to ask her to fly back with him, but he didn't. At the moment she was just grateful that he had chosen to spend the day with her.

As they dressed he filled her in on the children's activities of the past week, and they found themselves laughing like two doting parents. Mrs. Steele was working out beautifully, and the Holbrook home was running like clockwork. Wong's dance recital had been a great hit, and Slater was voted the best-looking grape there, he related proudly.

Sue and Arnold returned home shortly before six, and a birthday dinner was hastily put together. For dessert, since there was no birthday cake, bowls of chocolate pudding were served with brightly burning candles stuck in the middle.

While Arnold got the car out to take Slater to the airport, Slater stepped in Jillane's darkened bedroom and kissed her a long and lingering goodbye.

"I don't want you to go," she confessed, resting her head on his shoulder and fighting back tears. Today had been the most beautiful day of her life.

"Don't make it any harder for me, honey." His voice had turned husky with emotion as he squeezed her tightly. "I don't want to go, either, but I have to."

"Will you kiss the baby for me and tell Joey and Wong and Eben, I said hi . . . and don't forget Fleur and Caleb. Tell them I miss them."

"I will, I will." Once more their mouths captured each other's hungrily.

Their lips met twice more before he determinedly set her away from him and took a deep, cleansing breath. "We'll keep in touch. Take care of yourself."

With those few words he slipped out the door and back out of her life. Slumping weakly against the door, she heaved a long sigh and bit her lower lip. She finally let the tears that had threatened all evening finally escape.

You bet we'll "keep in touch," Slater Holbrook! Because the instant I'm over these rotten chicken pox, I'm coming home!

CHAPTER FOURTEEN

"Have you seen Slater Holbrook this morning?" A few days later Jillane sat opposite one of her co-workers, Nan Fuller, in the employees' lounge at the phone company.

"No, I haven't seen him today."

"He's surely here, wouldn't you think?" It was noon, and she still hadn't bumped into him in the halls as she usually did.

"I suppose he would be. Why the sudden interest in Slater Holbrook?"

"Oh, no particular reason," she dismissed hurriedly.

Obviously the word about her and Slater's marriage had not reached the grapevine yet, and she was grateful for that small stroke of luck. Especially in view of the fact that they might not even *have* a marriage any longer.

She had arrived back at her apartment late last night but decided to wait until today to let Slater know she was back . . . as if he really cared!

Once more he had failed to call her, and when Monday arrived without hearing a word from him, she had packed her bags and caught the first flight home.

"Well, speak of the devil," her friend said, interrupting Jillane's thoughts. "Isn't that Slater coming in the door right now?"

Jillane glanced up, and her heart nearly stopped as she saw her handsome husband stroll into the lounge with one of the sexiest-looking redheads she had ever seen. The lady was built like a *Playboy* centerfold, and all heads turned as she walked over to the coffee machine and picked up two paper cups to fill.

"*Who* is that?" Jillane demanded.

Nan surveyed the woman thoughtfully. "I think her name's Dagmar something or other. She's new with the company."

"Just what in the devil is she doing with Slater?" Jillane seethed, viewing the woman with growing jealousy.

"How should I know? Why don't you go ask him?" Nan stood up and gathered the remains of her lunch and pitched them in the trash can. "I have to get back early today. See you later."

What was he doing with that woman? Jillane continued to simmer, keeping her eyes glued on the couple, who chose a table across the room and sat down to drink their coffee.

Angrily wadding up her napkin, Jillane toyed with the idea of going over to her husband and joining the party. But after a second thought she realized that she didn't really have a right to barge in on Slater's personal discussion with anyone, even if they were redheaded and disgustingly attractive.

Fighting back the urge to go over and let him have it with both barrels, she picked up her purse and started out of the lounge in a huff. It was becoming abundantly clear why he hadn't called her. Obviously he was too busy at work to be concerned about his indecisive wife when he had something like *that* hanging on his every word.

Still, there was enough jealousy gnawing away at her that she chose to leave through the door closest to where her husband was sitting.

As she walked by his table she kept her eyes straight ahead, determined to give him a dose of his own medicine.

Glancing up in mid-sentence, his mouth dropped open in surprise as he saw his wife march past him.

"Jillane?" He sprang to his feet and cast an apologetic look in his companion's direction. "Excuse me a minute, Dagmar."

Rushing out to the hallway, he saw the hurriedly disappearing backside of his wife as she stomped angrily toward her department.

"Hey! Hold up a minute!" He broke into a sprint and finally managed to corner her just before she reached her destination.

"Jillane, what are you doing here?" he asked, his face breaking out in a wide smile.

"I work here," she snapped. "Remember?"

"When did you get back in town?" Noting the curious stares they were beginning to attract, he quickly pulled her into one of the empty offices and shut the door. "Why didn't you let me know you were back?" he coaxed gently, coming over to take her in his arms.

"I really didn't think you would be all that interested," she challenged.

Slater tipped her flushed face up to meet his, his eyes growing deeply concerned. "Am I in the doghouse about something?"

"Who was that woman you were with?"

"Dagmar?"

"Yes, Dagmar!" she mimicked. "Who is she?"

"She works here," he explained patiently, wondering what was upsetting her so. "My secretary decided not to come back to work after the strike, and Dagmar wants the position. . . ."

"She can't have it," Jillane cut in sharply.

"She can't?" He looked baffled. "Why can't she?"

"Because she just . . . can't!" she returned meekly.

He chuckled and ran his hands down her arms in a tantalizing gesture. "Well, okay. She can't have the job, but you're going to have to let me know why, so I can logically explain to the woman why she can't have a job she has all the qualifications for," he pointed out.

Jillane's gaze finally met his, and she became lost in the gray pools she loved so much. "Oh, Slater, she's . . . too beautiful," she confessed sheepishly.

"Is she? I hadn't noticed," he murmured, pulling her flush against him. "My taste runs more for young brunettes with sexy green eyes."

The familiar feel of him pressing intimately against her made her go weak in the knees as her arms came up around his neck. "I bet you haven't noticed," she chided.

"I didn't, and if it will make you happy, I'll have

personnel hire the first eighty-year-old they find with Dagmar's credentials," he promised.

"I've been meaning to tell you," she warned meekly. "I think I'm going to be very jealous of you, so you'd better be extremely careful about who you hire if you don't want me hanging around your office all day."

"That's nice to hear. I think I might like the idea of you hanging around my office all day," he accepted happily. The knowledge that she *did* care about what he did sent his spirits soaring. "Isn't there something else you forgot to tell me?" he challenged, letting a devilish grin tug at the corners of his mouth.

She knew what he was hinting at, and she was more than willing to give it to him now. "I love you, Slater Holbrook . . . although there have been times lately when I truly wished I didn't," she hastened to add.

He laughed at her distress and pulled her closer. "Why didn't you call me the minute you got back in town?" he chided, brushing his lips lightly across hers. Before she could answer, he captured her mouth hungrily and kissed her until she slumped limply against him.

"I just got back last night, so I thought I would wait and tell you today, but I haven't been able to find you all morning," she accused, allowing her anger to soften toward him. "Besides, you obviously didn't care when I returned, since you didn't bother to call after you left Sue's last week."

"I told you," he reasoned, seductively touching the tip of his tongue to hers, "there are other things I'd rather do with you than talk. I'll tell you what. You want proof of how much I've missed you? Let's you and I take a long lunch hour and go over to your apartment, and I'll be happy to show you just how much I care."

"No." She pushed away from him to clear her reeling senses. Maybe it was childish, but she was still more than a little hurt that he had not made one move to reconcile their differences. This time she wasn't going to appear so eager to get back in his bed.

"Honey, I didn't call you because I thought you needed the time to think this situation over carefully." He tried to pull her back in his arms, but she steadfastly refused to return.

Realizing that he was not going to be able to reason with her at the moment, he finally moved away. The last thing he wanted was for her to feel as if he didn't love her, but he just couldn't pressure her into coming back to him. It was important that she come back on her own accord, even if the wait was slowly tearing him apart.

"It wasn't because I didn't want to," he admitted softly. "You have to know that, Jillane."

Just as she opened her mouth to rebuke him, Lionel Miller decided to return to his office, only to find it occupied.

"Ooops! Sorry, I didn't know I had company," he said, apologizing.

Slater smiled and took Jillane's arm to steer her out of the confiscated room. "Thanks for the use of your office, Lionel."

"Oh, anytime. You were probably having a lot more fun in here than I do," he joked.

Stepping out into the bustling hallway, Slater

turned her around to face him. "Have dinner with me tomorrow night?"

"Tomorrow night?" Jillane's spirits sank. "Why not tonight?" She had hoped now that he knew she was back, he would at least want to be with her this evening.

"I can't tonight. I have to mow the lawn. . . ." His voice trailed off lamely as he saw the dark cloud begin to surface over her head. Realizing what a feeble, but completely honest, excuse he was making, he tensed as she glared at him. "But," he hastened to add, "I'll hurry through it as fast as I can. Maybe we can meet around nine o'clock or so—"

"Mow the lawn! Well! I certainly wouldn't want to keep you from anything that important!" she snapped. Turning on her heel, she started back down the hall. "I can't think of anything important we would have to talk about if we *did* see each other! By all means, stay home and mow your precious lawn!"

"Jillane . . . honey, I know that sounds crazy, but I've been so darn busy lately I haven't had time to fix the broken mower so that Caleb could keep the lawn work up. Now he's gone on a camping trip with friends and the lawn's gotten so high, it's a disgrace to the neighborhood. I promised Mrs. Steele I'd get it done tonight without fail," he pleaded helplessly as she flounced back to her office.

"You don't need to explain," she shot back. "I understand completely!"

He leaned against the wall disconsolately as she entered her department without a backward glance in his direction. It was clear she didn't understand, and he was going to have to do something about bringing the impasse between them to an abrupt end. But, he had to admit, he didn't have the slightest idea where to start.

Well, it had all come down to one question. Was she going to swallow her pride and go crawling back to Slater or spend the rest of her life regretting the fact that she hadn't? In the last two weeks her husband had asked her to do everything *but* come back to him, and now Jillane was beginning to grudgingly admit that she would have to be the one to plead for reconciliation.

And, she had to confess that it wasn't just Slater she had been missing. It was Caleb's dirty footprints, Eben's tuba, Fleur's smart mouth, Wong's unusual French-bread peanut butter and jelly sandwiches, Tara's never-ending messes, and Joey's accusing eyes she missed. Those children had become like her very own, and it had taken this painful separation to make her see that.

Mow the lawn! She fumed as she stepped in the shower to wash her hair. Slater certainly hadn't tried to make up any elaborate excuse for not seeing her this evening. She had to hand it to him. For the life of her she couldn't see how he was so interested in her in bed, and then, the moment they were out of it, he went merrily on his way without a thought about their troubled marriage.

The phone rang as she was still grumbling and trying to blow her hair dry. Glancing at the clock, she noted that it was close to nine.

When she picked up the receiver and heard Slater's voice, her heart did its usual flip-flops.

"Jillane, are you busy?" he asked in a tone she had never heard before. He sounded alone . . . and almost as if he were frightened.

"I was just doing my hair. What's wrong?"

"How did you know there was something wrong?"

"By the tone of your voice. Slater, what is it?" Her hand gripped the phone tighter, and she felt herself growing apprehensive.

"It's . . . it's probably nothing. I'm sure she's just wandered off somewhere—" His voice broke for a moment, and he paused to regain his shattered composure.

"Slater?" Jillane's heart began to pound erratically.

"It's Tara, honey. We can't find her anywhere," he finally managed to say.

Feeling as if her legs would no longer support her, she sank down on the side of the bed and tried to digest his words. "You mean . . . she's lost?"

"We don't know what's happened to her. She was out in the yard with me while I was mowing. The mower broke down again, and I took it around to the garage. Oh, God, Jillane . . . I should have watched her closer! She was right there on her swing set. I couldn't have been gone more than five minutes, and when I returned, she was gone."

"Oh, Slater . . ." Her hand went up to her chest protectively. "Have you notified the police?"

"Yes, first thing when we couldn't find her. The kids have scoured the neighborhood, but there's no sign of her anywhere. The police think she may have been abducted. There's so much of that happening these days."

Kidnapped! Hot tears sprang to Jillane's eyes. Her baby had been kidnapped!

"Jillane . . . can you come over here? I need you, honey. I need you so damn much right now—" He was unable to complete his sentence as he broke down completely.

"Hang on, darling. I'll be there in fifteen minutes."

Throwing the phone back on the receiver, her hands were shaking so hard, she could barely pull on her jeans and a blouse. Five minutes later she raced down the flight of stairs and out to her car, not even realizing that she still had her house slippers on.

There were three police cars and various other vehicles in the Holbrook drive and along the street as Jillane got out of her car and ran up the front walk. The sound of dogs barking caught her attention, and she noticed the canines being unloaded from a truck at the side of the house.

Slater met her at the front door and they fell into each other's arms. She held him tightly, her heart nearly breaking when she felt his strong body trembling with fear.

"They'll find her, darling, they'll find her," she crooned softly, holding him as she would a baby.

"It's my fault," he whispered raggedly. "I thought I was watching her . . . I swear I was . . . but I left her alone for just a moment . . ."

"I know, and I'm sure you weren't neglectful. She's around here somewhere, you'll see. They'll find her."

She wasn't at all sure they would, but he was so broken, so helpless. . . .

"Mr. Holbrook, I hate to bother you again, but we'd like to run over a few more things with you." One of the policemen had come through the doorway and paused before the couple expectantly.

Wiping guiltily at his eyes, Slater straightened up and put his arm around Jillane's waist. "Certainly. This is my wife, Jillane."

Extending a polite hand, the officer smiled sympathetically. "I know how upset you must be, Mrs. Holbrook, but we've called in some Civil Defense volunteers, and there are several neighbors out looking for the child right now. We've also brought in the dogs, and we'll be working them shortly. We'll conduct a house-to-house search, look in cars, behind bushes, under porches, in wells and cisterns . . . anywhere a child might crawl into to take a nap or possibly get their clothing snagged and caught." He began to write on a large pad he was holding. "Now, you said the child was about two feet four inches tall, has dark hair and blue eyes, and was wearing a yellow sunsuit at the time she disappeared?"

"Yes. She had on one of those one-piece things with straps. I guess it's called a sunsuit," Slater verified.

Jillane knew exactly the outfit Tara was wearing. "Yes, that's what it is. It's yellow and has tiny little green flowers embroidered on the front."

"She just got over the chicken pox not long ago, and she still has a few pink marks on her," Slater added. "She had her little teddy bear with her. I couldn't find it out in the yard anywhere, so she must have it with her."

"And you say she was playing on the swing set when you left to go to the garage to repair the motor?"

"Yes." Slater ran his hand through his hair and thought carefully for a moment. "I had been mowing, and the mower kept dying on me. My neighbor, Charlie Duncan, came over to the fence and talked to me a few minutes while I was trying to work on it. He was getting ready to leave for the weekend, and he wanted me to keep an eye on his house," Slater explained, trying to remember every minute detail of what had happened before the baby's disappearance. "I told him I'd be happy to, and he said as soon as he'd locked his storage shed he'd be on his way. He stopped to talk to Tara for a minute and gave her one of the pieces of peppermint candies he always carries with him. I figured while he was entertaining her, I'd take the lawn mower around to the garage and put a new spark plug in. I wasn't gone over five minutes, and when I came back, Charlie and Tara were both gone."

Jillane looked at Slater expectantly. "Do you think he might have taken her?"

"Charlie Duncan! No! Oh, I thought at first he might have taken her over to visit with his wife, Meridith. He does that a lot. They're an older couple, and they enjoy being around the kids. But when I went over there, Charlie and Meridith were just driving off down the street. They waved and honked, and I flagged them down. Naturally Tara wasn't with them, and Charlie said he had left her in the swing while he gathered up the rest of his

270

lawn tools. When he finished, he noticed she wasn't there any longer, but he just assumed that either Mrs. Steele or I had taken her in the house. They immediately wanted to cancel their trip to Meridith's sister's and help us find her, but I assured them that Tara had probably wandered over to one of the other neighbors." He looked at Jillane helplessly. "I really thought it was as simple as that."

"Well." The officer flipped his notepad shut and sighed. "You never know in these cases. She might have decided to follow some other child down the street, or a dog or a cat caught her attention and she wandered off. We'll do our best to find her."

The policeman went about his duties as Jillane and Slater walked back through the house arm in arm. All the children except Caleb were seated in the living room with Mrs. Steele. An unusual quiet prevailed as they took a seat on the sofa. Slater introduced Jillane to the new, motherly-looking housekeeper.

"The two of you need something cold to drink," Mrs. Steele announced firmly. "And you haven't eaten your dinner yet, Mr. Holbrook. I'll fix a tray of sandwiches."

"Had Tara eaten?" he asked worriedly.

"Oh, my, yes! She ate an unusually large dinner tonight," Mrs. Steele soothed. "They'll find her . . . don't you fret none. I've raised five children of my own, and I know how likely they are to just up and run off if they take a mind to."

Slater rubbed his eyes wearily. "I can't imagine someone coming along and just picking her up. I

271

was right there. Surely I would have noticed a stranger. . . ."

Wong started crying. Jillane stood up and went over to her. Gathering the child in her arms, she sat down on the sofa, and Eben edged closer to her. Moments later all seven of the Holbrooks were wedged on the couch, trying to comfort each other. It was a strange time to become a real family, but that's exactly what they did as they waited for word of the baby.

The hour grew late, and at about two, Slater sent the sleepy children off to bed. Both Slater and Jillane automatically went about tucking each child in and giving them a kiss.

"I'm glad you're here." Joey's arms came up hesitantly to encircle Jillane's neck and squeeze her tightly as she knelt beside his bed.

Giving him a big bear hug, she found herself holding him much longer than she had the other children, letting her tears flow freely for the first time since she had received word of Tara's disappearance. "I'm glad I am too."

"Baby Tara will be back, won't she?" His dark eyes peered at her trustingly.

"I don't know, Joey. We can only pray that she will."

When she turned off his light and closed the door a few minutes later, she still felt the touch of his arms around her neck. That was the first time Joey had ever hugged her.

Slater went on to the bedroom while she gently tapped on Fleur's door. "Hi. You still awake?"

"Yes. I don't think I'll be able to sleep. I keep thinking about her being out there all alone. . . ."

"I know, I do too. If you need me, just let me know."

"I will . . . and, Jillane, I'm glad you're here with Slater. He was a real basket case earlier."

Smiling, Jillane closed her door and went to join her husband. That was probably as close as Fleur would ever come to giving her marriage to Slater her blessing, and Jillane gratefully accepted the thoughtful gesture.

Slater was sprawled across the bed, his clothes still on when she entered the darkened bedroom. Jillane lay down beside him and drew him tenderly into her arms. At her touch soft sobs began to rack his body, and soon they were both crying as they tried to comfort one another.

What if someone *had* taken Tara and they'd never see her again? That thought kept going over and over in their minds as they held each other in their arms all during the long night. Or even worse . . . what if she were roaming around in the dark by herself? Was she cold and crying? Or had she fallen in a well or . . . the agonizing list went on and on.

At times they would both doze, or they would talk, just to hear the sound of each other's voice and know they were there.

A new day dawned, and there was still no encouraging word. The story had come out in the paper, and it was on all the television and news broadcasts. The yard was beginning to fill with curious onlookers, many of them combing the

273

neighborhood again and again for the missing two-year-old.

But for all intents and purposes, Tara Marie Covell had simply disappeared from the face of the earth.

CHAPTER FIFTEEN

"She's been gone twenty-four hours. They're not going to find her." Slater's speech was dull and lifeless as he sat at the kitchen table late Saturday afternoon and stared at his untouched meal.

One look at his exhausted features and Jillane knew he couldn't stand much more of the strain. He had not been able to eat or sleep since Tara disappeared, and she was helpless to do anything for him.

The police had depleted almost all means of trying to find the missing child. Both Slater and Jillane tried to bolster each other's sagging morale, but it was becoming increasingly hard to do. They were both aware that normally, in this amount of time, a missing child would have been found. As each hour dragged by without any luck in finding the two-year-old, they were forced to the heartbreaking conclusion that Tara had been abducted.

And so the agonizing hours of waiting dragged on.

Jillane reached over and covered Slater's hand with hers in reassurance. "We can't give up, Slater."

"We might as well!" He angrily shoved back from the table and walked over to stare out the patio doors. The lawn was filled with people. Television and radio had broadcasted Tara's description hourly, and there wasn't a person living in the town who was not aware of the missing child. "Look at them out there. What are they waiting for? Why don't they just go home!"

"Some are curious, but others are sincerely concerned," she said, trying to soothe him and lying her head down on the table for a moment. Every bone in her body ached, but she refused to give in until they had some word . . . one way or the other. "Your parents called again. They think they should be here. . . ."

"There is nothing they could do here but worry. They may as well be comfortable in their own home to do that. If we don't find her soon, I'll call them and ask them to come up."

Slater stood at the door watching the crowd outside, his hands jammed in his pockets. If only he had watched Tara closer, this nightmare would not have been happening.

Glancing upward at the darkening summer sky, he silently apologized to Fritz and Marie for not taking better care of their child.

Just then, Slater caught sight of his neighbor, Charlie Duncan, as he pulled into his drive and shut off the engine.

"Charlie and Meridith are back early," he noted quietly. "They are going to be upset to find out that Tara's still missing."

Jillane rose from her chair and came over to stand beside him. Slipping his arm around her waist, he pulled her close and tenderly kissed her on the forehead. All during their long vigilance, they had talked of everything except their problem.

"I love you. Have I told you that lately?" he asked softly. He knew he would have never made it this far without her by his side. She had been his only source of comfort during this nightmare, and he loved her so much, it hurt.

"Yes, but I never tire of hearing you say it." She lay her head on his shoulder and closed her eyes, letting his presence fortify her once again.

Slater turned his attention to the activity outside. Charlie was talking with one of the police officers, his weathered face growing deeply concerned over what he was hearing. Shaking his head in disbelief, he glanced toward the Holbrook house and sat down on his back steps, trying to digest the upsetting news.

"The police have told Charlie about the baby," Slater speculated. "What do you want to bet he starts mowing his lawn to work off the tension?"

Jillane laughed weakly. It was a known fact around the neighborhood that Mr. Duncan was a workaholic. And he seemed to relieve his tensions by gardening or working on his lawn.

Sure enough, five minutes later Charlie had changed clothes and was back out on the lawn, shooing people away with a stern lecture on the merits of allowing people a little privacy. Slater and Jillane watched as he headed for the storage shed where he kept his tools and inserted the key in the lock.

"Don't you think you should try to eat something?" Jillane coaxed, squeezing Slater's waist affectionately. "It isn't going to do Tara any good if you make yourself sick."

"I couldn't eat a bite, honey." His words suddenly faltered, and he stiffened apprehensively. "My, God, he has Tara!"

Breaking away from her hold, Slater slid the patio door open and shot out the back door as Jillane's feet flew to catch up with him.

Charlie was laughing and crying at the same time as he came running toward the back door, carrying the slightly grubby baby in his arms. "Look what I found in my shed when I opened it!" he shouted excitedly.

Slater reached him in seconds. His arms reached out, and he clutched the child to his broad chest, burying his face in her hair. He was mortified to find himself crying in front of all these people, but the tears of relief refused to be stemmed as he held her chubby body close, hardly daring to believe that she had been found safe.

"The little dickens must have slipped in the shed while I wasn't looking!" Charlie exclaimed. "She's been locked in there since we left yesterday! Am I glad we decided to come home early to see if you'd found her!"

Slater shifted the baby to Jillane, and she hugged and kissed her exuberantly. The baby didn't know what to make of all the joyful attention she was receiving. With a pout, as if she were angry at being neglected for so long, she told Jillane, "Food! I'm hung'y!"

"I'll just bet you *are* hungry!" The tears were nearly blinding Jillane as Slater, Charlie, and one of the policemen rushed Tara in the house to see to her immediate needs.

"Is she all right?" Slater's voice was shaky as the policeman checked every inch of the child to see if she had incurred any injuries during her long ordeal.

"I think she's fine." The officer grinned, tickling the baby's stomach playfully. "But we'll have a doctor take a look as soon as we can get one over here."

Mrs. Steele came in to see what all the commotion was about. She threw up her hands in relief when she saw the baby in Slater's arms. "Praise the Lord! I just knew he'd let us find her safe and sound!"

"She's been locked up in Charlie's shed all this time," Slater explained.

"I don't know why we didn't think to look there," Mrs. Steele agonized. "Mr. Duncan's shed is one of her favorite places to hide!"

"I'm afraid she might be dehydrated," Jillane cautioned as her hands shakily poured a glass of juice from the refrigerator and handed it to Slater. He couldn't stop hugging and kissing the child long enough to be of any help. "Make her drink this slowly."

"Juice!" Tara cried, taking big gulps of the cold liquid. With a big, toothy grin she burped. "More!" she demanded.

While Jillane and Slater settled her in her high chair, Mrs. Steele prepared a can of soup and shouted for the other children.

"Tara, were you afraid when you were in the shed alone?" Slater prompted, puzzled that no one had heard the child cry. The shed sat at the very back of the lot, but with so many people milling around, he was surprised that they couldn't have heard her trying to summon help. "Did you cry when no one came to let you out?"

Shaking her curls energetically, the child related proudly, "No! I don't cry."

The sound of pounding feet could be heard throughout the house as the kitchen door burst open. The children saw their baby sister sitting in her high chair stuffing crackers down her mouth as fast as she could.

The kitchen came alive with shouts of joy as they all crowded around for their share of the hugs and kisses. Slater and Jillane paused long enough to grab each other and hug tightly. Then they waltzed around the room hugging the other children. A slightly perturbed and extremely hungry Tara eventually pushed everyone away and authoritatively demanded more crackers.

There were whoops of joy coming from outside as the police told everyone the good news and tried to disperse the excited crowd. Two or three signs went up on the lawn, stating, WELCOME HOME, TARA! Even Charlie applauded as he walked outside and saw several large yellow ribbons draped around his shrubs.

It took another two hours to get the household back to normal. The doctor came by and checked Tara. He found her to be no worse for wear from her harrowing episode. She was bathed, fed again, and tucked safely away in her crib.

Caleb had returned from his camping trip, and

he was eagerly informed of all the excitement he had missed out on.

After assuring himself that the baby was indeed all right, he promptly asked what was for supper.

It was getting close to ten when Jillane realized that she should be going home. Slater needed his rest, and she was nearing a state of collapse herself.

Home.

She looked around the familiar living area and sighed wistfully as she prepared to leave. It would be so nice if this was her home again.

All of the children except Fleur, who had decided to go over to John's house, were gathered around the television, munching popcorn and eating oranges. They had kernels strewn all over the rug and peels overflowing the ashtrays . . . and it brought a warm surge of affection to her heart.

Slater was just coming down the stairs after taking a hot shower. He was pulling on a shirt over that broad, furry wall of muscle she loved so well.

"Well"—she picked up her purse and smiled bravely—"I suppose I should be running along and let you all get to bed."

A deathly hush fell over the room as the children's heads popped up expectantly.

"Running along?" Slater's voice turned guarded. "Where are you going?"

"Home."

"Home?"

"Yes. I know you must be exhausted." She started for the doorway before she could lose her nerve. The children began gathering around Slater at the foot of the stairs.

The wall of silence behind her was not very encouraging. Would he actually let her walk out without making one tiny effort to stop her? After all they had been through this weekend, didn't he realize that they were a whole unit . . . a perfect family that should be together!

The continuing silence assured her that he just might let her go. Her hand reached for the doorknob and paused. Was this what she really wanted? To go home to an empty apartment and spend the rest of her life wishing that she were part of the family once more?

She could feel the five pairs of eyes glued to her retreating back as she worked to swallow her stubborn pride.

Okay! If he wouldn't ask her, then she would ask him. All he could do was say no, and the matter would be settled once and for all.

Taking a deep breath, she turned around, forcing her gaze to fasten on the oil painting hanging over the fireplace.

"Listen, you guys. Would anyone have too many objections if I just stayed here? I mean, I know I was pretty rotten the whole time I lived here before, but I've had time to think about things, and I believe I have my priorities straight now," she said, rushing on eagerly. "I have a lot to learn about a lot of things, but if you'll let me share my life with you, I'll try my very best to do better," she pleaded with tears swimming in her eyes again. She found Slater's adoring gaze. "I really do love every one of you, and I'm truly sorry for all the trouble I've caused. . . ."

Slater finally spoke, his voice overflowing with

love. "Well, what do you think, guys? Should we let this poor little orphan back in Fort Holbrook?"

A loud chorus of yeahs! shattered the air, with Joey's voice booming the loudest of all.

Slater held out his arms to her, a lazy grin spreading across his face. "Looks like the 'yeahs' have it, babe. Welcome home."

Epilogue

Exactly two years later . . .

The babies had been collected from the new mothers for bed, and the maternity ward settled down for the night. The lights in the hallways were dimmed to a soft glow, and only the occasional swish of the nurses' polyester uniforms broke the hushed stillness.

Jillane was just beginning to grow drowsy when the door to her room cracked open and Slater slipped in.

Tiptoeing to her bedside, he leaned over and kissed her tenderly.

"Umm . . . hi! What are you doing back?" She stirred lazily and opened her eyes.

"I've been down the hall looking at our babies," he whispered.

"Again? The nurses are going to run you off." She smiled, thinking of how many trips he had made down to the nursery since the babies had been born early that morning. It had been a long and tiring labor, but the end results had been well worth it. Three perfect boys!

"They already have run me off," he confessed.

"But I wanted to see you one last time before I went home." He kissed her, long and lingeringly. "Thank you, my beautiful wife, for my handsome sons," he murmured against her mouth.

"You like them?"

"Almost as much as I like you," he agreed. "You know, I really feel sorry for those other new fathers standing down there looking in that nursery window. I bet they wonder how we came up with such cute babies and theirs turned out so homely," he noted sympathetically. "I started to reassure Hal Gray a minute ago that his baby would get better-looking, but I decided it might hurt his feelings."

"Oh, Slater!" She laughed. "You're not just a little prejudiced, are you?"

"Certainly not!" he defended quickly. "But I know exactly how Hal feels, honey. When our babies were first born this morning, I was really a little worried. There were a few minutes there when I wasn't sure what you had delivered, they were so . . . well." He patted her hand consolingly. "I don't want to hurt your feelings, but they were downright *ugly*," he confessed. "And when the nurses started wiping them off and they weren't improving one bit, I really began to get nervous! But, by this evening, they had really shaped up, and now they're the best-looking babies in the whole nursery," he confided confidentially.

"Is that why you've been hanging around down there bothering those nurses all day long?" she scolded incredulously. "To see if our darling little babies were getting any better-looking!"

"Oh, no." He hastened to defend himself. "I

wouldn't have cared if they had stayed that ugly. I would have loved them, anyway. But you have to realize, we're not just talking ordinary ugly, Jillane. We're talking *real* ugly. One of them had his nose smashed all over his face," he related in a conspiratorial whisper, "and the other one had cauliflower ears, and the third one . . . why, they had to use the salad spoons to get him out. . . ."

"You mean forceps?"

"Yeah. Is that what they're called? Anyway, they had to use those things to get him to come out!"

Laying a restraining finger on his lips, she smiled and sought to ease his anxieties. "All babies look like that when they're first born."

"No kidding?" He lifted a dubious brow. "Well, that's good to hear."

"The thought of having triplets doesn't scare you?"

"Not one bit."

She giggled and wrapped her arms around his neck. She sighed with complete contentment. "I don't know what it is about you, Slater Holbrook, but it seems like I always get more than I bargained for every time we get together."

"Hey, now wait a minute," he chided. "I'm not the one who had triplets in my family. *You* are."

"But I'm the one who has nine children now," she pointed out quickly.

"Yeah." He grinned and kissed her again. "And you love every minute of it."

"I do, I really do." She grinned back.

"And I'll bet you're even ready to start thinking about having more," he teased.

"And I'll just bet you're full of it too." She

frowned. "Nine children is absolutely, unequivocally the limit, fellow!"

"Well, Fleur's gone now, so you actually have only eight," he consoled.

"Oh, right . . . *only* eight." She settled back on her pillow. "Slater, you were about to tell me something about Fleur before I went into labor yesterday. What was it?" She yawned.

"Uhhh . . . you should really be trying to get some rest, honey," he said evasively.

"Oh, that's all I've done is sleep all day," Jillane protested. "What were you going to say about Fleur?"

Gently smoothing her hair away from her forehead, he chose his words carefully. "You know something? You are the prettiest thirty-year-old woman alive who has nine children and is about to become a . . . grandmother," he noted brightly.

"A grandmother!" She groaned helplessly. "I'm going to be a grandmother too?"

"Next January." He laughed sheepishly. "Fleur and John told me last night. But, don't worry, Grannie, I'll still love you when you're old and gray and . . . maybe even after you turn forty," he promised devilishly.

"Forty!" Dear heavens! He was trying to be obnoxious!

"It's not that far away, dearie." He decided to really rub it in while he had the perfect opportunity. "But what are you so worried about? Aren't you the bright ray of sunshine who's always running around spouting those corny soliloquies, like, 'The older the violin, the sweeter the music'?"

Looking up at him angelically, she made her

287

most corny pun to date. "I would have to have the right bow—beau—to make the music the very sweetest."

Slater's eyes grew loving as his humor subsided and his love for her overflowed. As his mouth descended slowly to meet hers he whispered in his sexiest voice, "You've got him, babe. You've got him."